THE REVENGE OF KALI-RA

Also by K. K. Beck:

We Interrupt This Broadcast
Bad Neighbors
Death in a Deck Chair
Murder in a Mummy Case
The Body in the Volvo
Young Mrs. Cavendish and the Kaiser's Men
Unwanted Attentions
Peril Under the Palms

The Jane da Silva Novels:

Cold Smoked
Electric City
Amateur Night
A Hopeless Case

THE REVENGE OF KALI-RA

K.K. BECK

THE MYSTERIOUS PRESS

Published by Warner Books

A Time Warner Company

Copyright © 1999 by Kathrine Beck

Mysterious Press books are published by Warner Books, Inc., 1271 Avenue of the Americas, New York, NY 10020.

Visit our Web site at http://warnerbooks.com

A Time Warner Company

The Mysterious Press name and logo are registered trademarks of Warner Books, Inc.

Printed in the United States of America

First printing: March 1999

10 9 8 7 6 5 4 3 2 1

Library of Congress Cataloging-in-Publication Data

Beck, K. K.
    The revenge of Kali-Ra / K.K. Beck.
        p.   cm.
    ISBN 0-89296-670-X
    I. Title.
PS3552.E248R48   1999
813'.54—dc21   98-35772
                                                                      CIP

This book is affectionately and respectfully dedicated
to the memory of Sax Rohmer, the Baroness Orczy,
H. Rider Haggard, E. Phillips Oppenheim, and many
others, who toiled ceaselessly for no reward
other than vast fame and massive fortune.

TABLE OF CONTENTS

BOOK THREE
In Which the Gong of Kali-Ra Summons the Faithful
to the Temple of the Chosen

THE REVENGE OF KALI-RA

✗

Valerian Ricardo selected a cigarette from the gold Cartier box with his initials in diamonds, fitted it into his ebony and silver holder, and strolled onto the balcony of his villa overlooking the Côte d'Azur. A tall, slim man of thirty-five, he had a strangely dissipated face for one so young. His fine brown hair was well oiled and combed flat against his egg-shaped skull, and he wore a maroon silk dressing gown over his white silk pajamas. His manservant, Lucien, proffered a lighter, and Ricardo gazed out over the Mediterranean. "It's too dammed bright," he said, retreating back to the dim recesses of the house.

He had really overdone it this time, he thought. Four or five cocktails with the duchess, then all those giddy debutantes and of course the cocaine, which never failed to energize and invigorate—that had been fine. But he'd had to go on and indulge later in copious amounts of opium more powerful than he had ever experienced, and Valerian Ricardo had experienced plenty.

He let out a world-weary sigh. At least, he thought, the drug had produced the desired result, a fantastic dream that could be swiftly tailored into one of his enchanting tales. It had been at least three months since the last book had been published, and if Valerian Ricardo was to continue living as he had become accustomed to living—indeed, as he *deserved* to live—he had better deliver another one by the week after next at the latest.

Eagerly, he rushed to his bedside and seized his leather-bound notebook. In the early hours of the dawn he had jotted down the main scenes, and there was certainly enough there for a real corker of a yarn. Thank God he had written it down, because now the details were hazy.

"Hero runs through thicket, pursuing naked girl with jeweled navel. Branches scratch his flesh." Good.

"Dagger. Cabochon emeralds and rubies. Plunged into bosom of sleeping woman in gossamer-fine negligee." Fine.

"Evil criminal mastermind, once a respectable member of society, now disgraced, directs his empire from a fetid tropical island, sending his minions to do evil." All right.

"Beautiful villainess disguised as serving girl." He'd done that one before but it never failed.

"Various people bound with stout ropes and locked in closets, etc." Okay.

But surely there was more! There had to be! The dream had been very well plotted. Better than anything he'd ever done in the previous twenty or so books.

Ricardo turned the page. Here were a few more jottings but they were less legible. He managed to make out "family secrets revealed," "lovers united," "all resolved," and "the end."

Disgusted, he flung the notebook down. There had been so much more in his dream! He must remember it all. And by next Tuesday at the latest.

Lucien coughed discreetly. "Has monsieur forgotten that Miss Nadi is coming to luncheon?" he asked, before leaving the room.

Oh yes. Vera Nadi, the screen vamp who had taken the villa next door. Last night she had lain beside him on the sofa, inhaling the magical fumes which had produced this wonderful novel, the details of which he had now, maddeningly, forgotten. As the hookah gurgled, she had charmed him with reminiscences of her harem childhood in Constantinople. She had been the daughter of the sultan's favorite, a proud beauty who later escaped to America with the young Vera. The story was slightly at odds with the movie star's thick New Jersey accent, but Vera had presumably learned her English in Newark where she and her mother had fled. Anyway, film actresses were of course not required to speak.

Suddenly, he remembered one more thing about his dream. Last night Vera Nadi had shown him a photograph of the sprawling villa she had just built in California. It was in that house, an Arabian Nights sort of house surrounded by dense and fragrant gardens, that his dream novel had taken place. He had brief images of a window, a parapet, large tiled floors. There were fleeting sensations of a moonlight swim, mysterious visitors whose errand was unclear, a gray-eyed girl of wisdom and a dark temptress—or maybe two dark temptresses. But these impressions fled as quickly as they had arrived, taunting him then running off, laughing cruelly, until he knew they were gone. Damn!

This was doubly vexing because it had all seemed so real. It was almost as if this dream had told a tale that had already happened, or that would happen in the future. Valerian Ricardo had been told by many psychics that he was a highly tuned entity, sensitive to truth from beyond earthly reality, with strong clairvoyant powers.

Lucien entered the room again. "Miss Nadi has arrived," he said.

Valerian Ricardo took a deep breath and slicked back his hair. "Tell her I shall join her shortly. The cream-colored linen lounge suit today, I think. But first, bring me a small absinthe, will you? I seem to have a slight headache."

Once Lucien had left, he tore the pages from his notebook to shreds and scattered them from his balcony, whence the gentle breezes carried them down to the Mediterranean.

BOOK ONE

In Which the Queen of Doom Awakens from Her Slumber

CHAPTER I

✗

Nadia Wentworth turned the slightly mildewed page. "God," she said. "This is so totally cool."

> Kali-Ra strode about the marble floors of the Temple of the Chosen with the gait of a jungle cat. Her green eyes narrowed and emitted a peculiar light, a light that the privileged few of her fanatic followers who had been permitted to bask in the heady presence of their mistress knew only too well. "I am displeased," she said in a purring, velvety tone. "I have been disobeyed, and now the meddling Englishman, Raymond Vernon, has been allowed to escape."
>
> Gasps of fear came from the mouths of the faithful in the temple. When it took on that purr, Kali-Ra's low, cruel voice was a precursor to the wickedest, the vilest, and the most fiendishly devised punishments and tortures.

Nadia, a small, dark woman in her twenties, and one of Hollywood's three most bankable female stars, shifted on the bed, producing horrible squeaks from the ancient springs, eager to learn just what the merciless Kali-Ra had in mind for those who had let her down.

Nadia seldom read actual books. If she was thinking of optioning one for her new production company, she'd get her personal assistant, Melanie, to tell her what it was all about. But the monsoon season had come early to the remote South Pacific island where she was shooting the remake of a forties South Seas picture in which she reprised

7

the Hedy Lamarr role of a sarong-clad Polynesian temptress. To update the work, the character had been rewritten as a literal as well as figurative man-eater. The picture was called *Cannibal.*

The joke among the crew was that if the rains didn't let up, they'd be forced to start eating each other. For the last three days, flights had been canceled, and even private planes couldn't get in or out. The crew had been killing time for a week and a half, holed up in the island's only hotel, a turn-of-the-century pile undermined by termites and filled with rickety rattan furniture and lizards.

Nadia had finished looking at the pictures in all her magazines, and had gone back and read every word. There was no TV, let alone cable or satellite dishes. The hotel's one VCR didn't track. Even the radio seemed to have just one station, and it had nothing on at all except crazed preachers lecturing people in static-ridden pidgin. Nadia couldn't even wash her thick dark hair because she'd run out of her special kelp shampoo and her defrizzing conditioning gel finish with healing aloe. Adding insult to injury, the bitchy set hairdresser pointed out that because she was working in a wig, he didn't have anything for her very special and chronic hair problems.

Nadia was sick of the picture, the crew, the director, her leading man, the island, and especially the Hotel Splendide, which provided really cheap shampoo in itty-bitty plastic bottles, and no conditioner at all.

"God," she'd said to Melanie earlier. "I can't even trash the hotel room because it was trashed before I even got here. Everything sucks. This is all somebody's fault. I have been totally screwed over by these so-called producers. I never should have done this picture. I had a weird feeling about it. Why didn't I say no? Why didn't we just shoot this in Hawaii, for God's sake? Why won't it stop raining? I am so fucking bored!" She scrunched her features into an angry knot. Her face usually wore an irritable expression, a petulant tightness not without a sulky charm. This tightness lost its grip primarily when the camera was on her. Then, her face softened and became dewy, open, receptive and enchanting.

Apart from the results of neglect, decay, and humidity, nothing much had changed at the Hotel Splendide since Somerset Maugham had checked in on his way to Tahiti. This included the collection of moldy books in the lobby provided for browsing guests. After Nadia's tirade, Melanie had sighed, and quietly left the room, reappearing some time later with a stack of these well-worn volumes.

Melanie, a tall redhead with intelligent grayish eyes and a calm demeanor unusual in someone so young, was Nadia's personal assistant, in charge of everything from acting as liaison with lawyers, publicists, accountants, and personal trainers to making sure that the Evian was room temperature. "There's an old Scrabble set down there too," she reported, "but the crew is using it. I can take it away from them if you want."

Nadia curled her lip. "Real tactful, Melanie. You know I have a genetic learning disorder that means I can't spell." She cast a sullen eye over the collection of books, and was drawn immediately to the cover of *The Wrath of Kali-Ra* by Valerian Ricardo. It depicted a tall, pale, exotic-looking woman with a cloud of black hair. She wore a diaphanous garment that revealed great breasts and legs, and some stunning jewelry, including bracelets on her upper arms and a band around her forehead in the shape of a snake. The woman had a haughty and cruel expression on her face, and carried a whip.

"God," said Nadia reverently. "She looks so totally empowered."

"Do you want me to read it and tell it to you?" asked Melanie pleasantly.

Nadia ignored her and opened up the book.

CHAPTER ONE

In the Web of the Queen of Doom

Raymond Vernon lit his pipe and leaned nonchalantly against the fireplace at his exclusive London club. Vernon was tall, lean, fit, and a wonderful example of the best of the Anglo-Saxon type. Only a few especially sensitive souls noticed, however, that there was something haunted and weary about his keen, steady, gray eyes. Here was a man whose fate it was to have lived as few men have lived, and to have seen much that was unspeakable.

Gazing into the distance, as if perceiving some private vision across the room, Vernon began. "There are places in the world where no white man has been, places where strange things happen, strange, mystical things.

"Often, when a certain occult power is awakened, a torrent of beautiful, deadly evil is unleashed. And, although only a handful of people know the terrible secret, this force is proven time and time again to be what drives a vast conspiracy with world domination as its inevitable end."

Colonel Bellingham looked up from his newspaper. "Come now, Vernon. You're not carrying on about this world domination business again, are you?" he said irritably, twisting the ends of his white mustache. "And this she-devil you claim is hiding behind every lamppost?"

"You may scoff if you like," said Raymond Vernon coolly. "But I have seen the face of Kali-Ra, and I have felt the terrible power she possesses. It is, Colonel Bellingham, a power with the beauty of a poisonous, waxy, night-blooming flower, alluring in its scent, yet somehow expressing also the evil that is all the more dangerous because of its seductive beauty."

"No, I'll read it myself," said Nadia. "The prose is so fabulous."

CHAPTER II

Nick Iversen pulled up outside the retirement home in sub-urban Minneapolis where his grandfather lived. He sat in the car for a minute, with the key on "accessory," until his song on the radio finished playing. He always stalled before going inside Manderleigh Manor. While he stalled, he looked through the windshield at a couple of old ladies with white fuzzy hair and glasses. They clumped along the concrete paths through carefully tended lawn with the aid of aluminum walkers. The women were smiling and chatting with each other and seemed to be having a good time. Why couldn't Grandpa have been one of those nice old people, the kind that donated their time making tapes of reminiscences for oral history projects?

Instead, Grandpa was the kind of person who gave old people a bad name. Since a series of small strokes, he tended to come out with blunt, irritable pronouncements and showed absolutely no interest in anybody else. Nick's mother said this was a cruel trick of nature, altering the personality of a wonderful man through the selective killing of brain cells. Nick, however, thought that Grandpa had probably always been basically crabby and selfish and all the strokes had done was impair his ability to mask these underlying flaws.

It had been a huge relief when Grandpa had finally agreed to move in here. After his retirement from the lumberyard, he had helped a little with household chores, always under the close supervision of his wife. But since becoming a widower, and especially after the strokes, he had simply abandoned any pretense of housekeeping. He preferred to spend all day on the sofa watching television.

Stacks of dishes in increasingly precarious piles had appeared on all the flat surfaces in the kitchen. Little nests of dirty clothes sprung up like mushrooms behind doors and in odd corners. Nick had helped his mother dig the old boy out about four times, before announcing that he wouldn't do it again, and that she shouldn't either—they'd have to get him into a home.

Now, Nick visited Grandpa because he felt guilty that he'd instigated the campaign to push the old guy in here. He also felt a residual gratitude for the fact that when he was a little kid, Grandpa had provided him with scraps of plywood and two-by-fours from the lumberyard for the construction of forts and tree houses. With a sigh, Nick forced himself out of the car and into the building.

The overpolished linoleum floors and the stainless steel elevators were pretty grim, but once you got into Grandpa's little apartment, things weren't so bad. After all, the furniture had come from the old house, and Nick remembered it all from childhood. The olive green sofa with the crocheted afghan across the back, the fake-colonial maple coffee table with his own baby-teeth marks on one corner, the brown braided oval rug laid over the wall-to-wall carpeting.

Nick knocked on the blond wood door and listened to the shuffle of slippers and his grandfather snapping, "All right, all right. Coming!"

"Oh. It's you," he said, staring up at his grandson as if he resented the intrusion. He'd seemed pleased enough when Nick had called forty minutes ago and said he was on his way.

"Hi, Grandpa," Nick said, trying to sound reasonably cheerful but not phony. "How are you?"

"Lousy." Grandpa collapsed back onto the sunken spot on the sofa across from the TV and his eyes drifted immediately back to the screen. Nick reflected bitterly that crotchety baby boomers were always accusing his own generation of having tube-fried brains, and here was someone who'd been in the Battle of the Bulge, using the television like electronic Prozac. "I always feel like hell," Grandpa elaborated.

"Sorry to hear that," said Nick breezily. He knew better than to ask what was wrong. That would just unleash a torrent of vague complaints about the food and the staff. Nick thought the food was pretty good for institutional fare, and that the people who looked after his ungrateful grandfather were incredibly kind and patient, if not candidates for sainthood.

"I brought you something," said Nick, handing over a box of Grandpa's favorite candy, chocolate-covered cherries.

"Thanks," said Grandpa, receiving the proffered box and flinging it to one side without ever removing his eyes from the screen.

Nick sighed, defeated. "What's on TV?" he asked.

"Oh, I don't know. It's all a bunch of crap if you ask me. Just a lot of junk, that's all there ever is."

Nick sat down next to the old man and figured he'd watch television for about half an hour, then clear out. It didn't matter how long he stayed. His grandfather always barked the same thing when Nick rose to go. "What are you leaving for?"

Grandpa appeared to be watching an afternoon talk show that featured a hostess with teeth that stuck out and a lot of lipstick. Nick was vaguely aware that her name was Sandy something, and that she dished up fluffy celebrity in-

terviews and cooking demonstrations. Next to her on a sofa
sat a famous actress, who was explaining that her new
South Seas picture, *Taboo,* had originally been titled *Cannibal,* until focus-group research revealed that people
thought it was a teen spatter flick.

"That's Nadia Wentworth, the movie star," Nick explained
to his grandfather.

Since graduating summa cum laude from the University
of Minnesota with a degree in philosophy, Nick had been
working as assistant manager at an arts cinema near the
campus and kept up on movies. Nadia Wentworth, he felt,
was a barely adequate actress who managed, nevertheless,
to make the camera love her. She also had lovely breasts,
which he had seen displayed in all their glory in *Primate!,*
the story of a crusading female ecology activist living topless among the sex-mad Bonobo apes who comes to grips
with her own sexuality when a trim game warden tries to
run the wildlife sanctuary his way.

"Movie stars!" snorted Grandpa. "I don't keep track of
any of them. Nice pair of bazongas, though," he added begrudgingly. Nadia was dressed a little provocatively for an
afternoon show, in a black transparent chiffon blouse.

Nick thought Nadia Wentworth was a lot less sexy when
she was being herself. Instead of letting her head fall back
with her signature wet-lipped, lust-glazed, panting look,
the star was wearing stagy horn-rimmed glasses and sat
hunched forward with a serious expression, stabbing the
air with her hands to make points. She was now explaining earnestly how a monsoon encountered during the filming of *Taboo,* which had at first seemed like a real downer,
had, in fact, been part of a divine, cosmic plan for her career. "You see, Sandy, if I hadn't been *trapped* there on
Boola Lau with nothing to do, I *never* would have found
this absolutely *fabulous* book. Since then I've learned that
Valerian Ricardo wrote a whole bunch of Kali-Ra books,

and I'm reading them, and I've already got a scriptwriter doing a final polish."

"Kali-Ra," repeated the hostess, apparently bemused.

"I'm *so* glad you asked me about my next project. Kali-Ra is this fantastic goddess-type woman, *way* ahead of her time. She has, like, masses of slave followers helping her to take over the world. It's powerful stuff and really deep. Valerian Ricardo must have really been an *amazing* guy."

"That gal is talking about Uncle Sid," Grandpa announced.

Nick was alarmed. The poor old guy was worse off than he'd thought. Now he was imaging that the screen he stared at all day was somehow hooked up with his early life. "What? No, Grandpa. You're confused. That's Nadia Wentworth. She's a famous movie star."

"You don't know a thing about it," snorted Grandpa. "You never even knew Uncle Sid. Neither did I, for that matter."

Nadia removed the horn-rims and stuck an earpiece thoughtfully into her pouty mouth for a pensive moment. "Valerian Ricardo was really a great thinker," she went on, clearly panicking the hostess by going off on a tangent. "What's so exciting is the way he tells these great stories, but there's a deeper level, a, like, *philosophical* thing about good and evil and how the universe isn't always in balance. Kind of like the dark and light sides of the force, you know?"

"The, um, George Lucas force thing?" Sandy suggested nervously.

"Yeah, but not exactly. The cool thing about Valerian Ricardo is that he gets it that you need some evil in the world too, and that evil can be way cool."

"She's talking about a crude form of Manichaeism," said Nick.

"She's talking about Uncle Sid," said Grandpa. "He called

himself that stupid name. Valentine Ricardo or something swishy like that."

"He did?" Uncle Sid was a shadowy figure in the family's past. All Nick knew was that jaws were clenched disapprovingly when his name came up, and that it was considered a blessing that he had left town never to return.

"That's right. Sid wrote those trashy Kali-Ra books. Mother wouldn't let me read 'em. She said they weren't suitable."

"I've been checking this all out," Nadia went on. "Apparently, Ricardo was born on a farm in Minnesota, but as a young man, he studied occult science in the East."

"Ha!" said Grandpa. "Studied chiseling and vice right here in Minneapolis, that's what he did as a young man. He was no damn good. Ended up like he deserved."

"So you'll be playing this Dalai Lama character. Interesting," Sandy said unconvincingly. She had apparently abandoned any attempt to control the interview.

"Kali-Ra," corrected Nadia with a finger held up in a schoolmistressy gesture at odds with the see-through blouse. "Kali-Ra, the Queen of Doom."

Grandpa snorted. "Uncle Sid made a lot of dough writing that trash. Ran around Europe, lived in the south of France, and never told anyone he came from Minnesota and that his real name was Sidney Gundersen."

"Really?" Nick was fascinated.

"He was kind of a dope fiend or something, and always in trouble. Women and girls weren't safe with him. Even when he was a kid he stole nickels and dimes from the Luther League missionary fund down at the church."

"Wow," said Nick. Finally, Grandpa had something interesting to talk about. "Was he really famous? What were the books like?"

"Say," said Grandpa, his eye settling on the box of chocolate-covered cherries. "Look at that!" He seemed to have forgotten that Nick had brought a gift, and acted as if the candy had appeared miraculously. "You know what? These are my favorites." He began tearing at the cellophane.

"Tell me more about Uncle Sid," said Nick.

"Uncle Sid? I don't know. Not much to say. Have one of these. They're my favorites, you know."

Nick gave up asking about Uncle Sid. Maybe Grandpa would be in the mood to talk about it next time. That would be nice. As far as Nick could tell, in a family characterized by unremitting dullness, shadowy Uncle Sid had been the only interesting thing that had ever happened.

CHAPTER III

The first Glen Pendergast heard about the Kali-Ra movie was in the faculty lunchroom. Carl Beckman, a Henry James expert who liked to sneer at Glen's scholarly interest in popular culture, rattled his newspaper and said, "It says here that Nadia Wentworth is a big fan of that Kali-Ra you're so hot for. I thought you were the only person alive who knew or cared who that depraved sicko Valerian Ricardo was." Beckman had taken it upon himself, out of what Glen could only assume was professional jealousy, to get his hands on and read a copy of Glen's Ph.D. thesis on Valerian Ricardo.

Glen tried not to let Beckman know how hurtful he could be. "Well," he said, "I'm not surprised. I always felt that Ricardo's work had potentially universal appeal. His themes speak to something deeply embedded in the culture."

Carl snorted, and said, "Yeah, stupidity," then flung the Arts section at Glen and addressed his attention to Sports.

Glen eagerly read the item, little more than a few lines in a showbiz column. Nadia Wentworth was producing and starring in a movie about Kali-Ra! He was thrilled. Maybe there was some way this project could enhance his career. After all, he, Glen Pendergast, was the greatest, the only, living authority on Valerian Ricardo and Kali-Ra, Queen of Doom. "This could be a good development," he murmured under his breath.

Beckman had apparently heard him and shot him a contemptuous look over the top of the paper. "Absolutely," he said. "Those cretins in Hollywood should stick to trash and leave poor Jane and Henry alone." Carl was always out to get him, intimating that Glen's boyish handsomeness was the only reason female students lined up eagerly for his office hours.

Finishing his grilled cheese sandwich in wounded silence, Glen went back to his desk. The Kali website, he figured, would have the latest on the movie deal. He sat in front of his computer, clicked on Netscape, and tapped out www.kali.com.

Dr. Glen Pendergast, associate professor of English and popular culture at Montana's Badlands State College, may have specialized in one of popular literature's more decadent writers, but he himself looked fresh and innocent. He had smooth skin, big blue eyes, and shiny brown hair receding just slightly at the temples.

He was glad about this last fact. Otherwise, he would have looked even younger. At the age of thirty-one, Dr. Pendergast was often asked to show his ID when ordering a beer. He felt sure that his lack of career progress was connected to his youthful appearance. That and the fact that his book, *The Whip Hand: Issues of Gender and Genre in the Work of Valerian Ricardo,* had never been taken seriously in the academic world.

If somebody like Camille Paglia had written it, he thought bitterly, it would have been a best-seller. No one cared what a white male had to say about images of erotically charged, powerful women in the popular consciousness. It was enough to make him give up on his latest project, a study of the fifties TV series *Sheena, Queen of the Jungle.*

From what Glen could figure, Valerian Ricardo, though a best-seller in his day, currently had about fifteen fans across the country. This, apart from library sales, was the approximate number of copies *The Whip Hand* had sold. The fans were devoted, though, and one of them, a shy computer programmer from Milwaukee named Les, with whom Glen had corresponded occasionally, maintained this website. Sure enough, Les had managed to get a transcript of the Sandy Shipley interview and had posted it.

Glen read it, feeling, as he often did, left out and neglected. There was Nadia Wentworth going on as if she'd discovered Valerian Ricardo, when actually he had. And now she would make a lot of money off it, and be even more famous, while he continued to rot away here in this crummy school for inbred descendants of pioneers too dim-witted to realize you can't farm a desert. Still, Glen was glad Nadia Wentworth would be publicizing Kali-Ra. That could only enhance his reputation.

And, he realized dreamily, he was glad she was going to play the part. He thought it was superb casting. Hadn't he always imagined Kali-Ra's breasts would look just like Nadia Wentworth's, which he had so admired in *Deep Body Rub,* the story of a topless masseuse with a heart of gold who wins the heart and hand, not to mention other body parts, of a fabulously wealthy tycoon with stuffy parents?

Sighing as the image of those breasts, round but perky, flashed upon his inward eye, Glen clicked onto the Kali-Ra chat room, which was abuzz with the news of the movie deal. Most of the fans were thrilled that the world would learn about Kali-Ra at last, although one contributor felt that "too many people would get involved and cheapen the whole thing." Some speculated that their collections of old copies of the Valerian Ricardo books would increase in value. One regular contributor, who exhibited troubling signs of the sadism found in the books, ranted on about the blasphemy of any mere mortal portraying the divine Kali-Ra. He suggested that Nadia Wentworth should be bound tightly to the marble Pillar of Pain centrally located in the Temple of the Chosen with stout ropes biting into her soft flesh and lashed without mercy if she didn't drop the project at once. Glen often wondered if this self-styled slave of Kali-Ra was the same creep who'd sent him those threatening letters when his book had appeared. Maybe he should have turned those letters over to some mental-health authorities, on the grounds that the writer was a danger to others.

And then, Glen saw with a shudder, there was a message from Lila. God! Lila online!

"I think those who appreciate Valerian's work," he read, and he could hear her imperious, genteel tones as if she were right in the room, "will appreciate that as Valerian's widow, I must act. I have demanded a meeting with Miss Wentworth. As many of you know, I promised Valerian on his deathbed that I would make sure his work was presented properly and in the best possible taste without betraying its inner spirituality. I may need the help of you, his many fans. I am an old woman, but I still have fight left in me. With your help, I will prevail. We must not let the legacy of Valerian Ricardo fall into the wrong hands."

Lila was up to her old tricks. That deathbed-scene routine was pathetic! Valerian Ricardo certainly hadn't died in bed, and she knew it. She'd never come clean about that.

Still, Lila's little screed gave Glen an idea. If she could get in touch with Nadia Wentworth, why couldn't he? He rummaged in the box under his desk for a copy of his book. Too bad it was a dull-looking, scholarly volume. The Badlands State University Press didn't run to splashy cover art. He opened it up to the title page and scrawled "To the woman born to play Kali-Ra, with best wishes from the author," and signed it Glen W. Pendergast, Ph.D.

CHAPTER IV

THE FLAME OF KALI-RA

Lila Ricardo sat across from Melanie in Nadia's huge living room, perched on the edge of the sofa like a bird, a small, bony woman of about eighty with bright blue eyes and crudely penciled brows that gave her a startled expression. She was wearing nineteen-fifties Doris Day career-girl attire somewhat the worse for wear—a beige suit with what looked like a cigarette burn on one lapel, yellowed and chipped plastic pearls, white fabric gloves, grimy at the fingertips, and a blue pillbox hat with a crushed chunk of veiling tacked to the front. She should have looked pathetic, but Melanie thought she looked scary. There was a horrible confidence and power in those bright eyes.

"It is so important that I convey to Miss Wentworth the importance of this project," she said in precise, stagy tones.

"Believe me, Miss Wentworth takes herself and her work very seriously," Melanie replied.

"It is a sacred trust," Lila went on breathlessly. "Valerian Ricardo died in my arms, and I promised him that those same arms would carry the flame of Kali-Ra."

"Yes, I see," said Melanie. Where the hell was Nadia? She was the one who'd wanted to meet the woman.

"It was my privilege to be his consort," continued Mrs. Ricardo. "The man was astounding. Such a fine mind, such sensitivity, such a fertile imagination." She leaned forward and whispered hoarsely, "I feel his presence so often." She

22

cast a startled look over Melanie's shoulder in the direction of the French doors. "He is with us now. In this very room!"

"Really?" said Melanie. Should she get up and try to find Nadia? She didn't want to leave the woman alone here. Melanie had noticed that upon entering the room, Lila Ricardo had scanned the whole place, her unsettling gaze resting greedily on various valuable knickknacks. Melanie could well imagine her popping the odd piece of crystal or silver into her capacious cracked vinyl purse if given a second or so.

Lila cleared her throat. "I need to find out just what Miss Wentworth intends to do in this film. I must give my approval, you see. That is how Valerian wanted it."

"Mmm," said Melanie. The Kali-Ra copyrights had expired. That was one of the few good things about this project. The original work was in the public domain.

"What's that dear?" Mrs. Ricardo was suddenly shouting.

"I just said 'Mmm,'" Melanie replied.

"Not you," she snapped, with a dismissive wave of her dirty white glove. "Valerian is sending me a telepathic communication. Be quiet. I must concentrate."

She threw her head back and stared up at the ceiling. "It's coming. His mind is so powerful," she muttered, then yelled, "Yes, dear, I'll tell them! Yes, my angel!" Presumably the extra volume was needed to get her message beyond the grave.

Her head snapped back into a level position. "Valerian says I should be a consultant on the film. Twenty thousand a week, my own trailer, and my own director's chair that says 'Mrs. Ricardo' on the back. And script approval too, of course."

Nadia walked into the room. She seemed slightly startled to see what looked like a genteel bag lady sitting on her sofa.

"This is Mrs. Ricardo, who wrote you that letter," prompted

Melanie. Despite the fact that this meeting was right there in today's schedule posted on the fridge, Nadia still looked blank, so Melanie added, "Valerian Ricardo's widow." She was tempted to add that the old boy himself was lurking around the French doors.

Nadia's face lit up and she rushed over to Lila. "It's wonderful to meet you. I am such an admirer of your husband's work."

Lila rose and put her hands on Nadia's shoulders. "Let me look at you."

Nadia, used to being looked at by fans, smiled indulgently.

Suddenly, Lila let out what sounded like a snort. "Ah, but you have the rawness of youth. How can you play a woman, a goddess, who is centuries old?" She allowed her hands to fall from Nadia's shoulders.

Nadia gave Lila Ricardo a look Melanie had last seen when her employer had chewed out Manuel, the gardener and pool man, for overchlorinating. Her eyes blazed, her nostrils flared, her lip curled. "I am an *actress*. I can be any age or I can be ageless. I was born to play this part. I am Kali-Ra!" She thumped her chest and stuck out her chin in a way that always reminded Melanie of old newsreels of Mussolini posturing on his balcony.

Lila clasped her hands together and closed her eyes. "Yes! I see it now. You have the sacred power that some would call cruelty, but which Valerian learned from the Enlightened Ones was an essential part of the cosmic whole." Her eyes opened again, and Melanie noted the maniacal light in them just before the old lady, apparently overcome, tottered and fell backward, the result being that she reassumed her sitting position on the sofa.

"Wow," said Nadia, sitting down cozily next to her. "Tell me more about these Enlightened Ones."

"It may cost you," said Melanie. "Mrs. Ricardo wants twenty thousand a week as a consultant to the picture."

"We can work something out," said Nadia, giving Melanie a dismissive wave. She turned eagerly back to Lila. "Did these, like, Enlightened Ones sort of guide him? I feel I have Spirit Helpers from another plane who led me to the Kali-Ra books."

"Of course they did," said Lila. "Nothing happens by chance. It is all part of the twisted skein of fate. You and I, Miss Wentworth, were meant to meet and work together, so that the world might know the strange, alluring power of Kali-Ra and all she stands for. Valerian will assist us from beyond the veil."

"Well, if that's settled, there's some filing I should do," said Melanie, eager to get away from Lila's presence. She'd give a heads-up call to George, Nadia's business manager, and let him know that Nadia was once again being played for a sucker by some greedy leech, and this time she was swallowing the pitch whole.

CHAPTER V

AN UNEXPECTED LEGACY

The next time Nick went to Grandpa's apartment at Manderleigh Manor was a few days after the funeral. The old man had had one great big stroke. Nick's mother had said this was a blessing, as his last years had been so sad. The funeral had been very nice and seemed to cheer her up a lot. Some of Grandpa's old cronies from the lumberyard were there and told Nick and his mother how much everyone loved Bill and how he was always a solid guy who could estimate board feet to the inch with a mere flick of the eye. An old neighbor lady said that after her husband had died, Bill Johnson had mowed her lawn every Saturday during the summer for years.

Now Nick and his mother were going through Grandpa's things. It was pretty depressing folding up all his clothes and putting them in boxes to take to the Goodwill—the plaid shirts and work pants he used to wear to the lumberyard, and his old worn-out slippers.

"There's really not much, thank goodness," said his mother with a sigh. "We got rid of a ton when Mom died, and then more when he moved in here." She gazed over at the wall. There were two black-and-white framed photographs—a wedding portrait of Grandpa and Grandma and a picture of Nick's mother as a baby—and color pictures of Nick and his sister taken when they were two and eight. "I'd like that picture of Mom and Dad, and that's about it."

"Whatever you want," said Nick apologetically. Grandpa had astonished everyone by leaving everything to his grandson. The will had explained that Bill Johnson had taken care of his only daughter during his lifetime. This he had done by turning over his house to her in some weird scam Nick didn't understand so that Manderleigh Manor wouldn't get it all and Medicare would have to pay for more of Grandpa's nursing home or something. The will had also noted that Nick's older sister was doing well, which was true. Elizabeth was a dentist, married to another dentist.

At first, Nick felt embarrassed by his status as sole heir. After thinking about it for a while, however, the whole thing gave him a nice warm glow. Grandpa must have liked him, must have appreciated, in some way, his awkward visits. Unfortunately, it turned out Grandpa didn't really have much. Just the contents of the apartment here, a little cash, and a few municipal bonds that added up to seven thousand dollars. Seven thousand dollars didn't seen like a lot for a guy who had worked hard all his life. You couldn't buy a new car with that or anything. Nick hadn't decided what to do with it yet, although he was tempted to use it to travel to somewhere warm. With palm trees.

"What should we do with the furniture?" asked his mother with a sigh. "The Goodwill too, I guess. Although maybe that colonial stuff is coming back in style. Everything does eventually."

To Nick, the maple coffee table, the green sofa with the wooden arms and the flounce, the flowered chair with matching footstool, all had a certain charm associated with an era he imagined as safe and cozy—an era when parents didn't get divorced, when mothers wore aprons and were unharried instead of unmarried, and kindly dads were on hand to play catch in the backyard. It was an era Nick was sorry he had missed, experiencing it only vicariously in television reruns.

"I'll keep the furniture for now," he said. "I think it looks kind of homey."

Mom sighed. "I remember how much I hated it when they bought this stuff when I was in college," she said. "I wanted them to get a Parsons table and big cushions for the floor. I was such a pretentious little thing." She began to weep a little.

Nick put his arm around his mother, and she leaned her head on his shoulder. "It feels weird not to have parents anymore," she said. "Even at my age."

"I can imagine it does," said Nick, patting her shoulder and feeling helpless and inadequate, as he often did when she turned to him for emotional support. It was at times like this that he felt like calling Dad and yelling at him for ditching out and leaving Mom alone.

And where was Elizabeth? She should be here helping Mom. She claimed she couldn't afford to, because her time was so valuable and she and her husband had to keep about eight chairs going at once, just to pay the interest on their student loans. Nick, who had loved and admired his big sister when they were children, felt distant from her now. He reflected sadly that if there had been anything in Grandpa's estate worth squabbling over, Elizabeth and Dan would have dropped their drills and raced down here as fast as their silver Lexus could carry them.

Nick's mother sniffed bravely, wiped her eyes, stood up straight and looked around the little apartment. "I don't know how much of this I can take."

"Listen, Mom, we don't have to do all this now. Let's just

do one load now. Then I'll come back and get the rest later. We can go through it slowly. Okay?"

Nick's mother agreed. They loaded up as much as they could fit in the back of her old Volvo station wagon, including some mysterious boxes that had once held canning jars, and took everything over to Nick's basement apartment in St. Paul. Then Nick took his mom out for a pizza and a movie, which, with his employees' courtesy pass, cost him nothing.

It was the next day, while all by himself in his apartment, that Nick opened the canning jar boxes and found bundles of letters, all neatly folded in their envelopes. The first batch was from World War Two—letters his grandparents had exchanged while Grandpa was overseas. Nick read them with fascination. Here was this guy who could die at any moment, and a couple of people who were madly in love, at least they were engaged, but neither of them seemed to sense the drama of it all. "How's the prettiest girl in the world? I'm counting the days, honeybunch, 'til we can be together. Can't wait to sit on that porch and smooch. Say hi to your folks." "Dear Billy, We pooled all our butter coupons and made a couple of pies today. Mama's leg is better. I miss you too."

There were also letters his mother wrote home from college and his own misspelled crayoned missives and letters from camp. What Nick found most interesting, however, was the one letter from Uncle Sid.

Los Angeles, California
August 15, 1962

My dear nephew Bill,

Life's a queer thing. Who would ever have thought that I, Valerian Ricardo, once lionized by the masses and

the companion of dukes and duchesses, would have to
throw myself on the mercy of a stranger, a man I have
never met, but to whom I am connected through the
most sacred of human ties—that of blood? I can only
hope and pray that some remnant of family feeling still
exists.

Although I have never been fond of children, I remember your mother as a pleasant child. She must
have been about eight when I left Minnesota for good.
I don't know what your mother told you about her
uncle Sid. I'm afraid the family was never open-
minded. Anyway, I left, vowing never to return, and
led a life devoted to literature and the study of the Es-
oteric Secrets of Hidden Masters. I regret nothing and
believe my destiny was cast long before I entered this
earthly plane.

Unfortunately, while my astral life is very satisfac-
tory, materially speaking, I have never been as low as
I am now. I'm afraid, Bill, that your great-uncle is a
lonely old man, living alone with his memories, and
hounded by unfeeling creditors. The sad truth is that I
find myself in considerable (although temporary) fi-
nancial distress, and I would be very grateful if I could
borrow some money to tide me over. That an artist of
my stature should find himself in this position reflects
poorly on the kind of world ours has become. A few
thousand dollars should take care of my most pressing
obligations.

It seems to me that it isn't too much to ask, seeing
as under the present circumstances, you will inherit
the rights to all the Kali-Ra books after I have passed
over into the Beyond. I have no will, and you are my
only living relative. Frankly, the family was never very
kind to me, but I am willing to forgive and forget all
if I sense you have the kind of family feeling that will

move you to take some responsibility for my situation.

Ah, perhaps you are you sneering now. Perhaps you are saying, "The world has forgotten Valerian Ricardo! Those copyrights are worth nothing!" It is true that my work is out of print at the present time, but I believe with all my heart that the world will come back to its senses and appreciate truth and beauty once more.

Do you think you could see your way to wiring the funds? Time is of the essence.

Sincerely,
Valerian Ricardo (Uncle Sidney)

CHAPTER VI

ON THE SPOOR OF KALI-RA

The ad in the Yellow Pages for the House of Seven Genres Booke Nooke read "For the Discerning Connoisseur of Yesterday's Sensational Literature. Mystery. Science Fiction. Fantasy. Horror. Suspense. Adventure. Collectibles. Book Searches. Mail Order. We Buy Libraries. Ask about Our Cozy Mystery Tea Time Book Discussion Group. Subscribe to Our Thuvia, Maid of Mars Newsletter. Visit Our Gothic Cellar—If You Dare. Visa. MasterCard." The ad also included a website address and a 1-800 number.

When Nick telephoned, he was delighted to learn they had five Valerian Ricardo books for sale and what the nasal clerk of indeterminate sex referred to as "some other Kaliana. But you'd better hurry. There's going to be new interest in this area because of the Nadia Wentworth movie."

Nick hoped that the clerk wouldn't be erasing the old prices and penciling in new ones in the time it took him to find the store. The Booke Nooke was wedged between a Laundromat and a martial arts school in a drab strip mall in the suburbs.

Through dingy glass, Nick observed a jumbled window display. A listing nineteen-seventies department store dummy with sideburns and a white painted grin dressed in a Sherlock Holmes cape and deerstalker. A poster showing a pneumatic science-fiction babe in hubcap bra and chain metal

G-string crouching aggressively. Some curling old black-and-white movie stills, scattered at artistic angles. Plastic *Star Wars* live action figures.

Inside, behind the counter, there was a young, strapping female clerk who looked as if she could eighty-six five rowdy guys from a truck stop. She gave him a curt nod and continued reading a mystery called *Marcel Proust and the Missing Madeleine.*

The phone rang, and the clerk grabbed it. "Seven Genres." She listened for a moment, then said, "Hamsters and gerbils? No. Just cat and dog mysteries. Mostly cats," and hung up.

"Hi! I called about the Valerian Ricardo books and the Kaliana," said Nick. He had already decided to go ahead and splurge and buy everything they had. After all, he was Valerian Ricardo's great-grandnephew. Uncle Sid may have been a sleazebag, but he was a romantic figure, the only interesting relative Nick had ever come across. Uncle Sid had had the gumption to get out of Minnesota and run off to Europe and lead a glamorous life before hitting the skids in Los Angeles. He'd *lived.*

The clerk put down her own reading with an air of reluctance. "Here," she said, pushing a stack of books across the counter.

Eagerly, Nick opened the one on top. Opposite the crumbling yellow title page, *The Temple of Kali-Ra, A Tale of Evil and Intrigue by Valerian Ricardo, author of The Wrath of Kali-Ra, The Curse of Kali-Ra, The Sins of Kali-Ra, etc.,* was the following dedication:

> *To all who yearn for adventure, may the spirit of Kali-Ra*
> *take you far away from shop and farm, from provincial town*
> *and grim little village, and transport you to a realm where*
> *life is lived to the fullest and the feelings of pain and pleasure*
> *are keen, if only for a little while. V. R.*

He opened the novel somewhere in the middle and, noting the musty smell of the old pages, began to read:

"So, you stubborn Englishman, you try once more to foil my plans. Your foolish attempts are in vain as always." The woman was transforming before his horrified eyes. The mocking green eyes with their hypnotic light, the cruel, sensuous mouth twisted with twisted pleasure replacing the sweet, innocent face he'd barely noticed at the doorstep. Raymond Vernon felt the cold steel of the manacles cutting painfully into his manly wrists and ankles.

The trim little French maid with the demure lace cap who had let him into this house of horror had been yet another of her uncanny disguises! For he was looking once more into the face of the Queen of Doom—Kali-Ra!

"You!" he said. "Still up to your old tricks, I see. World domination! Well, you won't get away with it." But even as he said these bold words, doubt crept into his soul. Could she be stopped? But she must! It had to be done. All of civilization, everything that was good and decent and civilized hung in the balance.

Yet there was something about her cruel beauty that touched a darker place in Raymond Vernon's soul, a place tainted, he realized with a shudder, by this very creature, part woman, part goddess, complete fiend.

She laughed cruelly, a chilling but strangely exciting sound, like the pealing bells of some pagan temple. "Perhaps I shall keep you alive. For a while. For my amusement. Ah! I see you still bear the mark of the lash from our last encounter." She stepped forward and drew the tip of her finger across the scar on his temple, the scar that mocked, yet strangely excited him every time he looked in the glass and observed his clean-limbed Anglo-Saxon face.

Nick could see why Grandpa's mother had said the books were trashy. Whips. Manacles. Dungeons. It read like a low-rent *Story of O*. And the writing was incredibly bad. Could a face be clean-limbed? And should a mouth twist with twisted pleasure? The idea that Uncle Sid had alienated his stolid relatives by getting rich off this sleazy stuff amused him, and he smiled.

When he looked up, he saw that clerk was sneering at him and his apparent pleasure in the sadomasochistic text. "Valerian Ricardo is a specialized taste," she said.

"It's pretty crappy stuff, isn't it?" Nick said, with a little laugh that he hoped didn't sound as forced as it was. "Actually, Valerian Ricardo was a relative of mine, and I was curious about his work."

The clerk shrugged her beefy shoulders and said, "Whatever," adding with a hint of envy, "I guess you'll get some money from the movie, and they might reprint in paperback."

Nick had already investigated this possibility after finding Uncle Sid's begging letter to Grandpa. Unfortunately, in Uncle Sid's day, copyrights lasted twenty-eight years. His last book, *The Lash of Kali-Ra,* had been published in 1926, remaining in copyright until 1954. Uncle Sid could have extended the copyright. Judging from the letter, dated 1962, he had. But he could only renew for another twenty-eight years, or until 1982.

"They're out of copyright," said Nick as he checked out the other books in the stack. Four more moldy novels and a scholarly-looking modern work from some university press, called *The Whip Hand: Issues of Gender and Genre in the Work of Valerian Ricardo.* There was also a volume in a tattered dust jacket protected by a plastic library wrapper, called *My Life with Valerian Ricardo: The True Story of the Fabulous, Forgotten Genius and Master of Metaphysics Who Created the Sensational Kali-Ra, as told by his life's companion, Lila Lamb Ricardo.*

"That biography is from some vanity press," said the clerk with contempt. "The author sold it out of the back of her car at fan conventions."

Nick examined the Valerian Ricardo portrait on the cover, a sepia-toned studio shot of a dissipated-looking Uncle Sid.

The eyes were haunted, the mouth sensuous but weak. His hair was carefully oiled and slicked down and his long-fingered hand was wrapped around a smoldering cigarette. Actually, though, he also looked vaguely familiar. Nick had the same slightly cleft chin. On the back of the dust wrapper was an author photo of a glittery-eyed woman of about sixty with a white pageboy, high cheekbones, and too much makeup.

"I'll take them all," said Nick, removing his MasterCard from his wallet. He had decided for once in his life not to look at prices. He'd be getting his inheritance any day now, and had already planned to pay off his MasterCard balance then. This was fun.

The clerk had written down all the prices by hand on an old-fashioned receipt, and now she was running the card through the scanner in a put-upon way, eyeing the Marcel Proust mystery with longing. The phone rang. She sighed and answered it as the receipt inched its way out of the machine.

"Seven Genres." A pause. Her scowling face suddenly took on a beatific light. "Wow! Really?" she said. "The real Nadia Wentworth?"

Nick felt an exciting leap of his heart. The glow of celebrity emanated from the stack of his relative's books and now from the phone receiver in this grungy little store. Suddenly, it seemed, life could be glamorous.

"As a matter of fact, we do," the clerk was saying. She sounded, perhaps for the first time in her life, eager to please. "I have them right here!"

With a circular sweeping motion, she scooped away the books from where they sat in front of Nick and slid them to her side of the counter. "We've got five of the novels. *The Temple, The Blade, The Spear, The Gong,* and *The Lash of Kali-Ra.* No wrappers but all in good condition. *The Spear* is a first. London 1923. We also have a book of criticism, *The Whip Hand: Issues of Gender and Genre in the*

Work of Valerian Ricardo, and," here she lowered her voice dramatically, "a very rare, privately printed memoir with original dust jacket: *My Life with Valerian Ricardo* by Lila Lamb Ricardo, Long Beach 1978. Do you want them?"

"Hey!" said Nick, reaching for his purchases. The clerk kept her arm wrapped around them like a mother bear protecting its cub, and glared at him.

"I just bought those," he said.

"What? Oh, there's another customer here who's interested in the books," she said into the phone. "But I'll explain to him that Nadia Wentworth wants them."

Nick was usually a polite young man, slow to anger. Once in a while, however, when feeling pushed, he could be very adamant. "Tough!" he said. "My money's as good as hers." He grabbed the credit card receipt out of the machine, tore it off neatly, grabbed a pen from an Edgar Allan Poe coffee mug on the counter, and defiantly scrawled his signature at the bottom.

"You can't do that!" said the clerk, aghast.

"Here's the merchant copy," snarled Nick, peeling it away from his own yellow cardholder's copy and flinging it at her. Now he had to figure out how to separate her from the actual merchandise. She had leaned over the books on the counter, and they were hidden beneath her large bosom, the perimeter guarded by her muscular arm. If he touched her, especially her chest, which was the chief barrier between him and his property, he'd probably end up being booked for sexual assault.

He leaned in toward her and put his face close to hers. "Give me my books," he said.

Still clutching the phone, she wrapped her other arm around the books. "No way!"

He made a darting, open-handed gesture, meant to indicate she should give the books to him. "But I bought them!"

Her arm shot out in a quick jab toward his face, and he saw that her fist was closed. He grabbed her wrist and pushed her arm away.

"Oof," she said, dropping the receiver.

In her office at Nadia's home, Villa Vera, in Beverly Hills, Melanie had heard a muffled, angry male voice in the background and then became vaguely aware of what sounded like a scuffle going on at the other end of the line, followed by a clunky sound, as if the receiver had hit the counter. Was there some crime in progress? Should she hang up and call 9-1-1? She wasn't even sure what city she was calling. All she had was a 1-800 number.

"Hello! Hello!" she said, alarmed.

A slightly breathless male voice came on the line. "Listen, I just bought these books. The credit card receipt is signed. I own them. But the clerk here seems to think that because you're famous you get first dibs."

"I'm not famous," said Melanie. "I'm Miss Wentworth's personal assistant." Her efficient mind clacked away. The guy didn't sound stupid, and the fact that he'd signed the receipt sounded as if there might be some contractual thing going here that could lead to some nuisance lawsuit. That's all she needed. Another greedy hand held out.

She modulated her voice and tried to sound very sweet, the way she used to sound before she'd started working for Nadia. "But really, Miss Wentworth is very interested in anything about Valerian Ricardo. Maybe you'd be willing to sell them to her."

There was a pause. "Valerian Ricardo was a relative of mine," he said. "There's sentimental value there."

"I see," said Melanie, instantly wary of anyone who shared the blood of that creepy old hack. She glanced up at the wall where Nadia had insisted they hang an old photograph of Valerian Ricardo, bought from an antique store in Santa Monica. Every feature, except perhaps for the manly chin, spoke of perversion and debauchery. Melanie could well believe that such a creature could have produced the thinly disguised sadomasochistic, protofascist porn that made up the Kali-Ra series.

The guy on the other end of the line sounded apologetic now. "I mean, frankly, I think the books are probably not exactly great literature, no offense, but I've never read any of them, and I'm curious."

Melanie thawed. After constant exposure to Nadia and Lila Ricardo, who was a regular visitor to the house these days, it was refreshing to talk to someone who suspected that the books weren't masterpieces.

"Well, we already have that work of criticism," she said. "The author sent it to us. And I can probably find the novels somewhere else. But I'd sure like to take a look at the biography." Lila had never mentioned this work, which was uncharacteristic. Maybe she had something to hide.

"So would I," said Nick. "But maybe after I read all this stuff I could sell some of it to her. I can't promise anything, though."

"Listen," Melanie said, "I'll give you my phone number and you can let me know."

"Okay," said Nick.

"And give me yours, if you don't mind," she said, dangling a carrot in front of him. "Who knows? Maybe Nadia will want to invite you to the premiere, or even let you visit the set. Seeing as you're a relative of Valerian Ricardo and all. She might even want to meet you." In Melanie's experience, the hope of meeting a famous movie star got all kinds of people to roll over and grovel in the most disgusting way.

"Oh," he replied, and despite his nonchalant tone, she thought she detected excitement in his voice. "As a matter of fact, I'll be in L.A. on business next week. Maybe I can deliver any of the books she might want then."

CHAPTER VII

THE TREASURE OF KALI-RA

Quentin had always heard that in any encounter, the clothed had a psychological advantage over the naked. This presumably is why doctors forced patients into those skimpy robes that fell open at the back, then came in to the examining rooms wearing their own long white coats. It never worked this way with Maurice, though. Quentin, in his pale linen suit, felt small and weak and somehow over-dressed sitting here on Maurice's poolside terrace while a large black man in an English butler's uniform adjusted the large umbrella over the nearly nude Maurice.

Since coming to this Caribbean island nation thirty years ago, one step ahead of a criminal investigation and before his in absentia disbarment proceedings, Quentin's boss, Maurice Fender, had conducted all his business clad in a small black Speedo swimsuit, accessorized by a Rolex watch, a few gold chains, and a pair of Ray-Bans. It was a rather bold choice for a man with his three-hundred-pound-plus frame, most of it in the form of a huge, hairy stomach, with more Michelin-man rolls here and there.

"What have you got for me, Quentin?" he said wheezily from under the shadows of the umbrella. He'd taken to the shade after a melanoma scare a few years ago that had left his bald head dotted with brown spots.

"Nadia Wentworth. She's in preproduction on a big picture starring herself. It's a done deal. A lot of studio money, part of a three-picture deal she has with them. The work-ing title is *The Revenge of Kali-Ra*. Based on the series char-acter Kali-Ra, Queen of Doom, from the novels of Valerian Ricardo."

"Never heard of him," said Maurice.

"No one has. He died in the early seventies. The books are crap."

"So? We make a lot of money on crap. Do we own him?"

"Yep. Never made a nickel off him. He's just been lan-guishing in the files." Quentin ventured a smile of triumph. Maurice grunted.

"He was in the public domain for years," Quentin con-tinued. "But he's Uruguay. I've checked it out pretty thor-oughly. According to the files, his name came up a few years ago with some professor who wanted to quote a few lines in a scholarly work."

Maurice nodded thoughtfully, and sipped what looked like a gin and tonic. As usual, Quentin hadn't been offered anything. "And no one talked to us about this? Nadia Wentworth thinks it's out of copyright?"

"Apparently. Most people would assume that. Valerian Ricardo's books went out of copyright in 1982, but when the European Union changed its rules last year, British copyrights were extended to match longer German ones. Ricardo was an American but his books were all published in England first. So now he's back in copyright in England, and under the Uruguay treaty, where we acknowledge British copyrights, that puts him back in copyright here too. We can file with the Copyright Office right away and make it clear we own the rights."

"Let's not be hasty," said Maurice thoughtfully. "How did we get a hold of this guy? I don't recollect a guy named that."

"According to the records, we picked him up acciden-tally with a bunch of doo-wop artists from some little tax lawyer about twenty years ago. He was part of a package with Carla and the Cleartones and Little Bopping Bobby."

"Yeah. I remember that guy. His clients had big problems with the IRS and he took over their rights in lieu of legal fees after he'd represented them unsuccessfully, then sold them to me."

"What do you want me to do?" asked Quentin. He didn't want to prolong his stay. The reptilian Maurice loved the sun, but it was too damn hot out here for mammals. He longed to get back to his little air-conditioned office.

"I'm thinking," said Maurice.

Quentin gazed out over the manicured lawn fringed by palms. To his horror, he caught sight of a tall black man in a black suit and sunglasses lurking in the bushes and staring at them.

"Jesus, Maurice," he whispered hoarsely, reaching over and shaking Maurice's fat, hairy shoulder. He kept his eyes on the man, who now leapt out from behind the fronds, assumed a crouched, legs-apart stance, and reached into his suit and pulled out a large silver gun of some kind, which he was pointing at them.

"That's okay, it's just Mike," said Maurice offhandedly. He gestured to the man, who resumed a normal stance, replaced the gun, and strolled elegantly back into the shrubbery. "One of my bodyguards. He's a little overzealous. He worked for the last president of the republic here, and he's trained to leap into action if anyone lays a hand on whoever he's protecting. You shouldn't a touched me."

"Right. Okay," said Quentin, quickly withdrawing his hand, which he was horrified to discover was still clutching Maurice's shoulder. "Sorry, it kind of rattled me."

"Hey, it's a different way of life down here, but you get used to it," said Maurice. "Mike's a good guy. Machete Mike, they call him, but he handles a gun pretty good too."

Quentin's temples began to throb with one of his tension

headaches. He wanted to get out of here and back to the office. It was the only place on the island he felt safe. Lately, he'd actually found the rackety sound of the cockroaches being chopped up by the air-conditioning unit there rather soothing.

"I can go back to the office and file an NFI right away," he said. "That way we can make it very clear we own the rights."

"Don't do anything yet. Snoop around. See how it's shaping up. See what the traffic will bear. I'd rather hit them when they've already sunk some more money into the thing, maybe started principal photography," said Maurice. "That way, they'll figure what's another million for rights. Meanwhile, make sure there's no doubt we own this Ricardo guy and his Queen of Dread character."

"Doom. Queen of Doom. Kali-Ra, Queen of Doom."

"Go to L.A., hang out, find out what you can. Give me a full report on where the project stands, who the players are. Then stand by for the kill."

L.A.! Quentin's heart soared. He'd been trapped here for six whole months, ever since he took this horrible job in a spasm of desperation. He would call Margaret as soon as he landed! They'd walk hand in hand on the beach. He'd explain everything. Then his heart sank again. "Are you sure it's . . . safe?"

Maurice waved a pudgy hand in the air. "They haven't even indicted you. The case is probably rotting away somewhere in a drawer. But if you're really nervous, you can travel under another name."

"But my passport—"

"Jesus, what kind of an outfit do you think we're running here? I need you to go to L.A. Go to L.A. I'll get you a passport. A real one, from my pals at the Foreign Ministry."

"Okay," said Quentin nervously. At least it wouldn't be a fake American passport. Anyway, the risk was worth it.

He'd been so claustrophobic lately on this damn island. He suddenly had a whiff of the clean smell of Margaret's hair and remembered the light dappling of freckles on her nose with a surge of affection.

Maurice coughed raspily. "But don't mess up with that Doom thing. That little tax guy we got the rights from was a real scumbag. God knows how *he* got the rights. Anyone else who figures this Uruguay angle and pops up and gets greedy, like any relatives or whatever, make sure they meet their own personal doom. Buy 'em off, scare 'em off, whatever. I don't want to get tied up in litigation and see the whole project go down the toilet."

"Oh," said Quentin. "According to the correspondence we had back in 1990 with the guy who wanted to quote from the works, there was a widow. At that time, she had apparently been representing herself as the copyright owner. She was pretty aggressive about it."

Maurice nodded. "Find out if she's still alive. In that case, I'll send Machete Mike over to soften the old broad up. He might be getting bored just hanging around here in the yard."

"I'm sure that won't be necessary," said Quentin, horrified, the headache pain plunging deeper into his skull.

"I'll be the judge of that," said Maurice.

Quentin rose to go. "I'm looking forward to getting back to L.A.," he said, trying to end the meeting on a less sinister, more conversational tone.

"Good," said Maurice. "While you're there tell the whole goddamn town to fuck itself from me."

It was dark in Minneapolis, and Nick was sitting up in bed, telling himself to stop trying to read. He was clearly falling asleep. He'd read the same passage from *The Spear of Kali-Ra* about three times.

"I will always walk among you, often disguised as the humblest of serving girls, but in truth my power is constant and my slaves numerous and ever loyal. And even you, Raymond Vernon, you who mock me and pretend to think I can be stopped, you are truly one of my slaves as well."

Her eyes shone with a strange amber light. He had just about worked the knot loose. He knew he must make haste as her voice, with its strange, hypnotic powers, was beginning to lull him into a queer state of mind. God! It must have been that voice that had been the end of poor Carruthers.

A moment later, his efforts were rewarded and he had unbound himself. He leapt to his feet, seized her by her smooth golden shoulders, and cast her rudely aside as he prepared to flee, taking only a moment to admire her crumpled form on the stone floor. She looked more beautiful than ever when she was defeated, her hair disarranged, her diaphanous garments slipping from her fabulous form, her color high and her eyes flashing. For a moment an ignoble thought crept into his crazed mind. There was one way to know whether she was truly a goddess or if she was a real woman of flesh and blood, and she was helpless to prevent it here in this remote cave far from her slaves.

But a better part of him came to the fore and he realized his duty was to escape and warn the others of the awful plot he had discovered and which she had revealed to him when he was bound up, never realizing he would be able to escape her cruel clutches as he had so many times before. As he ran out into the dark desert night, he heard her cry after him: "I will still walk this earth long after you are gone, Raymond Vernon."

Finally, Nick managed to drop the book on his bedside table and turn out the light. As he lay in the dark, half dreaming about Kali-Ra, he realized that Uncle Sid's books were eerily addicting. He was on his third one in a row, and he told himself he should stop. He'd better quit while he was ahead, he thought groggily, or he might start thinking they were real.

In a time zone farther west, the long-limbed, golden-skinned young woman stood at the edge of the Pacific Ocean, staring out at the setting sun, now reduced to little more than a golden streak on the horizon.

A queer light came into her green eyes, and ocean breezes lifted her long dark hair, giving her the alarming appearance of some ancient sorceress, or perhaps even a goddess. She wore a white, filmy garment tied around her hips, which she had knotted in such a fashion as to allow herself to bathe her feet in the cool water.

She stared dreamily down at the lapping wavelets and made an impression of her small, neat foot in the firm, wet sand, only to watch the water surge back and make the sand smooth again.

In a low, husky tone, she murmured, "The vanishing footprint of Kali-Ra," and then laughed a strange, thrilling laugh. "Yes, I shall succeed, I know I shall. The treasure will be mine, all mine, and I will have riches and power as is only fitting for the one and only Kali-Ra."

She turned and ran up the beach, unknotting and smoothing her garment as she reached the wooden steps of the low bungalow. She sat on the first step and brushed the sand from her feet, then slipped on the pair of sandals she had left there. *I must go to the places where I feel the emanations. I must will myself through time to learn the truth and bring it to the world,* she thought.

Her reflections were interrupted by a voice from the top of the stairs. "Are you still on break? We're totally jammed."

"Sorry," she replied. "My feet were killing me."

A moment later she had entered the building and stood before a table carrying a sheaf of leather-bound menus. "Hi," she said. "I'm your server, Callie, and I'd like to tell you about some of our specials today." She flashed a broad smile and began explaining how the Chilean sea bass was flame-broiled and basted with a lemongrass-based reduction on a bed of pureed parsnips topped with fresh ginger and zucchini chutney with chili peppers. As she went on by rote to recite the other choices, her inner voice carried on with heady thoughts of its own. *Be patient, my slaves! Soon the gong will strike and you will come forth to serve me, your cruel but powerful mistress, she whom it is a joy to serve, the Queen of Doom!*

In a lonely rooming house in another part of the metropolis, a slave of Kali-Ra lay on a narrow bed, consumed with longing. It has been years, thought this wretch, gazing up at the naked lightbulb and the cracked plaster ceiling. I have waited so long to hear the sacred gong. But surely my mistress knows I await her summons. I must not lose my faith. Sighing, blinking back tears, the pathetic figure rose and went to the closet to admire the things that had been prepared for so long and that never failed to produce an exciting shiver. The coils of stout rope and lengths of fine chain from Home Depot, the yellow silken garment in which to appear at the holiest ceremonies in the Temple of the Chosen, and most thrilling of all, the sacred dagger, encrusted with jewels, little more than a narrow spike, but strong enough to penetrate armor and sharp enough to inflict a fatal wound in the blink of an eye. Like the Queen of Doom herself, this weapon was as deadly as it was beautiful. How wonderful it would be to wield it in the service of the one whom it was a joy to serve. Surely this day would come soon! The idea of this dagger doing its work, being pushed into human flesh, was intoxicating.

CHAPTER VIII

THE SLAVE OF KALI-RA

Melanie sat in her office going through the mail. First, she opened this week's packet of clippings from the service. Nadia had them delivered here to the house, on the assumption that her publicist, Karen, was dishonest and would destroy anything negative.

There were some local newspaper stories about Nadia's attendance at an adult literacy benefit and the pale green Armani she'd worn to it. There was also an article on Beauty Tips of the Stars in a downmarket women's mag that said Nadia made her own skin-care products out of things from the fridge for just pennies, a homey little fancy dreamed up by Karen and approved by Nadia. There was also, Melanie noted with horror, a tabloid story with a picture of Nadia biting her knuckles while wearing a black negligee. It was a still from the infamous weed-whacker scene in Nadia's very first movie, the low-budget cult classic *Terrorized Three: The Slaughter Continues.* The tabloid headline read "Sad Saga of Sexually Frustrated Beauty. Desperately Lonely, Nadia Wentworth Tries and Fails to Seduce Pool Man."

Oh, hell, thought Melanie, reading on. "Screen legend Nadia Wentworth may be every man's dream date, but the sad fact is the sultry star hasn't had a real date in six months. Hot and bothered, the negligee-clad beauty burst into the servants' quarters and tried to climb in bed with her startled young pool man. Engaged to his childhood sweetheart, he failed to give in to her hysterical demands for sex."

This was not good. In fact, Melanie could hardly think of anything worse. It would have been better if they'd said the pool man had been unable to resist and would now die happy.

Sighing, she telephoned Karen. "Did you see the same tabloid story I saw?" she asked.

"Those bastards never called me for a comment or anything," said Karen. "There's no way in hell I could have known. Am I fired again?"

"Yeah. I'll call you when you're not."

"Okay. Meanwhile, I'll make some calls and see where this came from."

"I'd be pretty surprised if it came from Manuel. His English isn't good enough and he's smart enough to know he'd be fired. In fact, I think I will fire him for a while too. Talk to you soon, Karen."

Sighing again, she hung up and opened another letter. It was written on an old-fashioned typewriter with a carbon ribbon. It began primly enough, *Dear Miss Wentworth,* but then quickly escalated to full rant. *You dare to portray Kali-Ra—she whose very name is too precious to be uttered by mere mortals in any tones but those of adulation and worship! When you speak her name, you must tremble. Kali-Ra, the beloved, the powerful, has seen your performance on the Sandy Shipley Show, and is displeased. Her willing slaves will reach out and smite any such as you who have the arrogance to think they can imitate her! Stop now, you foolish woman, or prepare to suffer such exquisite tortures as only the Queen of Doom can invent.*

At the bottom of the letter was a drawing of an Egyptian scarab, presumably the same one tattooed on the left breast of Kali-Ra and all her slaves, and some strange writing that

Melanie guessed was probably an example of what Valerian Ricardo referred to as *those ancient symbols, words from a tongue that goes back to the mists of time and has been kept alive only by the initiates of Kali-Ra*. To reveal its secrets would, needless to say, result in lingering death by unspeakable torture.

Melanie smiled. It was hard to be terrified by a displeased Kali-Ra when you were informed at the same time that the Queen of Doom watched daytime TV. Melanie imagined Kali-Ra taking in the *Sandy Shipley Show,* putting her tired feet up on an ottoman and sipping a Diet Coke, perhaps in some Orange County home for retired arch villainesses. In Melanie's vision, Kali-Ra's once beautiful but now haggard face was heavily made up with rouge circles and circumflexed eyebrows, there was an artless dye job on her thinning hair, and she had become one of Southern California's large contingent of old gals who tarted themselves up well into their eighties so that they looked like retired prostitutes instead of dignified old ladies.

But then Melanie remembered that according to Raymond Vernon, Kali-Ra possessed the secret of eternal youth. She had been running her sordid operation for centuries, never quite managing to take over the world completely. Through it all, her skin had remained perfect, "a luminous, creamy alabaster"; her lips were "soft and red and curved into a smile both cruel and full of promise"; and her hair was "abundant, fine, and black as a raven's wing."

Melanie knew all this because she had been asked to make a file of all the physical descriptions of Kali-Ra so Nadia could work out a look for the character. Nadia was particularly fond of the passage where it was explained that Kali-Ra *had the freshness of youth and the slim and supple body of a young girl, with the carriage of a goddess who was also a woman. It was only in her remarkable eyes, eyes which seemed to change color with her every mood, radiating simultaneous passion and wisdom, that one could see she was ageless, that she had seen more pleasure and more pain than anyone else alive on earth.*

"See!" Nadia had said. "You were trying to say Valerian Ricardo was a shitty writer, but he had it figured out all along. The eyes change. Kind of like the screen saver on your computer."

Until stumbling across the passage from *The Punishment of Kali-Ra* describing the mutable eyes, Melanie had taken satisfaction in pointing out that Valerian Ricardo had never managed to get his character's eye color consistent. Sometimes Kali-Ra's eyes shone with a cruel green light. At others they exhibited an inky darkness like a bottomless pool of evil. Once they had flashed with the coldness of sapphires, and several times they were described offhandedly as *an unusual color, as violet as an amethyst or the dawn.* Old Valerian had probably come up with that lame story about her eyes changing in response to complaints from irate readers.

Melanie wished that her job had not made it necessary for her to become an expert on Kali-Ra. She wished she had never dragged the damn book upstairs back at the Hotel Splendide on Boola Lau. Why couldn't there have been some Dickens or Trollope or something in the lobby?

Nadia padded into the office in bare feet. This morning, she looked nothing like Kali-Ra. She wore tights and a sports bra, her face wasn't made up and it seemed a little blotchy, and her hair was pulled back from her face and scraped into a frizzy ponytail on top of her head.

She was carrying her morning postworkout mango flip in one hand and a spray bottle of mineral water for continuous skin hydration in the other. The tightness in her features softened momentarily, as Nadia glanced fondly up at the portrait of Valerian Ricardo.

Melanie followed her glance and tried not to shudder. "We got a letter from one of the followers of Kali-Ra," she said.

"Really?" said Nadia, clearly interested, setting down the mango flip. "Let's see." She snatched the letter and began to read. Melanie watched her silently moving lips.

"Wow," said Nadia. She pointed at the writing beneath the drawing of the scarab. "I wonder what these letters mean."

"It's supposed to be in that weird language . . ." Melanie began patiently.

"I know. The one only Kali-Ra and her followers speak," said Nadia solemnly.

"It's a made-up language," said Melanie, feeling just a little snappish. "It doesn't mean anything."

"How do you know that?" demanded Nadia.

Melanie sighed. "Even in the books Raymond Vernon says scholars from all over the world couldn't crack it."

"Yes," quoted Nadia dreamily. *"Wise men from all over the world, the finest scholars, men of genius, all were baffled yet strangely intrigued by this language like no other, but those few who had heard it spoken remarked on its queer, hypnotic power to thrill."*

She looked back at the drawing. "But maybe there's someone who can translate it," she said.

Melanie heard her voice rising and forced it back down to a normal register. "It's all made up! Valerian Ricardo made all this Kali-Ra stuff up, for God's sake!" She stopped herself from adding that Nadia sounded just like the nut who wrote the letter.

"People can speak Klingon, can't they?" said Nadia triumphantly. "They have Klingon dictionaries at Barnes and Noble and everything. If people can speak Klingon, a language of the future, why can't they speak the language of the Ancient Ones?" With a victorious air, Nadia flung the letter back at Melanie, then slouched out of the room. "When my aromatherapist arrives, send him to the cabaña," she said over her shoulder.

"All right," said Melanie, glancing back down at the letter. That reference to "exquisite tortures" made it clear they were dealing with a hard-core Valerian Ricardo fan. It also made Melanie uneasy enough to put the letter right into the stalker file. It would be forwarded to Tom Thorndyke, the security expert who was paid a retainer to protect Nadia from various drooling psychopaths, incarcerated killers, demented suitors, people who thought she was their long-lost daughter, and an old classmate who kept insisting, more and more forcefully, with unkind references to her reputation in high school, that she invest in his ostrich ranch.

Melanie returned her attention to the more pressing tabloid story. With the aid of a dictionary, she drafted a memo to Manuel in her strange, self-taught Spanish, based in part on the Latin she had studied. "I know you are upset with the way Miss Wentworth has been angry with you a lot," she said. "She is sorry and wants to send you on a vacation back home to visit your family. Please accept her apologies and this check for the airplane ticket. Don't thank her in person in case she changes her mind. We know how unpredictable she can be."

To the clipping itself, she attached a Post-it note that said: "Nadia: Look at this trash! I got a hold of Karen and Manuel and fired both their asses immediately."

Then, sighing, she reread the latest fax from the production manager in Costa Rica. "When do we get a final script? Is the handmaidens' bedchamber set in or out? What about the torture of the tiny chains? The chains have to ship by next week at the latest. And what do we tell the tarantula wrangler? He's getting unpleasant."

CHAPTER IX

AN INVESTIGATION BEGINS

A week later, Duncan Blaine, a lean, tanned, and ravaged-looking Englishman of forty-two who appeared much older, sat in his black convertible Jeep in Nadia's circular driveway. He reached into the glove compartment, removed a bottle of Stolichnaya vodka and a Styrofoam cup, and poured himself a stiff one. He was having another script meeting with Nadia Wentworth.

He would have preferred gin or whiskey, but Nadia was one of these American health fascists. If she caught a whiff of booze on his breath at ten in the morning, she would not only fire him but probably also follow up with a court order forcing him to check into the Betty Ford Clinic against his will. It had to be scentless vodka. One had to adapt to the customs of the country.

Melanie Oakley let him in. "I liked the last draft a lot," she said over her shoulder in her usual rushed sort of way as she led him through the dimly lit hall toward the terrace. "Very lively and fun."

This was good news. Duncan hoped Nadia felt the same way. But Melanie continued ominously, "I think Nadia may take the material a little more *seriously* than I do." She stopped for a moment, put her hand on his arm, and giving him a level gray-eyed gaze, said, "The trick is in the pitch. You've got to pretend you don't know the stuff is crap. She'll miss most of the irony you get into the script. We've got to get a final script as soon as possible."

Duncan replied with a noncommittal "Mm."

"I think you'll also find," Melanie continued, "that Lila Ricardo is still very much involved." As he emerged through the French doors from the living room he saw that both Nadia and the ghastly Lila creature were waiting for him on the brick terrace by the lily pond with its gurgling fountain of fat dolphins. The two women were eyeing him like a pair of carnivorous birds, ready to peck at his flesh and gnaw on his bones. He sat down in one of the hideously uncomfortable cast-iron lawn chairs, and gave them both a big smile.

Back in her office, Melanie sighed. At least she'd warned him. Poor Duncan. It was a pretty good script. But how long could it stay that way?

Taking advantage of the fact that Nadia was in conference and wouldn't be bursting in, she called Tom Thorndyke and asked him for an update.

He sounded more serious than usual. "First of all, this Kali-Ra thing seems to have set off a real wacko who's been obsessed with the character for years. This is a potentially dangerous situation."

After the first threatening letter with its scarab symbol, Nadia had received three more. All were written in florid Valerian Ricardo style and suggested that various punishments should be meted out to anyone connected with the picture, especially Nadia.

"I'm concerned for two reasons," he went on. "The frequency of the letters and the fact that they're mailed from Los Angeles right to the house.

"This individual is obviously following things closely. They seem to be reading the trades. They know about casting, script rewrites, location scouting. This indicates a

pretty deep obsession that may be moving from Kali-Ra to
Nadia.

"And finally, there's a quality to the letters that goes beyond just that. In this business you sometimes hear bells
ring and you're not sure why."

Melanie nodded. "I know. I've been freaked out myself
by the intensity of the writing. This nut believes Kali-Ra is
for real."

"I was kind of hoping you could give me some background. I want to come up with a profile. I need to be able
to think the way this individual thinks, and it seems clear
to me that all they think about is Kali-Ra. Know anything
about it?"

Melanie sighed. "I'm afraid so. Nadia had me research
every aspect of the character. I've read about twenty of the
novels. It's driving me crazy, to be honest."

Tom cleared his throat. "I kind of figured from the letters
that the books are way out there."

"No kidding," said Melanie, rolling her eyes. "Kali-Ra is
some kind of cruel dominatrix with a lot of slaves. The
books keep talking about the beauty of evil, and there's a
strong sadistic erotic element."

"I guess your boss is no fool. With material like that she'll
probably make millions."

"To tell you the truth, she *is* kind of a fool," said Melanie,
who appreciated the fact that the success of Tom's business
relied on his complete discretion and he would never repeat
anything she said about Nadia or sell any dirt to the media.
"I mean," she went on, "she's bought into the whole thing
herself, just like the fruitcake who's writing these letters."

"Nothing would surprise me. I work with a lot of these
creative-type people."

Tom was always so reassuring. Melanie promised to
FedEx him a few of the books.

"Great," he said. "And is there any organized Kali-Ra fan

club or anything? Maybe they'd know about someone who's just a little too far into the whole thing."

"Valerian Ricardo has been mercifully forgotten for years. But there is a website with a chat room, www.kali.com."

"I'll check it out. I also talked to that professor you told me about, Dr. Pendergast. He says that when his book came out he had some weird letters from someone who sounds just like our guy. He didn't keep them. He thinks they came from Moose Jaw, or it might have been Saskatoon, Saskatchewan. Apparently, they petered out. But stalking a college professor isn't nearly as much fun for these kinds of folks as going after a movie star. I'm recommending increased security for Nadia. How would she feel about having a guy on the premises?"

Melanie sighed. "You know how she is. No problem spending thousands on that old fraud Lila Ricardo, but if it's anyone else's idea, she thinks we're trying to bleed her to death."

"Well, it's your call," said Tom. "But you're paying for my advice."

"Oh! I know how to do this without bothering Nadia," said Melanie. "We can get him to replace Manuel, the pool guy. He's on a little vacation. Manuel doesn't live in, but your guy can have the apartment over the carriage house. He has to mow the lawn and supervise the other gardeners who come by twice a week and keep the pool clean, though."

"No problem," said Tom. "I've got a real sharp young guy. Former Navy SEAL. Completely trained. Putting himself through graduate school working for me. I'll have Kevin over there in a day or two."

"Great," said Melanie, who found herself wondering what this Kevin was like, and what kind of degree he was pursuing. In the three years since she'd come to Hollywood to work twenty-four hours a day for Nadia, she hadn't met any guys outside show business. Even Tom Thorndyke,

who seemed reasonably down-to-earth, had capped teeth
and a hundred-dollar haircut, and was rumored to sleep
with a lot of the gorgeous actresses he protected.

Melanie lowered her voice conspiratorially. "And what
about that other thing? What have you found out about
Lila?" Because Melanie felt that Lila was a menace, both fi-
nancially and as far as the script went, she'd asked Tom
Thorndyke to do a background check on her. The last
straw had been a few days ago, when Nadia had suggested
Lila move into the guest cottage because "she's really cru-
cial at this stage, creatively speaking." The last denizen of
the guest cottage, a nasty piece of Eurotrash named Guido,
who had staked out a claim as Nadia's fencing coach when
she was considering a lady pirate script, had managed to
live rent free for more than a year.

"It's done," said Tom. "I'll fax it over to you."

"Is she Valerian Ricardo's widow for sure? I mean we
only have her word for it. She could be anybody."

"I haven't come across any record of a marriage, but it's
clear she's who she says she is. They lived together as man
and wife. Professor Pendergast told me she knows all about
Valerian Ricardo and he has no reason to doubt she's gen-
uine."

Melanie was disappointed, but read Tom's report carefully when it came through on the fax machine a few minutes later. Maybe there was something in here she could
use to discredit Lila in Nadia's eyes.

*Lila Ricardo a.k.a. Lila Lamb a.k.a. Ethel Mae Lasenby.
Lila Lamb is a stage name. Born in Rumford, Maine, circa
1915, where her parents ran a dry goods store.*

*LR apparently arrived in Hollywood in 1937. Member of
Screen Extras Guild, and later Screen Actors Guild. SAG
records indicate that Lila Lamb had two credited parts in B
movies: hatcheck girl in* The Lady Cracks Wise *Twentieth*

*Century Fox, 1939, and a jitterbugging switchboard opera-
tor in* Victory Canteen *RKO, 1942.*

*According to Dr. Glen Pendergast of Montana's Badlands
State College, and the author of a book about Valerian Ricardo, LR says she met VR in 1942 when he was a writer at
RKO and they married. They moved into the penthouse of
the Scheherazade Apartments in 1944.*

*VR's career fell flat after the war and the couple had fi-
nancial and legal problems. In 1948, he was arrested in a
raid on a printing company that was publishing porno-
graphic novels. He was apparently there to pick up a check
for a work entitled* Naughty Spanking Nuns Confidential,
*but beat the rap when he offered to testify for the prosecu-
tion against his editor. He was also charged, very briefly in
1952, with statutory rape in a case involving a teenage girl
living in his building, but the victim recanted and the
charges were dropped. The Ricardos had tax problems in
the sixties, which dragged on for years, and Lila set herself
up as an elocution teacher.*

*Economically pressed, they moved from the penthouse
into a series of smaller units lower down in the building,
ending up in the caretaker's apartment in the basement.*

*In 1972, VR was found dead of a heart attack in the
boiler room of the Scheherazade. There were a few small
obituary notices, noting the fact that VR was once a best-
selling author, and alluding to mysterious mechanical
equipment of unknown purpose, in which Ricardo's partially nude body was found entangled.*

*Because tenants at the Scheherazade had complained
about juvenile drug use in the boiler room, there was a brief
police investigation into the case. According to the detective
in charge, now retired and living in Oregon, Valerian's
body had been found by a tenant who had come to complain about the malfunctioning heating in the building.*

Ricardo was tied up to some sort of bondage apparatus of

his own design and manufacture. Lila told the police her husband regularly insisted she tie him onto this framework, make small adjustments with a series of cranks and read passages of his works to him, although occasionally he simply asked her to come back in half an hour or so and release him.

Recently, she said, he's been hanging out with a bunch of hippies who'd been providing him with hashish, opium, and cocaine, drugs he had used previously during the years right after World War One. Lila wanted these youths to be held accountable for his death, and produced some hashish they had left behind.

It was the detective's opinion that the heart attack could well have been brought on by a coke binge, but it would have been difficult to make a case against Ricardo's juvenile associates.

"I told her to forget about it," he said. "She was a respectable woman in her late fifties or early sixties, and she'd suffered enough with that husband of hers. He got what was coming to him, many years too late, in my opinion, and there wasn't any point in exposing the poor old gal to a lot of ugly publicity."

Lila moved to West Hollywood soon after Valerian's death, and found work as a manicurist at a department store hair salon. She appears to be living on social security and a small pension.

According to Glen Pendergast, she has litigious tendencies and in 1992 made many attempts to extort money from him on the basis that she owned rights to VR's works. She threatened him with legal action and demanded the right to edit his book. Pendergast expressed concern about her sanity, telling the interviewer, "That crazy woman is one of the scariest people I know."

CHAPTER X

THE VISION OF KALI-RA

The last line gave Melanie an idea. Maybe the professor's presence around here could undercut Lila's influence. She'd pitch it to Nadia that the guy was a great intellectual with terrific insight into the work of Valerian Ricardo, and suggest they hire him as a consultant. Maybe he could stop Lila from ruining Duncan's script.

Nadia would probably buy it, and Dr. Pendergast would too, if his gushy inscription was any indication. She took his book down from the shelf and read a passage at random.

> Even stylized phallic symbols such as the Sacred Dagger and the Pillar of Pain can thus be reappropriated ("re-gendered") by Eternal Woman defined, unlike Goethe's *Ewig-Weibliche*, not despite but through her sex(d)uality. In Kali-Ra, the vagina dentata becomes a textual black hole creating a parallel "she-male" universe in which pain/pleasure, power/humiliation, good/evil are fused in post-Manichaean bliss (cf. Lacan, op. cit.).

It was, Melanie thought, pretentious bullshit, but a lot classier than the stuff Lila was dishing out. She would definitely try to get the professor on board. It shouldn't be too difficult. Judging by his agitated prose, Dr. Pendergast hadn't had a date in some time.

Out by the pool, Duncan Blaine clutched his lemon-papaya spritzer, feeling badly in need of something more stimulating. The old girl was banging on about Kali-Ra's moonlight soliloquy to the bound and gagged Raymond Vernon, which she felt needed beefing up. "In short, I'm sorry to say that you don't seem to grasp the depths behind all this," she said.

He suppressed the urge to say depths couldn't be grasped, and weren't behind anything, while she fished around in what looked like a knitting bag and came up with some sheets of lined notebook paper covered with crabbed, penciled writing. "I've put together a few of my own thoughts, with more emphasis on the metaphysics. This is where we can deliver Valerian's insights from the Enlightened Ones to the common people. But it takes time. It's not something you want to rush through."

He put down his glass and scanned the pages, pretending to skim, although he couldn't have deciphered her scrawls even if he had chosen to. The lines seemed to run into each other at odd angles.

"Hmm," he said with fake reluctance. "I don't know. This looks pretty long. We can't stop the action for five minutes while Kali-Ra gives us some kind of occult sermon."

Nadia chimed in. "Maybe it could be really dramatic. Get in closer and closer on me until you see just my eyes. And then they can change color, like a mood-ring thing."

"Yes, yes," said Lila enthusiastically. "Nadia, darling, a moving soliloquy with the wisdom of the Enlightened Ones as its subject! It's your chance to show the world what a powerful actress you are."

"Well, we're still running pretty long," said Duncan. It had been his idea to cut this scene by half through the simple expedient of literally gagging Raymond Vernon, and tying him up too, of course, then reducing his lines to a few muffled groans. But then Nadia had wanted to shoehorn in about a million temple rituals in which her followers lay prostrate before her in dumpy robes her while she pranced around modeling kinky goddess gear.

"I've been thinking about running-time issues," said Nadia. "I think we should cut the virgin handmaidens."

"Cut the priestesses of Kali-Ra?" said Lila, aghast. "That's like making a movie about Jesus without the apostles."

"I kind of like what we've got going with the handmaidens," said Duncan. "A little postmodern referential thing that goes back to the Goldwyn Girls." He appealed to Nadia. "The critics will realize how sophisticated and witty it is." Duncan also thought the virgin handmaidens cavorting around their living quarters at the temple together, handled properly, could work on another level. The way he'd written it, it was pretty saucy stuff. His take had been to interpret the label "virgin" only in its heterosexual sense.

"This project is not about exploiting female sexuality," said Nadia with a pout. "A bunch of bimbos' tits take away from the central focus."

Yeah, thought Duncan. Which is *your* tits. He cleared his throat and decided it was time to try to get back out to the glove box-cum-drinks cabinet. "Listen, you ladies have given me a lot to mull over. What I want to do now is get back to the hotel and have a really good drink. Er, think." He flapped the notebook pages. "And of course go over Lila's notes."

"They're not *notes*," said Lila huffily. "I've written the whole scene. Or actually, Valerian did. He guided my hand while I was in a trance state."

"Wow," said Nadia her eyes widening. "Maybe we should give him a writer's credit."

"What?" Duncan felt himself losing it. "You want me to share credit with a dead man?"

"Dead is a relative term," said Lila.

"Not to the Writers Guild," snapped Duncan.

Lila's eyes took on a glassy opacity. "Valerian is speaking to me now, Duncan," she said in a husky voice. "You're not a very evolved entity. And he's worried about your spiritual emanations. You may be blocked."

"We can't have anything like that," said Nadia. "We're shooting next month, for God's sake. Duncan, you better move in here and we'll put in twenty-hour days or whatever it takes until we get it right."

"All right," said Duncan, making a mental note to clear out the minibar, stash all those little bottles in his luggage and bill it to the picture before he checked out, and then stop by the liquor store as well to make sure he was adequately supplied. He rose to go but Nadia stopped him. "Stay right here. I'll have Melanie or someone drive down there and get your stuff."

CHAPTER XI

"Margaret? Is that really you? God, I'm so glad you took my call."

Quentin Smith lay on his hotel room bed, stared at the sprinkler heads on the ceiling, and reveled in the sound of her voice.

"Morbid curiosity, I guess," she said bitterly.

"I'm really glad you did."

"I think I wanted a chance to tell you just what a jerk you are."

"I know I'm a jerk," he said.

She sighed. "I wrote you a bunch of letters telling you in precise terms just what a jerk you are, but I never sent them."

"I wish you had. Any letter from you, no matter how abusive, would have comforted me in my horrible exile." This would have been easier in person. He could have showed contrition through body language and with a spaniel-eyed look.

She continued with her narrative. Quentin had the feeling she might have rehearsed it. "At first I didn't send those letters because I thought they made me sound hysterical and unattractive," she said.

"Oh, Margaret," he said tenderly.

"Later I didn't send them because I didn't care what you thought anyway," she snapped.

He produced a doglike whimper.

"So," she said briskly, changing key, "just what brings you to town?" Apparently, the personal part of the conversation was over.

"Um, a little research. About a Nadia Wentworth project. Your firm did some business with her a while back, didn't they?" he asked.

"That's right. I wasn't involved, but Lou was. Remember him? He handled it and he started doing painkillers and had to go into rehab and his marriage broke up. Nadia Wentworth has an ego the size of an aircraft carrier and she's about as maneuverable."

This didn't sound good.

"She's also very stupid," Margaret added thoughtfully.

"Really?" This sounded better.

"The word is, ever since some disastrous experiences early in her career, Nadia Wentworth has displayed a reckless disregard for the advice of her attorneys and her business manager. She wants to handle everything herself."

"I see."

"So far, it seems to have worked. A few years ago, she hired a young personal assistant, Melanie Oakley, who seemed to have arrived in town off the bus from college. Rumor is her last job was pulling lattes at a Starbucks somewhere, but now she handles Nadia's entire career and her production company, and she seems to be doing a fantastic job."

"Interesting."

"Well," Margaret said curtly. "We've talked business. Is that why you wanted to see me? To pick my brain?"

This wasn't going well. In a huge spasm of helplessness, Quentin decided to blurt out the whole truth. If she wasn't moved, at least she'd be disarmed. "Margaret, I wanted to see you because you're the only woman I have ever loved and could ever love. I want to spend the rest of my life with you. Go ahead. Laugh."

After a little pause, she did laugh, then said calmly, "You

should have written that on the postcard you sent me, instead of that glib invitation for me to throw away my chance at a partnership, give away the cat, sell my condo and come join you on some Club Med–type island."

"It was a very confusing time," he said.

"You got that right," she said, sounding hard and cold and proud of herself because of it. "So how *are* things in your tropical paradise?"

"I hate islands," he replied with a shudder. "I feel like a prisoner."

"I take it you're still working for that scumbag who makes Sammy Glick look like Mahatma Gandhi."

"I'm afraid so."

"I'm sure you're learning a lot."

"I'm learning my lesson," he said. "I'm learning how much I had to lose. I'm learning what it feels like to turn into someone you don't like very much, doing things that you wouldn't want your mother to know about."

"Quentin, for God's sake. You talk as if you have no choice! Quit. Come home."

"I can't," he said.

"You didn't seem to have much trouble quitting your old job, packing your bags, and leaving town six months ago."

"I might have had more trouble if I'd stayed," he said.

"What? What kind of trouble?" She sounded concerned now.

"Legal trouble."

"Quentin! Is it the McCorkindale matter?" He winced. How he wished he'd never heard the name McCorkindale. "I always wondered if you were in that deeper than you let on!" She sounded shocked.

"I filed this document with the Securities and Exchange Commission that—" he began.

"Stop! Don't tell me!" she said.

"But I *want* to tell you! Oh, Margaret, marry me. If you marry me, you can't testify against me."

"Ha! Now *that's* a real winning proposal."

"I know I sound crazy," he said urgently.

"I've got to go," she said.

"What? Can't we at least have dinner?"

"No. Anyway, I have a date. That's why I have to go."

"Who is this guy?" Quentin felt helpless and angry. "Someone from your firm?"

"No. He's a lawyer, but not an entertainment lawyer. I've sworn off sleazebags. Actually, he's a federal prosecutor."

Quentin's head started pounding and he put a trembling hand on his forehead.

"Don't worry," she said sweetly. "I won't mention the McCorkindale matter."

"When can I call you again?" he asked plaintively.

"As soon as the statute of limitations runs out," she said, hanging up on him.

He replaced the receiver, consulted the room service menu, and was about to pick up the phone to order a French dip sandwich and fries, when the phone rang again. It was Maurice's secretary, asking him in her clipped tone to stay on the line for Mr. Fender.

Quentin went over the details in his mind. He'd learned all about the project and reported back to Maurice a few days ago. It wasn't anything Maurice couldn't have learned from the trades. *The Revenge of Kali-Ra* was ready to start shooting in a month. They had a pretty decent director who was in Costa Rica right now, along with the production staff, nailing down some final locations, and a writer, who although washed up at the moment, had written a screenplay about disaffected young people in Thatcher's Britain that had won a Golden Bear at the Berlin Film Festival a decade ago.

Quentin had also learned that the studio was frantic because Nadia Wentworth was still in town screwing around with the script. Her screenwriter had green card problems, and couldn't risk leaving the country now, so he couldn't be in Costa Rica doing the rewrites. They were powerless, however, because her deal had a creative-control clause that was about as good as what Orson Welles had had on *Citizen Kane*. Quentin had told Maurice that now was as good a time as any to produce proof of copyright and screw a million or so out of the producers of *The Revenge of Kali-Ra,* who would be glad to pay up in order to avoid the costly holdups that would result from litigation. Maurice had finally agreed, and Quentin had duly filed with the Copyright Office and mailed a letter to Nadia's production company, Apple Blossom Productions, pointing out that the works were no longer in the public domain and that Maurice's company owned the rights.

Maurice came on the line. "Quentin!" he said frantically. "Did you send them the letter yet? You know. The Doom Queen people?"

"I sure did," said Quentin chirpily. "Letter to the lawyer and a copy to her business manager went out on Thursday. Haven't heard yet, but it's the weekend."

"Shit," said Maurice. "I want immediate results!"

"I'll rattle their cage on Monday." Quentin was more than slightly indignant. Just a few days ago Maurice had wanted to stall until the thing was actually shooting. Now he was bitching because things weren't happening fast enough.

"Get to another phone," Maurice said tersely. "A secure line. Get yourself a mess of dimes and find a phone booth somewhere. Don't use the credit card."

Jesus, the old man was sounding even more paranoid than usual. And had he been away from the States so long he didn't know pay phones took more than ten cents these days?

Twenty minutes later, Quentin was standing outside a Taco Time in a graffiti-covered phone booth with malt liquor bottles on the floor, pumping coins into a slot and hitting the country code for the nation that had provided Maurice Fender with a safe haven for so many years.

Maurice answered and told him to fax him the phone number of the booth, and go back and stand there, while he, Maurice, moved to another line on the island.

The old man was clearly nuts, but Quentin said okay, wrote the number down, got back in his rental car and hoped to God that this particular booth took incoming calls. Maurice presumably didn't know that the war on drugs had changed the way public phones operated. Quentin cruised along Sunset until he found a liquor store with a neon FAX sign in the window. This was no way to live, he thought bitterly.

When Quentin finally got back in communication, the first thing Maurice said was "It's that bitch Carla."

"Carla?"

"Carla and the Cleartones," said Maurice impatiently. "You know. Ever since k. d. lang did that cover of 'Shebang Dulang Wamma Wamma Baby,' Carla's been after us."

Quentin knew that Carla Lomax, songwriter and lead singer of a one-and-a-half-hit fifties girl group and now a retired high school music teacher in Oakland, California, had been trying to get her rights restored. Carla Lomax, like a lot of young R & B artists in the fifties and sixties, had been fleeced by an unscrupulous manager. "Yeah. So? Her manager sold those rights to that tax lawyer a long time ago, and we got them from him."

"Sure," said Maurice impatiently, "but he had a heart attack in his hot tub about ten years ago, and he's not around for her to sue, and her manager's in the charity ward at some old folks' home."

"That's right, and we wrote her lawyer a letter explaining that they didn't have a leg to stand on and they went away," said Quentin. Was Maurice's memory going too?

"They came back. Carla's hungry little shyster working on retainer won't quit. And *he* found someone in the FBI who's an old Carla and the Cleartones fan. Carla and her lawyer are getting this guy to leak some stuff about me right out of my files. If I were still an American citizen, I'd be outraged. The stuff's not good enough for a criminal prosecution, but good enough for Carla to use in a civil matter. It could open the floodgates. Shut me down."

For a moment, Quentin hoped Maurice would get shut down. Then he'd be free.

"What really steams me is the lack of integrity here," continued Maurice. "Her original deal, okay, so maybe it was unethical, exploitive, and unfair, but it was legal. And so was my subsequent acquisition of her rights. The way I run my business is irrelevant. Her coming after me is just a shakedown. There's no honor left in this sad old world."

"How much you gonna buy her off for?"

"We're negotiating," said Maurice tersely. "Obviously, they expect the rights back and plenty extra for Carla to keep her mouth shut. But the problem is I got those rights in the same package as the Valerian Ricardo thing. If it gets around that Carla's deal was no good, it's going to screw up this Kali-Ra thing too, seeing as it was part of the same deal. I was counting on at least a million from Nadia Wentworth. I could sure use it to pay off Carla."

"What do you want me to do?" said Quentin.

"Try and put together a deal with Nadia Wentworth right away."

"Like in the next few days?"

"Like yesterday, goddamn it!"

Quentin remembered what Margaret had told him about Nadia not trusting lawyers and turning over her business decisions to her personal assistant, Melanie Oakley, and he relayed the information to Maurice. "Maybe there's a chance I can get to this Oakley woman over the weekend and try to ram something through and we can get it all drawn up and signed early next week." He realized suddenly that this was ridiculous. No one would be so stupid as to negotiate a million-dollar rights deal directly, even the eccentric Nadia Wentworth and her naive little personal assistant. He began to backtrack. "Of course it would be highly irregular. I mean I can't imagine that she would—"

"She might," said Maurice in a menacing tone. "If we can scare her."

"Scare her? Like how?" Surely Maurice wasn't going to set Machete Mike on Nadia Wentworth.

"I'll get Vince Fontana on the job," said Maurice.

Vince Fontana was a seventy-eight-year-old crooner whose nostalgia albums, *Vavavoom! The Best of Vince, Serenades for Swingers* and *Ave Maria and Other Sacred Hits,* sold briskly to the Geritol set through a 1-800 number advertised on television. Lately, twenty-year-olds had discovered him along with Tony Bennett, Frank Sinatra and martinis. Fontana had been doing business with Maurice for fifteen years, ever since he'd run into tax problems. He was also rumored to be well connected with what was left of the Mafia.

"Vince can drop a few hints," said Maurice with a growing confidence Quentin found alarming. "He'll let this Oakley woman know she should get with the program or some of his associates might stir up trouble with the unions on the Doom Queen set. Cranes will fall over, that kind of thing. He can pitch it like he's trying to do her a favor."

"But you told me those Mafia rumors about Vince were baseless," protested Quentin.

Maurice made an unpleasant, contemptuous hooting sound. "Don't believe everything I tell you."

Unleashing a geriatric lounge act who had once partied with Bugsy Malone to deliver hints about cement overshoes seemed like a desperate move. Something snapped, and Quentin heard himself say peevishly, "I don't know, Maurice, it sounds kind of flaky to me."

"Flaky!" thundered Maurice. "It's fucking brilliant. You little twerp, I saved your sorry ass *and* your law license. I gave you a job just when you were about to get nailed, disbarred, screwed, blued, and tattooed. Who cleaned up the fucking mess you made? I did! If it weren't for me, you'd be teeing off at the ninth hole in one of those white-collar-crime federal slammers right now. So just do what I tell you and *don't screw up.*"

"Okay, Maurice," said Quentin. His head was pounding.

"Listen to me," said Maurice in a low, slow way that chilled Quentin's blood. "If Carla Cleartone tries to sell me to the feds, I'm gonna make it easy on myself. I'm gonna leverage whatever *I* got. Which includes you. If you don't pull this off and keep me in business, it's your problem more than it is mine. They can try to cut off my life's blood but I still got friends here on the island and assets where no one can find them. All you got is my goodwill, which can be revoked at any time. Got that through your pointy little Ivy League brain?"

"I got it, Maurice," said Quentin.

"Okay, what about the widow who tried to make trouble for the professor? Is she gonna be a problem?"

Quentin, unwilling to do anything to encourage Maurice to send out his own personal Tonton Macoute assassin, had until now been less than frank about Lila, but felt that refusing to answer a direct question about her could backfire badly. "I was just about to tell you, Maurice," he said. "Apparently, Mrs. Ricardo is alive and well. In fact, she's staying with Nadia Wentworth and serving as some kind of consultant on the picture."

"Fine," said Maurice. "I'm glad I took the precaution of sending Mike out there. He should arrive tonight. He won't be in touch directly, though, unless it's absolutely necessary. It's better if you aren't seen together."

"Good thinking, Maurice," said Quentin feeling queasy. "I don't want to know any more than I have to."

CHAPTER XII

A BEAUTIFUL STRANGER

The following afternoon, Nick Iversen got out of his frigid, air-conditioned rental car and felt the close heat hit him in the face. He stood across the street from a condominium complex that had once been the Scheherazade Apartments, a U-shaped Moorish folly in cream-colored stucco with dark-stained wooden trim and a red tile roof. The three sections of the building surrounded a charming garden full of festive palm trees and geraniums. A low wall was covered with a jumble of jasmine. He double-checked the address in his copy of Lila Lamb Ricardo's book. Yes, this was definitely the place.

The building had the air of having been recently restored to its thirties splendor. Nick tried to imagine what it must have looked like in 1972, when Uncle Sid had died there. In *My Life with Valerian Ricardo*, the place had sounded like a real dump. Uncle Sid's widow had been pretty clear about that in the final chapter, in which she lamented that a great artist had sunk so low. According to her, Uncle Sid had managed, through inner spiritual strength, to have survived the humiliations of stoking the boiler, fixing stuck windows and leaking faucets, setting rat traps and trying in vain to kill the armies of cockroaches that called the place home. Lila had been especially bitter that all his efforts had been unappreciated by the lowlife tenants, none of whom gave him so much as a fruitcake at Christmas.

At LAX, Nick had bought a cheap throwaway camera. Awkwardly juggling the book, he took a few shots of the building now. As he did, he became uncomfortably aware that someone had sidled up next to him. He felt instantly on his guard. He'd seen a lot of scruffy homeless people around, and although homeless people didn't scare him in Minneapolis, he was worried that the California variety were more likely to be hearing voices and might stab him or engage him in irrational conversation. He stepped sideways and turned warily, only to be confronted by the sight of a stunning young woman who was staring at him.

She was tall and aerobicized in the way he expected California girls to be, but instead of being a tanned Barbie blond, her skin was a very pale gold and she had thick dark hair to her shoulders. She was wearing a black swimsuit top that showed off impressive cleavage, some kind of ankle-length flowered sarong arrangement wrapped around her hips, revealing a flat stomach and a navel pierced with a jeweled ring, and a small woven pouch on a leather thong that crossed her bare torso diagonally.

Against his will and his better judgment, Nick checked out her entire body, including one long leg partly exposed by the slit in the sarong, and ending with feet in gold lamé high-heeled sandals, the toenails painted bright blue.

"Are you interested in this building?" she asked. He was reassured by her voice, with its immature Valley Girl tinge, at odds with her spectacular appearance. Nick told himself that she was real.

"Yeah, it's great," he said, putting the cheap camera in his pocket, suddenly wishing it were some expensive matte black model with a brace of lenses.

"I know. I'm writing a paper on this building for a history class. This used to be the Scheherazade Apartments. Some famous people lived there. Not like the Garden of

Allah or anything, but still, it's part of the cultural heritage of Southern California."

Nick caught a whiff of some exotic perfume. He wasn't sure if it came from her golden skin or the nearby jasmine. "Well, my uncle Sid lived there and he was kind of famous in his day," he said with a modest downward glance. "He wrote books under the name Valerian Ricardo."

He heard her take in her breath rapidly and her eyes widened. They were green, fringed with dark lashes and flecked with little bits of gold. "Wow, really?"

"You mean you've heard of him?"

"Well, yes. I came across him in my research. He wrote those Kali-Ra books that Nadia Wentworth is making a movie of. He died in weird circumstances in the boiler room in there."

"He did?" Lila had poignantly described Uncle Sid's death in a large, carved bed with Egyptian motifs. *Whispering "Au revoir," he slipped gently beyond the veil, my arms still around him.*

"Valerian Ricardo. Wow. How are you related to him?"

"He was my grandfather's uncle."

She appeared to make some rapid calculations. "Then he's your great-great-uncle."

"Yeah. I guess so."

"I'd really like to interview you for the paper I'm writing," she said. "Get some family history and all."

"No problem," said Nick dizzily. "Shall we go get a coffee or something?" But then he remembered he had an appointment with Nadia Wentworth. Here was the most incredible girl he had ever seen in his life, and she wanted to talk to him, and he had a schedule conflict because he was due at the Beverly Hills home of the woman with the best breasts in America. He felt he had to lean against something while he composed himself, and backed up against his rental car.

"Are you all right?" she said with a look of concern. It suddenly occurred to him that she was as good-hearted as she was beautiful. She had to be. Anyone who looked this good had to have an equally lovely soul.

"Sorry," he said. "It's the heat. I just got here from Minneapolis."

"You are a little overdressed," she said, fingering the lapel of his tweed jacket and shifting her weight thoughtfully from one foot to the other. The result was a spectacular curvature of her left hip.

"Listen, I really want to talk about Uncle Sid," he said urgently, "but I just remembered, I'm supposed to go see Nadia Wentworth." He consulted his watch. "And I'm not sure how long it takes to get there. I'm not used to the freeways and all that."

"*The* Nadia Wentworth?"

"Yeah. I have some material for her about Uncle Sid. But I'd really like to talk to you. About Uncle Sid. I'm kind of fascinated by the old guy, to tell you the truth."

"I know, so am I," she said. "Take me with you to Nadia Wentworth's. I'll drive, so you won't get lost. And we can talk in the car."

"Oh," he said, worried. Would Nadia Wentworth mind if he brought someone else?

His new acquaintance seemed to be telepathic. "Just tell her I'm your girlfriend or something. Is this your car?" She opened the door and slid into the driver's seat.

"I'm Nick," he said, stumbling around to the passenger's side. "Nick Iversen."

"Callie," she said, flashing a smile and holding out her hand for the keys. "Callie Cunningham."

He handed them over. "Kali? Like Kali-Ra?" Maybe she was making some kind of a joke.

She laughed. "God, no. It's short for Caroline."

"Um, this is a rental car," he said. "I'm not sure the thing I signed said anyone else could drive it."

"Chill, Nick. I've got my driver's license and everything." She revved the engine and barreled out into traffic. "Wow. I think it's a fabulous coincidence that we met. A real kismet thing, you know? So where is this place?"

She drove very fast, but quite expertly, and soon they were winding up a curved road past an architectural hodgepodge of French châteaus, Spanish missions and Gothic castles. Nick was startled to see little metal signs stuck in bright green lawns that read PREMISES PATROLLED. ARMED RESPONSE.

"Back at the Scheherazade you said Uncle Sid died in weird circumstances. What do you mean?" asked Nick.

"Didn't you know?" she said, raising an eyebrow but keeping her eyes on the road.

"No. The family never had much time for the guy. There's no one left who remembers him."

"He was over eighty and doing some heavy partying with a bunch of hippie chicks. He was found tied up to some bizarre bondage device in the boiler room of the Scheherazade surrounded by drug paraphernalia."

"Oh really?" said Nick. He held up Lila's book. "His wife says he died peacefully in bed in his striped silk pajamas, full of tender thoughts for her."

Now Callie did turn around. "That book looks interesting," she said. "I noticed it under your arm at the Scheherazade. I've heard about it but I've never seen a copy."

"Apparently, it's very rare, and Nadia Wentworth wants it," said Nick. "I arranged to sell it to her, but I Xeroxed it first." Nick had had a hard time doing this. Kinko's had refused to help him, saying it was copyrighted material, so he'd sneaked into the office at the theater every night for a few weeks and done it bit by bit.

"Wow! Could you make me a copy too?"

"Sure," said Nick, absolutely thrilled. He now had a reasonable excuse for staying in touch with this fascinating creature. "It's amazing I ran into you," he said. "I can't believe you've heard of Valerian Ricardo. I never had until Nadia Wentworth got interested in him. All I knew was that there had been some no-account Uncle Sid that no one liked to talk about."

She nodded. "Like I said. Kismet."

"To tell you the truth," said Nick, "when I found out about Uncle Sid, I had this little fantasy that I owned the movie rights and Nadia Wentworth would have to buy me off. But then I did some research and realized the copyright had expired. Anyway, I consoled myself with the thought that it would be interesting to meet a movie star." He looked over at her solemnly. "And I got to meet you too," he added.

She favored him with a sly smile.

"But of course," he continued, "since then I learned he was married to this Lila person, so I guess even if the rights hadn't expired, she'd own them. If she's alive."

"She's alive," said Callie with a hard edge. "She left a big message about the movie on the Kali-Ra website."

"Kali-Ra has a website?"

Callie fluttered her eyelids for a second, opened them, then said in a low, thrilling voice, now free of any Valley Girl intonation, "The power of the Queen of Doom reaches everywhere, my friend, even into cyberspace. Come, Raymond Vernon, surely you do not think Kali-Ra, she who has toiled forever without sleep, would not seize any opportunity to extend her evil power over the hearts and minds of mortals."

BOOK TWO

In Which Kali-Ra
Wreaks Havoc by Moonlight

CHAPTER XIII

COCKTAILS AT VILLA VERA

✗

"What did you say?" said Nick, stunned at her transformation. It had been so sudden. He wondered if he had imagined it, if his brain had been fried by reading too many Valerian Ricardo novels. In any case, she was now sounding like a mall rat again. "Wow, here we are. I can't believe I'm going to a real movie star's house." Brakes squealing, she turned the car into a driveway and stopped in front of forbidding wrought-iron gates.

After they buzzed an intercom and spoke to someone inside the house, the huge gates moved slowly apart, as if opened by invisible hands. Nick told himself to pull himself together. When that spooky voice had come out of her and she'd called him Raymond Vernon, she had just been kidding around.

Callie drove through a dark glen of rhododendrons and the house loomed up at them. It was a huge cream-colored stucco pile in which Moorish, Romanesque, and Tudor elements struggled for dominance. Set at the top of a hill, it seemed to reach far into the sky, like Mont-Saint-Michel. Palm trees jutted out from around the massive structure bursting with gables, turrets, balconies, cupolas, and bay windows. Large swathes of wall were smothered with bougainvillea.

"Nobody but a movie star could live here," said Nick. "My God, look at it!"

83

"It's totally *Sunset Boulevard*," said Callie appreciatively. "It must be worth millions."

They parked on scrunchy gravel and walked up to the enormous planked door trimmed with black square nail heads and heavy ornamental hinges. "Wow," said Callie, squinting up at a balcony railing bearing a row of giant green ceramic jars like something from Ali Baba and the Forty Thieves. "It's all authentic twenties stuff."

Nick rang the bell, which resonated from behind the door like church bells. A second later, a red-haired young woman with an intelligent face and gray eyes opened the door. She wore jeans and a white T-shirt.

"Hello," she said. "Welcome to Villa Vera."

"Villa Vera?" said Nick.

"Come in. I'm Melanie Oakley. And you're Nick." She turned to Callie inquiringly.

"I hope it's okay that I brought my girlfriend," mumbled Nick. To carry out this fiction, Callie gave his shoulder a possessive little squeeze, then thrust out her hand to Melanie and gave her a handshake more appropriate to a business suit than a bikini top, sarong, and navel ring. "Caroline Cunningham," she said.

They followed Melanie into the hall. "It was built by an old silent movie star, Vera Nadi," she explained.

"Villa Vera," repeated Nick as he glanced around a large, dim entryway with a sweeping staircase and a chandelier that looked like something from a Spanish cathedral. "Villa Truth."

"Rather ironic, seeing as the architecture is completely fake," said Melanie.

"Maybe she should have called it Villa Falsa," said Nick, who had taken Latin in high school.

Melanie laughed. "Villa Adultera would be like Villa Fake. Villa Falsa would mean the house itself was lying."

"You must have been one of the stars of the Junior Classical League," said Nick.

She looked pleased. "Actually, I was. Were you?"

"Not really, but I tied a mean toga," said Nick, slightly embarrassed. Callie would know he'd been a nerd in high school, bouncing through the Midwest with other overachievers on an old school bus to JCL conventions in cheap motels. He glanced at her but she wasn't listening. Instead, she was staring at the furnishings in a way Nick felt looked just a little crass, as if she were conducting an inventory of the place. But perhaps she was simply absorbing the exotic atmosphere. After all, she was interested in the cultural heritage of Southern California, a phrase that until his arrival a few hours ago Nick would have dismissed as oxymoronic.

"Nadia and I were hoping you'd stay for dinner," said Melanie. "It's a regular Valerian Ricardo reunion. Lila Ricardo is here, and Duncan Blaine, the screenwriter on the project, and Doctor Pendergast."

"He wrote that book about Uncle Sid, didn't he?" asked Nick.

"That's right." Melanie turned to Callie. "I hope you won't be bored by all this Valerian Ricardo talk."

"I'm really interested in Valerian Ricardo myself," said Callie. "We'd love to stay."

Nick thought maybe he should apologize for bringing an extra person, or Callie should apologize for tagging along, seeing as they were staying for dinner, but then he imagined Nadia Wentworth wouldn't care. She must have servants. It wasn't as if she'd have to run out to the store for an extra pork chop, or tell the family to hold back.

"What do you eat?" asked Melanie.

Nick was confused. Maybe an extra guest was an imposition. "Just, um, food," he said. "But I had a big lunch."

Callie said, "I do chicken and fish but no red meat, very little dairy, and low sodium."

Melanie nodded. "Fine. That's what Nadia does. Our housekeeper, Rosemary, is also our cook, and she's strictly macrobiotic herself but she's open-minded."

"Here's the book, by the way," said Nick.

Melanie took it. "Thank you. I'll put it in the office," she said. "I always read everything for Nadia. Can I write you a check for it?"

Nick waved his hand expansively. "Oh, I wouldn't dream of selling it to you. Think of it as the bottle of wine I would have brought if I'd known I was staying for dinner." He felt like an idiot. He couldn't imagine Nadia Wentworth would have been impressed with the kind of wine he would have brought—a $5.99 bottle of Chardonnay he'd picked up at Cub Foods.

They followed Melanie down a murky corridor to a large sunny room, full of modern office equipment—a phone with lots of buttons, filing cabinets and a big desktop computer with, Nick noted, a screen saver of an eyeless Roman bust. This room, with a view through French doors out onto sweeping lawns edged with cypresses, seemed decades newer than the rest of the house. Melanie put the book in a desk drawer.

Callie gazed up at the wall and said, "There he is. Valerian Ricardo." Hanging there was the same publicity shot of Uncle Sid that Nick had seen on the wrapper of the book he'd just handed over.

"Nadia put that there," said Melanie with a defensive little edge.

Nick looked up. "I don't think I look a bit like him. Except for the chin, maybe."

Callie reached over and ran two fingers across his chin, feeling the shape of it. "Maybe," she said dreamily. This was the third time she'd reached out and touched him, if you counted fingering his jacket down in front of Uncle Sid's old apartment house.

Because Nick had billed Callie as his girlfriend, he tried to look as if he were on regular terms of physical intimacy with her, all the while fantasizing his own hand touching her gleaming shoulder and then sliding down her bare arm. He pulled himself together and said, "I was noticing your screen saver, Melanie. Isn't that Marcus Aurelius?"

"Yes, it is," she said, sounding pleased. "There are eight rotating Romans. In a second, you'll see Suetonius."

"Cool," said Callie politely.

Duncan Blaine sat out on the brick terrace with Lila, Nadia, and Glen Pendergast. He clutched the gin and tonic that had appeared at two minutes past five, the hour Nadia allowed the bar to be cracked, and scowled. It wasn't enough that he'd been dragooned up to this Hammer House of Horror to ruin his own script by a jumped-up little tart who'd been given carte blanche by the studio because of her moneymaking mammaries. He was also expected to collaborate *and* socialize with a loopy, aggressive old harridan with the artistic judgment and charm of a newt. And now there was this twit Pendergast who'd been brought in to muddy the waters some more. Presumably he'd want a credit too.

The academic was now holding forth about the real meaning of Kali-Ra. "Of course, Mrs. Ricardo, I understand completely that the popularity of the series rested, er, rests, on philosophical ideas that many find attractive. The question is, why do people find these ideas attractive? What *basic human needs* are met by the desire to believe that evil is a rampant but beautiful force with erotic implications?"

God, thought Duncan contemptuously, what basic human needs? It was pretty obvious to any reasonably astute person who'd read those Kali-Ra books what kind of basic needs we were talking about here. They were the kind of needs that were met by whores who posted little notices in London telephone boxes saying, "You have been a disgusting, naughty boy. Mistress Brenda, second floor up, will treat you as you deserve to be treated."

Now Lila was snapping back in her vicious way. She was on the defensive when confronted by even so sketchily educated an opponent as Glen Pendergast, holder of a doctoral degree in literary trash and a lecturer at some cowboy college on the prairies. "All this talk about sex," she was saying. "That's such a *shallow* interpretation. Valerian was misunderstood in his day by narrow-minded puritans, but I wouldn't expect a learned professor such as yourself to miss the high-minded, spiritual aspects of the work."

Duncan turned to Nadia, who was following this exchange with a furrowed brow and a confused light in her lovely, stupid eyes. "What do you think, Nadia?" he asked maliciously. "What's your take on this central point?"

She looked thoughtful for a moment, then her brow smoothed and she produced a half smile. "I think there's something to be said for both points of view."

"In that case," Duncan replied, "I think we should keep the scene with the Torture of a Thousand Tiny Golden Chains." This had nothing to do with anything the nasty old bat and the weedy little wanker were saying, but Nadia wouldn't know that. Duncan had already reluctantly given up on the sapphic revels in the bedchamber of the temple handmaidens. It had been made abundantly clear to him that there was only room for two fabulous breasts in this picture, and that these appendages were firmly attached to the chest of the executive producer.

Melanie Oakley appeared, trailing a couple of people, an agreeable-looking young man and a stunning specimen of half-naked California womanhood with a tight body. Now, at least, there would be something pleasant to look at. Duncan's eye roved over the flat golden stomach and the navel ring. Piercing, he felt, was a clear signal that you were offering the world a body eager for penetration.

Initially, Duncan had enjoyed leering discreetly at Nadia, but he had grown to loathe her to the point where he actually found the sight of her physically repulsive. There was something menacing about her big teeth, an aggressive example of the American obsession with dentistry, and occasionally there was a slightly rodentlike twitch to her features. He fantasized telling her so. Combining vanity and stupidity as she did, an insult to her sex appeal was the only insult that would ever have the power to wound her.

But of course he couldn't. He couldn't fuck this one up. Handled right, he'd be able to get a sole credit on a huge moneymaker. A moneymaker that, with the sly, postmodern jokes he'd slipped in, would also impress the European critics. He had so much to gain.

And even more to lose. After a string of flops, his agent had come right out and told him that this picture was his last chance.

CHAPTER XIV

A STRANGE ACCUSATION

Melanie had impulsively asked the Ricardo nephew and his girlfriend to dinner because she felt the party needed diluting. A couple of extra people, without agendas, would lower the stress level. This afternoon's script conference had been ugly and feelings were running high. Duncan was irritable, although he might mellow out now that he had a drink. Melanie had been hopeful that Dr. Pendergast would undermine Lila's influence with Nadia, but so far all she'd been able to detect was politely veiled hostility between them.

"This is Nick Iversen. Caroline Cunningham." She introduced everyone sitting around the patio. Duncan Blaine pulled out the chair next to his and gestured for Caroline to sit in it. When she did, he smiled lecherously. Melanie glanced over at a disapproving Nadia, who didn't like other women to be admired.

Caroline goggled at Nadia and gushed, "It's so exciting to meet you. You have a really great place." She gestured vaguely at the lily pond and its fountain of porpoises. Nadia, instead of doing her usual gracious-celebrity-being-nice-to-the-little-people thing, gave the girl a frosty smile.

Much to Melanie's annoyance, Tom Thorndyke's undercover operative, Kevin, now appeared on the lawn next to them with a noisy, gas-powered leaf blower. Didn't he realize the devices were illegal in the interests of smog control and shouldn't be used in front of people? She gestured him away and he ambled off. Kevin had been a big disappointment. He seemed to be out of shape, with greasy hair and glasses that slid down his nose, and he breathed through his mouth, but presumably he was more effective as an undercover operative if he looked like an idiot.

It seemed Melanie would never meet any interesting guys. Why couldn't Kevin have looked like this Nick Iversen, for instance? Tall and healthy-looking, with an intelligent face. But of course, he was hooked up with this half-naked model-actress-whatever with the ditzy voice.

Melanie found another chair for Nick and fit him in between Nadia and Lila, saying cheerfully, "Nick is actually Valerian Ricardo's great-nephew."

"Great-great, I think," said Nick, smiling at Lila.

Lila had ignored both of them, but now she peered at Nick intently. "There's no resemblance," she said flatly. "So you're one of those Minnesota farmers, eh? I've always felt that the fact that Valerian sprang from such stock is clear proof of reincarnation."

Nick, the philosophy major, who had aced Logic 101, was tempted to lecture the old babe on what would actually constitute clear proof of her metaphysical whimsy. Instead he said, "I'm glad to meet you." Should he call her Aunt Lila? "I'm kind of curious about Uncle Sid."

"Uncle Sid?" said Duncan Blaine.

"Valerian Ricardo's real name was Sidney Gundersen," explained Nick. He didn't like the way the Englishman had leered at Callie, so he added patronizingly, "You didn't really believe anyone would be named Valerian Ricardo, did you?"

Duncan snorted a laugh. "In this country, anything is possible." He turned to Callie. "It's refreshing to meet someone with a pretty, *real* name like Caroline in these parts. The place is teeming with Crystals and Tiffanys and Buffys."

Lila said stridently, "Valerian Ricardo was *too* his real name. It was given to him in young manhood by his spirit guides."

Glen Pendergast seemed to be feeling left out. He cleared his throat and announced, "It's worth noting that Ricardo's protagonist, Raymond Vernon, has the same initials as Valerian Ricardo."

Nadia looked puzzled.

"But reversed of course," he explained.

"Wow," said Nadia. "That's so deep. I never thought of that."

Melanie took drink orders and went off to the kitchen to ask Rosemary to bring them out. On her way back, she heard the office phone ringing and she went in and picked it up. It was Nadia's business manager, George, and he sounded terrified, but managed to get his story out, ending with a pathetic, "Will you explain it to her? Tell her we're working on the problem."

"Okay," said Melanie. "I'll tell her." Melanie said this a lot to all kinds of people. Lawyers, agents, producers, accountants, even Manuel the pool man—none of them liked to bring Nadia bad news.

"I really appreciate it," said George, his voice trembling pathetically. "Listen, Melanie, when you do tell her, I hope you'll make it very clear that it's not *my* fault. There was absolutely no reason to think the damned things weren't in the public domain. Tell her I'm acting aggressively to check out their claim. Tell her not to panic." He sounded as if he were doing just that.

"Okay. Who are these people exactly?"

"The corporation is registered on a small island in the Caribbean with unusual banking and tax laws. The letter

said they have a lawyer who'll be in touch. I'm faxing you
a copy, and a memo explaining how the Uruguay Round
and recent changes in European copyright law affect all
this."

Melanie hung up the phone. So, there was a possibility
that Valerian Ricardo's wretched works were under copyright after all, and that they were owned by a bunch of unfeeling businessmen who wouldn't be the least bit
impressed that they were dealing with a movie star. This
would slow Nadia down a bit. By blabbing to everyone
who would listen that she was born to play Kali-Ra, she'd
managed to jack the price into the stratosphere.

Melanie had mixed feelings. She didn't want to see millions go down the tubes as the project ground to a halt
while the lawyers got into it. This would be bad news for
Nadia's credibility as a producer.

At the same time, there wasn't much of Nadia's own
money at stake. Maybe during the months or years the
agents and lawyers thrashed around wasting a lot of time
and money, Nadia would lose interest in the whole thing
and get monomaniacal about something else. Maybe a new
man, for instance. Nadia was between men now, and in
one of her careerist phases. Melanie sighed. Life was a lot
easier when Nadia was in love.

She'd better tell Nadia about this new development as
soon as she could get her alone. She would, of course,
go ballistic. Melanie found herself thinking a few of the
lines from the latest version of the script, lifted directly
from the canon. *The Queen of Doom is displeased by
this latest blunder. She must be paid in blood. A suitable
sacrificial victim must be brought to the altar of the
temple!*

Yes, someone would have to pay. Melanie imagined that
George was figuring out just who in his organization
would be an appropriate victim for Nadia's altar. The trou-

ble with life imitating art was that when the art in question was written by Valerian Ricardo, the results were kind of sleazy.

Back on the terrace, Rosemary, wearing her white uniform, bare legs, and sandals, and smelling more strongly of patchouli oil than usual, flicked her heavy gray braid back over her shoulder as she handed around the drinks and hors d'oeuvres. Melanie sat down quietly and tried not to look preoccupied.

There seemed to have been a slight lull in the conversation, and now Caroline Cunningham leaned across the table, flashing cleavage, and said eagerly to Lila, "I'm kind of interested in Valerian Ricardo myself."

Lila stared at Callie, apparently noticing her for the first time. "You!" she shrieked. "You've come back! You sly little minx with your wicked emanations!" She rose, shaking, and made a bony fist, then collapsed unconscious onto the bricks of the terrace.

"My God!" shrieked Nadia, throwing herself down beside the old woman with the same hair-tearing gesture she'd used in *Frederic and Georges,* the musical biopic, thereby stealing the scene where Chopin, weakened by tuberculosis, sinks to the floor.

Melanie was pretty sure that Lila had just fainted, but with someone her age, it seemed prudent to call the doctor. She asked Glen Pendergast to put some cushions under Lila's feet so the blood would go back to her head, and went into the kitchen to phone.

The operator from the doctor's service was just explaining that he was out of town and that another doctor was backing him up when Nadia rushed into the room and said, "She came around, but I'm so worried. God, I need her! The picture needs her! She's our pipeline to Valerian Ricardo. I want a doctor here right now! She should have round-the-clock nursing care!"

Despite Nadia's hysterical flapping around, Melanie ran down the backup doctor at a restaurant with some friends. Since he hadn't driven his own car, Melanie arranged to send a car and driver around to pick him up. She gave Rosemary instructions to buzz in the limousine when it appeared on the gate video monitor immediately, and went back to the terrace with Nadia.

There, Lila was sitting upright, and although she looked perfectly all right, Dr. Pendergast was fanning her with what looked like pages of the script. Nadia rushed to Lila's side. "The doctor is on his way," she said. "I'm *so* worried about you." Duncan Blaine sat drinking and looking put out that Lila had regained consciousness. Nick Iversen and his girlfriend seemed to be having an agitated conversation at the edge of the terrace out of Lila's line of sight.

Caroline approached Melanie and whispered, "I don't understand. I've never met the woman before in my life. I don't know why she said those things. God, I'm really sorry!"

"Don't apologize," said Melanie kindly. "She's very old, and to be honest, she's come out with some other things that are pretty, well, eccentric."

"Maybe we should go," said Nick beside her.

Melanie patted Caroline's shoulder. "Please don't leave unless you want to," she said. "I invited you to dinner, and I'm not going to have our guests driven away by the ramblings of a querulous old woman." Lila was *not* going to be allowed to call the shots around here. If she'd taken an instant dislike to another guest, that was just too bad.

"Well, maybe it would be awkward . . . ," began Nick.

Callie interrupted him. "Wow, that's really nice of you, Melanie," she said. "We'd love to stay."

Duncan, glass in hand, drifted across the terrace and turned to Callie. "Well, my dear," he said, "you certainly made an impression. The old girl went pale and keeled right over at the sight of your beauty. Real Kali-Ra stuff." He drained his glass and said hopefully to no one in particular, "Maybe it's her old ticker."

Callie's features took on a cast Nick hadn't seen before. The sight gave him a strange frisson. There was a faraway look in her eyes, which had taken on an uncanny, greenish glow. Dreamily, and in that same low tone that had startled him so before, she said, as if to herself, "It seems that old woman has displeased the Queen of Doom. If so, I fear she may not last the night."

CHAPTER XV

TAKEN FOR A RIDE

The unsmiling young man standing at the door to Quentin's hotel room had a neck the circumference of a beer keg, an off-center nose with the uneven contours of a root vegetable from the organic section of the produce department, small eyes set close together, and a bodybuilder's physique squeezed into a black suit. He didn't look like someone from the hotel staff who'd come to inventory the minibar.

"Mr. Fontana's waiting for you in the car downstairs," he announced in a voice out of *Guys and Dolls.*

Quentin put on his jacket and reknotted his tie, then grabbed his briefcase, thinking vaguely that as a prop it made him look and feel less like some chump being taken for the proverbial ride and more like a player. He followed the man down to the lobby and into a very long black car with tinted windows. This sinister-looking vehicle was parked out in front of a sign that said TAXIS ONLY. ALL OTHERS WILL BE TOWED.

Some German tourists peered at him as he climbed inside. Inside sat a tan, fat Vince Fontana. The dim lighting, reminiscent of a nightclub, illuminated his still-handsome chiseled jaw and his gleaming, oily black curls, considerably darker than his gray sideburns. He wore a silk suit and an open white shirt. Chains and religious medals nestled in silver chest hair.

"Okay, kid," Fontana said in a wheezy baritone. "It's all set." The car pulled out into traffic, and the old crooner patted Quentin's knee. "Anything for Maurice, ya know. He's a pal, and a pal's gotta help a pal. Now me and him went over all this, and I got it all down. You just sit there, and after I soften 'em up, you jump in with the paperwork."

"You mean we're going to talk to Nadia Wentworth now?"

"Sure. Swing into action immediately. That's the way Vince Fontana does it."

"I see," said Quentin uneasily. "Did you talk to Melanie Oakley? What did she say when you made the appointment?"

Fontana smiled, flashing a lot of capped teeth, and gave Quentin a playful slap on the cheek. "Appointment? Ha! Vince Fontana doesn't need an appointment."

Suddenly, Vince Fontana's slow-tempoed, heavily orchestrated version of "Que Sera, Sera" surrounded them. Fontana closed his eyes. "Doris was cute as pie, but she never got the real feel for this song," said the old man in a confidential tone. "Fate. That's a powerful thing. *My* people understand that. You gotta put more feeling into it. Phrase it like you get it. *Destino.* A kind of impending doom thing, ya know."

"I know just what you mean," said Quentin. The headache had started again. He leaned back in the leather seat and closed his own eyes.

Vince began to sing, accompanying his burnished youthful voice with the raspier one he had now, the voice of a slightly swacked traveling salesman at a karaoke bar. Quentin became aware of the sound of rattling ice cubes under this bizarre duet and opened his eyes to see that Vince was wielding glasses and a bottle of Chivas from the backseat bar. "You seem tired. You need a belt. God, these kids today, I'm telling you. No stamina."

He handed over a scotch on the rocks. Quentin accepted it, thinking it might numb the pain in his head. He didn't dare ask for soda or water. Vince Fontana would probably make disparaging remarks about his manhood and throw him out of the car.

"Hey, that Nadia Wentworth's something else," mused Vince, firing up a Chesterfield. "Great boobs and they look real. Maybe me and her will hit it off tonight." He exhaled extravagantly. The resulting blue cloud made the space seem even more like a nightclub. "Anyway, I need a photogenic date for the Golden Globes."

Fontana jabbed Quentin in the ribs and gave a phlegmy laugh. "Maybe you'll get lucky too, kid. You can have the other broad. The assistant. Melissa Oakland or whatever the fuck it is."

"I don't know if we should mix business and pleasure," murmured Quentin, wondering how Nadia Wentworth would feel about being pawed by this tubby old man with a Brylcreemed toupee and nicotine-stained fingers. This was shaping up very badly. Maurice had been away from the center of action for too long. Vince Fontana might have been a good friend to have back in the Sputnik era, but now he was just quaint. Presumably, though, his Sicilian associates still had seriously menacing people on the payroll whom he could unleash. Quentin began to hope frantically that there was no one home at the Wentworth place.

Quentin was astounded when the gates to Villa Vera opened magically and the limousine slid right past the buzzer and speaker box. "Trust me, kid," said Vince, knocking back his third scotch on the rocks. "Vince Fontana never needs an appointment."

The driver pulled up to the front door. For someone so muscle-bound, he leapt with remarkable agility from behind the wheel and around to open the car door.

A middle-aged woman with her long gray hair in a

braid down her back and a white nylon uniform covered by a tie-dyed chef's apron was waiting for them on the doorstep. "Please come right in," she said. "Miss Wentworth is freaking."

Fontana gave Quentin a what-did-I-tell-you look of triumph. To the housekeeper he said benevolently, "Hey, if she's a smart broad and plays ball, Vince Fontana will see she's got nothing to worry about. Lead me to her."

Quentin looked over his shoulder to see if the beefy chauffeur would be following them into the house to loom menacingly, perhaps cracking his knuckles in a forbidding way, while Vince gave his pitch. Instead, the big lug had put on a pair of glasses and settled in the front seat with a book.

"But how did they know we were coming?" said Quentin as they followed the housekeeper down a long, dimly lit hall. "You said you didn't make an appointment."

Vince's eyes narrowed. "My associates have ways of getting the message across to people they do business with," he said. "Don't ask so many questions, kid."

Quentin stumbled after him out some French doors onto a sunny terrace, where a group of people were looking up at them. He had a vague impression of a pale old lady and a dark, sultry girl with what looked like a bedspread tied around her hips, before picking out Nadia Wentworth, who rushed toward them.

Fontana flung his arms out in a hammy way and said, "I guess you all know who *I* am. Allow me to introduce, um, hey, kid, what the hell's your name?" He snapped his fingers impatiently.

Quentin started to mumble his name but Nadia Wentworth ignored him. Instead, she gave Fontana a pitiful look and said, "We're so scared!"

"Hey, nothing to worry about, sweetheart," said Vince, taking her hand and giving her an oily smile. "That's why

I'm here. We want to avoid unpleasantness, right? I'm here to tell you how you can do that."

He looked around at everyone else who seemed to be waiting for him to do something. "Let's go somewhere where we can have some privacy."

Quentin wondered who all these people were. The old lady with white hair startled him by standing up and saying adamantly, "I'm perfectly all right and I'm not taking off my clothes." Vince Fontana gave a tight smile but there was confusion in his eyes.

From over by a square lily pond, a rumpled middle-aged man with a red face stared at Vince and said in an English accent with a slightly slurred tone, "I do believe it's that funny little dago who flogs records on the television." He proceeded to quote from the ad, in a reasonably success-ful American accent. "Act now, and I'll include my Christmas album, *Carols for Lovers,* absolutely free." The Englishman closed his eyes, stepped up on the raised brick border of the lily pond, and began singing "roasting chestnuts on an open fire . . ." with a wide-armed gesture.

"Wow! It's Vince Fontana," said the girl in the bedspread. "Cool."

A collective "ah" of recognition went around.

A guy with a baby face standing next to Nadia Went-worth cleared his throat and addressed Fontana in formal tones. "You were a symbol of a certain kind of postwar suaveness, continuing the Latin lover tradition pioneered by Valentino but with a more blue-collar take." He added, "My mom is one of your biggest fans."

A crisp-looking young woman with red hair, who Quentin imagined must be Melanie Oakley, stepped for-ward. "I'm sorry for the confusion, but we were expecting a doctor."

"I'm not a doctor," said Fontana, who was eyeing the singing Englishman in a murderous way. Duncan Blaine had run out of lyrics, but continued the song with some scatlike syllables and swayed to the music. "Da-da-da-da-dad-da-dum."

Fontana made his hands into fists and lurched over to him. "But you people are gonna need a doctor, 'cause I'm gonna knock this limey asshole's teeth down his fucking throat. No one calls Vince Fontana or any other Italian-American a dago!" He went over and pushed his clenched-jaw profile into the Englishman's face.

The Englishman stopped singing and blinked. "I beg your pardon," he said. "Perhaps I should have said wop."

With a little squealing noise, Vince grabbed him by the collar and started shaking him. Quentin, his briefcase still in hand, rushed over to the enraged old man and tugged at his sleeve. Nadia Wentworth screamed, and Melanie Oakley yelled, "Stop it!"

Fontana had now pulled back his elbow in a pistonlike movement, and appeared to be deciding whether to pepper Duncan Blaine's face or punch him in the gut. The Englishman seemed to have belatedly realized that he was being assaulted and had begun to wriggle. Quentin clambered around Vince's burly form next to the Englishman so now he was facing the angry old man. "Listen to me," he said, grabbing Vince's shoulder. "Calm down. This is not helpful!"

"Aw, shut up," said Vince, turning his attention briefly to Quentin. He put a big hand in his face and gave him a push. Quentin lost his balance and teetered on the brick edging for a second before falling backward into the lily pond.

CHAPTER XVI

TWILIGHT ON THE TERRACE

Nick and Callie took the brunt of the splash. The undignified dousing made Nick mad and that galvanized him into action. He rushed at Vince just as Duncan managed to writhe and duck, so that when the fist landed, it landed on Nick's cheek.

"Ow!" he said, getting even angrier and pushing at the old man. Apparently emboldened by the better odds, Duncan gave Vince a kick to the shins, as if repelling a dog. By now, the guy in the lily pond had emerged dripping wet and festooned with bits of slimy greenery. He lurched toward Vince and put his arms around him. "Forget it," he said. "Calm down."

"Don't touch me when you're all wet like that," screamed Vince. "This is pure silk, not some drip-dry suit. Jesus!"

"I'm sorry," said Quentin.

"For Christ's sake! It says 'dry clean only' right on the label!"

At this point, Melanie noticed Kevin waddling up the steps from the pool carrying a leaf skimmer. She rushed over to him. "We've got a situation," she said.

"A situation?" he repeated stupidly.

"We seem to have a fight breaking out. Bust it up, will you?"

"Oh. Okay," he said hesitantly, following her onto the terrace where things had now seemed to have reached

103

some kind of a standoff. All combatants were stepping backward from the wet guy.

"This is our security man," announced Melanie. Kevin stood there with the leaf skimmer like a spear-carrier in an opera and made no move to take charge.

"No he isn't. That's the pool man," said Nadia, undercutting his authority further. "What happened to Manuel?"

"Ask them to leave," said Melanie to Kevin.

"Okay, you heard her. All of you guys go home," said Kevin unconvincingly.

Melanie stamped her foot. "No, not all of them, just the wet guy and Mr. Fontana." For the first time she wondered why the two of them were here in the first place.

"I don't get it. Did Manuel quit or what?" said Nadia.

"Why should *I* leave?" asked Fontana poutily. "I was the one that was insulted. By him." He pointed at Duncan.

"I'm sure Mr. Blaine will apologize," said Melanie, giving Duncan a fierce look. "I don't think he realizes how offensive ethnic slurs are."

Duncan smiled. "Sure, sure. Sorry. Keep forgetting how sensitive you Americans are. I hope your leg will be okay where I kicked it."

Fontana turned to Nadia. "Whaddaya doing hanging out with a lowlife like him anyway?" he demanded.

"He's a writer," said Nadia.

Fontana nodded with a look of comprehension, and Rosemary came in followed by a middle-aged man with dark hair, gray at the temples. "Another doctor's here," she announced.

"Thank God!" said Nadia, rushing up to him and leading him over to Lila's side. She dragged Glen Pendergast along too, presumably because he also bore the title doctor.

The wet man sidled up to Melanie. "We'd better go," he said. "I'm sorry for the misunderstanding."

"Not so fast, kid," said Fontana. "We got business to take care of here. Are you the assistant? Melinda, Melissa, whatever." He snapped his fingers at Quentin as if trying to get him to jog his memory for him.

"Melanie Oakley," mumbled Quentin.

"What kind of business?" asked Melanie.

"We're here giving you a word to the wise," began Fontana. "Is there somewhere more private where we can talk?" He glanced meaningfully over at Nick and Callie, who were standing there listening. Duncan Blaine had collapsed in his old chair by the table and was smoking a cigarette and gazing glassily into the middle distance. "Private? I suppose so," said Melanie, thoroughly confused, "but you'd better tell me what it's about."

"I know it may seem unusual just dropping in like this, but I'm representing an unusual party," said Quentin. "The owner of the rights to the Kali-Ra novels by Valerian Ricardo." With as much dignity as he could muster, he went over to the edge of the lily pond, squatted there and fished out his briefcase. When he rose holding it, water streamed noisily out the bottom around the hinges onto the brick terracing.

Kevin interrupted. "So do you still want me to throw them out?" he asked.

Nick said to Callie, "But Uncle Sid's books are in the public domain!"

"Things are not always as they appear," she replied, sliding her green eyes over the dripping form of Quentin Smith, who in turn stared at Nick and said, "Uncle Sid?"

Rosemary came onto the terrace, folded her hands and said, "Dinner is ready." She turned to Vince, then eyeballed the soggy Quentin. "Are they staying?"

Vince Fontana smiled. "Sure, that'd be nice. Just to show there's no hard feelings."

"Okay," said Rosemary coldly, "so two more places."

Vince Fontana slapped her heartily on the back and said, "My driver's parked out in front. Maybe you can feed him in the kitchen or something."

"Yeah, okay." Rosemary turned back to Melanie. "What about Mrs. Ricardo? Is she sick or what?"

Melanie glanced over to where the doctor seemed to be giving some instructions to Nadia and Glen. Lila still looked pale. Maybe she could be talked out of joining them at the table where she would no doubt harangue Duncan, snipe at Glen Pendergast, and shriek at Nick's girlfriend. Melanie took in the rest of the assemblage, including Duncan, who now seemed to be draining the dregs of other people's drinks from the table in front of him. The chances were good that a sit-down meal with this cast of characters would end in disaster.

It was time for some command decisions. To Rosemary she said, "Things are a little confusing tonight. Maybe we should have a kind of casual buffet thing. Set it up in the dining room, okay?"

She now addressed Vince Fontana and his waterlogged friend. "I can't think what we have to talk about but I will give you a few minutes in the office."

She asked the doctor how Lila was and he told her that it looked as if she had just fainted and should get some rest. She could come to his office tomorrow for some tests. Melanie thanked him and asked Rosemary to show him out.

To Lila, she said firmly, "We'll bring you dinner on a tray in the guest cottage."

"We can't leave her alone," protested Nadia.

"Why don't you go with her and make sure she's comfortable," said Melanie. "Let me just see what Mr. Fontana here wants."

Kevin was still hovering around, and as she left with Fontana and Quentin Smith, she said over her shoulder, "Thanks a lot, you can go," though what she was thanking the phlegmatic security guard for she couldn't imagine. If there were any real trouble around here, she'd have to handle it herself, as usual.

CHAPTER XVII

THE DISAPPEARING DINNER GUESTS

After Melanie had left with Vince Fontana and his drenched associate and Nadia had led Lila away to the kitchen to get her a plate of something, there were only four people left on the terrace.

Duncan Blaine, still seated but listing a bit, seemed to be approaching a comatose state. Glen Pendergast, clearly uncomfortable at the prospect of making small talk with him, sidled over to Callie and Nick. "Well," he said nervously, "I guess we wait until someone calls us for dinner."

Nick shrugged and said, "I guess so." He cleared his throat. "You know a lot more about Uncle Sid than I do. I assumed all his stuff was out of copyright, but that guy with Vince Fontana said he represented the copyright holder. What's the deal?"

"Beats me," said Pendergast. "I was told the novels were all out of copyright when I wrote my book a couple of years ago. Frankly, Lila here tried to convince me otherwise, and when that didn't work, she threatened to sue me for mental anguish."

"You're kidding," said Callie.

Glen Pendergast rolled his eyes. "She had some lawyer make a big deal out of the fact that the guys who invented Superman got a lot of cash when the movie was made, even though they had no immediately apparent legal claim to the material, and said I could get creamed in a jury trial with a hysterical, impoverished little old lady sobbing on the witness stand.

"I got so paranoid I tracked down the last copyright holder, and wrote them asking if I needed permission to quote from the books. Some outfit in the Bahamas or someplace like that. I got back a short, polite note saying it was in the public domain. Lila denies it, but she or Valerian Ricardo must have sold the copyright."

"But what does Vince Fontana have to do with it?" said Callie. "This is all too weird." She turned toward the professor. "So you never found out exactly what happened with the rights?"

Pendergast shrugged. "My book was a literary and cultural study, not a biography. As far as the copyrights went, I wasn't interested in anything other than avoiding trouble with quoting the material. And believe me, the combination of loony Lila and her lawyers seemed like big trouble." He suddenly looked concerned. "I'm so sorry poor Nadia has gotten into her clutches. I know it's only because she's such a sweet, kind, trusting person."

Suddenly, Duncan Blaine, ambulatory once more, loomed up behind them. "That Ricardo woman is trouble all right," he said. "She should be put down like a dog. It's disgusting to think that an old bitch like that is in a position to destroy the career of a sensitive and gifted artist!"

"Oh," protested Glen Pendergast, "I'm sure Nadia's career is safe. She's a powerful icon in today's popular culture."

"She's a silly cow," said Duncan. "It's *my* career I'm talking about, you twit! Don't you know who I *am*?" He lurched toward Pendergast in a menacing way.

The professor flinched. "I just remembered I have to make a phone call," he said, beating a retreat through the French doors into the house.

Blaine turned to Callie and Nick and said in a surprised tone, "I believe that I am drunk."

"Maybe you should lie down or something," said Callie.

"Nonsense. I should work. I do my best work when I'm completely pissed. I'm a prisoner in this fucking house until I finish this screenplay. I shall go to my room and write my way to freedom." He zigzagged his way across the terrace toward the house.

Alone with Callie, Nick felt suddenly overwhelmed. Dusk had fallen and above them a few stars and a sliver of moon had emerged. The air was heavy with that scent of jasmine again.

He turned to her, and heard himself say, "I know this sounds nuts, but you know, you actually remind me of Kali-Ra."

She brushed a strand of dark hair from her face and smiled at him.

"I don't mean that I think you're the personification of evil or anything," he added hastily. "It's just that here, in the moonlight, with that outfit and everything, and when you joke around sometimes in that voice—"

"I *am* Kali-Ra," she said. "Await me here. I have work to do." She started to flit away.

"Wait!" he said. "Where are you going?"

She turned and raised a slim, pale hand. "It is not yours to ask, Raymond Vernon," she said dramatically, then sprinted, gazellelike across the lawn and around the corner of the house.

He stood there for a moment wondering whether to follow her. She really was a fascinating person. In this atmosphere, Nick began to feel, anything could happen. He could run after her, catch her, roll around with her in some bosky corner of the estate, make mad passionate love to her under the starlit California sky—

These thoughts were interrupted by Rosemary, who came out to say, "Okay. Dinner's all set up in the living room. Where did everyone go?"

"I'm not sure," said Nick.

CHAPTER XVIII

A SCREAM IN THE NIGHT

✗

Meanwhile, in her office, Melanie was explaining to Vince Fontana and the man with him, who appeared to be named Quentin Smith, that under no circumstances was she prepared to negotiate anything until the lawyers had a chance to look things over.

"Listen, Vince," said Quentin nervously, "we can't approach anyone directly without their attorney. I mean—"

"Hey!" said Fontanta, "I'm not talking about the actual deal. I'm here as a goodwill gesture to say that certain associates of mine who have strong ties to show business are interested in these negotiations going off without a hitch."

"Just what is your interest in this matter?" asked Melanie. "I'm afraid I don't understand."

"Hey!" barked Vince, "I'm trying to warn you." Quentin wished he wouldn't begin all his thoughts with "Hey!"

"Warn me about what?"

"About maybe some bad shit happening if the party Quentin here represents is crossed. These are fair people but they're hard people. I grew up with these people. They're my people, *capisce*? That's why I'm in a position to know how tough they can be. But if I tell them that I spoke to you and you're willing to pay what these rights are worth, no bad stuff has to happen."

"What kind of bad stuff did you have in mind?" said Melanie.

He shrugged and raised a knowing eyebrow. "Accidents on the set. Maybe a lot of downtime. Union troubles. You know how that can all add up. My friends are very powerful."

"Who are your friends exactly?"

"Hey, do I have to spell it out to you? Didn't you ever go to the movies?" He began to hum the theme from Francis Ford Coppola's *The Godfather.*

Suddenly they heard a scratchy sound at the French windows, as if a branch were scraping against it. The men had to turn to look, but Melanie was facing the garden and she alone saw the shadowy figure moving quickly away from the window. "Look!" she said. "Did you see that? There was someone lurking in the shrubbery."

"Hey, I tried to get them to wait until I talked to you," said Vince in a sad voice. "Be reasonable! Make a deal with the kid here."

Melanie ignored him and reached for the phone to call Kevin in the carriage house. She frowned. There was no answer. She put in a call to Tom Thorndyke with the speed dial.

Quentin's head was pounding again. "I'll be right back," he mumbled, staggering out of the room. He was going to check and see if Vince Fontana's muscle-bound chauffeur was still at his post or if he was cruising the grounds and thrashing around in the bushes, trying to scare Melanie Oakley. He had to be stopped, or they'd all be put in jail for extortion.

The long black car was still parked in front of the house, but the driver was gone. Quentin peered nervously into the front seat. The book the driver had been reading was lying there. It appeared to be some kind of physiology textbook, open to a page illustrating the skeletal structure of the knee. Quentin had a horrible feeling the thug was reading up on how to maim people.

He also noticed a car phone. The car was open and he slid into the front seat and picked it up. He felt compelled to call

Margaret. She'd probably still be out having dinner with that prosecutor, but he could call her machine and at least hear her voice. It would be so soothing to hear Margaret's voice.

When confronted with the fact that all the dinner guests had disappeared, the housekeeper had simply shrugged and led Nick into the living room, a vast space filled with pale sofas and chairs and low tables and lit by candles in silver candelabra. Above the fireplace was a huge portrait of Nadia in a black evening gown holding an ostrich feather fan. After examining the room with a certain amount of awe, Nick went over to the buffet table along one wall where a meal was laid out.

This was a hell of a note, he thought. Here he was at a Hollywood dinner party and he was eating all alone. It was weird, but what else was he supposed to do? Anyway, he was starving.

He filled himself a plate of some kind of sauteed chicken thing with mushrooms and a salad of avocados and yellow tomatoes and set it down on a coffee table by a picture window overlooking the garden. He supposed Callie would reemerge at some point, and the others too. He went back to the buffet and helped himself to wine.

In a way, it was rather restful to be alone. He had been reeling at the day's events and a little quiet time was welcome. He couldn't believe he'd woken up in Minneapolis this morning. It seemed a lifetime ago. Since then, so many strange things had happened, and now he was sitting here all by himself in a movie star's living room, staring into a moonlit garden with the odd feeling that anything could happen to him. And it was all because of Uncle Sid.

Just then, Nadia and Lila walked slowly by the window. Nadia was carrying a tray. Presumably they were headed toward the guest house. Lila had certainly been a disappointment. She hadn't told him anything of interest about

Uncle Sid and then she'd turned on poor Callie in that irrational way. She was clearly nuts. That nice Melanie Oakley had come right out and said so, and Duncan Blaine and Glen Pendergast had said she was big trouble too.

One of Uncle Sid's books lay on the coffee table, and Nick picked it up and began to read as he ate his chicken.

> "I don't like it," said Raymond Vernon, as he smoked a Balkan Sobranie and paced in front of the huge fireplace. "I sense a strange presence here at the Old Priory. Can't you sense it, inspector?"
>
> The detective sipped his brandy. "Steady, old chap," he said. "I know you've had a bit of a scare, but we captured the queer leopardlike creature with the jeweled collar that was roaming the grounds. Odd business, I agree, but it's all quiet now."
>
> "Too quiet," said Raymond Vernon with the grim fatalism of one who has faced evil personified, not just once but many times. Suddenly his head rose and he stood as still as a deer in the forest. "There it is, that strange scent. A musky, Oriental sort of scent. Inspector, she is here, I know it! Up to her old mischief." His heart began to race as it always did when he sensed he was soon to come into the presence of the Queen of Doom. That scent was as much her signature as the sacred gong with which she summoned her slaves.
>
> "Nonsense, old man. Your nerves are shot," said the inspector.
>
> Just then, the deadly quiet of the night was rent by a woman's terrified scream.

As he read these words, Nick heard a shattering crash, followed by a woman's terrified scream, and he froze for a second. He must stop reading these damn things. They were beginning to seem real. But then it occurred to him that he had heard an actual scream and that it had come from outside.

CHAPTER XIX

THE INTRUDER'S CLUE

He ran back out onto the terrace. There were more screams now, and muffled hysterical sobs coming from farther away in the garden. He ran toward the sound.

A moment later, along a gravel path, he encountered Nadia Wentworth clutching Lila Ricardo to her chest and pointing up at the roofline. At their feet lay a fallen tray and dinner plate surrounded by a massive pile of ceramic shards, glazed in jade green. He peered up in the direction she was pointing. There was a balustrade with a row of giant Ali Baba–style jars high above them. One of the row was missing.

"There's someone up there," she said. "I swear I saw someone moving around up there. He tried to kill us."

"I was worried about the emanations around here," said Lila, her eyes glittering in a way that made Nick feel she'd gotten some kind of sick thrill from her experience.

"We'd better go inside," he said. "And call the police."

"Could it be," Nadia gasped, "one of the slaves of Kali-Ra?"

"Calm down," said Nick, who began to wonder if she actually had seen anyone. "You're in shock. Maybe it was one of those earthquakes they have here."

"My dear," said Lila to Nadia, "the slaves of Kali-Ra aren't real in anything other than a spiritual, symbolic sense. Although I have sometimes wondered if Valerian knew more than he let on."

"For heaven's sake," said Nick impatiently, "get inside. There are a lot more of those jars up there waiting to fall or be pushed!" He led the two women back up the path, where they encountered Melanie Oakley, trailed by Vince Fontana, who seemed to be puffing a little to keep up with her. Melanie stared with horror at the jagged remains of the heavy jar and glanced back up at the balustrade.

Now, Callie and Glen Pendergast were coming down the path toward them. "What happened?" asked the professor. "I heard a scream. Nadia! Are you all right?" Nadia began sobbing quietly, and Pendergast surprised Nick by putting his arm around her in a protective way, while Nick explained what had happened.

"Nadia says she saw someone up there," he said. "Somebody should call the cops." He turned to Pendergast. "Meanwhile, let's go up there and check it out."

"Absolutely," said Pendergast, who released Nadia and looked surprised he'd had his arm around her in the first place.

At the same moment that Nadia Wentworth's scream had rent the night air, Quentin Smith was sitting in the front seat of Vince Fontana's car, babbling hysterically into Margaret's voice mail about how he had been taken against his will to Nadia Wentworth's house by Vince Fontana and his chauffeur, who seemed to be psychopaths. "Jesus, Margaret," he said. "I just heard a woman scream. That thug must be working over Nadia and her assistant. I gotta go."

Quentin encountered Nick and Glen Pendergast in the main entry hall, just as they were running up the steps to the second floor. Sensing that this was some kind of posse and that they knew where they were going, he followed them. "Is everyone okay?" he asked.

Over his shoulder Nick explained that a huge vase had fallen at Nadia's and Lila's feet, and that they were investigating. Nick and Quentin followed the professor up the carpeted stairs leading from the main entry hall and down a long second-floor corridor to another set of steps at the far end of the house, presumably the servants' staircase, which led still higher into the complex architectural mass that was Villa Vera.

"I thought I saw someone in the bushes outside my office," said Melanie as they settled uneasily back down in the living room. She glared at Vince Fontana. "Mr. Fontana here seems to think the Mafia is after us." He seemed not to have heard her and was browsing around the buffet, helping himself to chicken and wild rice.

Callie looked flustered and said, "Um, actually, that was me outside your office. I'm really sorry. I took this walk in the garden and I sort of mixed up all those glass doors to outside and I tried to get back in through your office. When I realized what I'd done, I was embarrassed and I just went back until I found the fountain again. I'm really, really sorry."

"Well, that's a relief," said Melanie.

"I still think someone tried to kill me!" said Nadia.

"Or maybe me," said Lila, sounding as if she felt left out.

"I suppose we'd better call the police," said Melanie.

"Oh, please, no!" said Nadia. "If it gets out that the slaves of Kali-Ra are after me, the insurance company won't let me do the picture. You know how they are."

"The slaves of Kali-Ra? Like, for real?" said Callie.

Vince Fontana examined the wine label and poured himself a glass.

"She doesn't mean literally," said Melanie in a worried voice. "She's gotten some letters from some crank. I've already called Tom Thorndyke because I heard Caroline here and thought she was a prowler. He's on his way. But he'll tell us to call the police, Nadia. I'm sure he will."

Anxious for Tom to arrive and desperate to do something, anything, Melanie looked around at all the candelabra. Dining by candlelight was a pretentious affectation of Nadia's, but in the present circumstances, Melanie also found it made the room look spooky. "Let's turn on some real lights," she said, then proceeded to bustle around clicking on the lamps and blowing out the candles.

High above them, in an atticlike space full of unused servants' bedrooms, Nick, Quentin, and Glen had made their way to a door that led to the long balcony. Outside, the row of jars stood in silhouette, and Nick was startled by the sheer size of them. They must each weigh a ton. It was dark up here and the three men fumbled around, feeling their way along a space that by its narrowness seemed to indicate that the balcony and its huge jars were nothing more than decorative, like part of a movie set.

As their eyes adjusted, Nick was horrified to see Quentin lose his footing and lurch toward one of the vases. As he struck it, he gave out with an audible "Ow!" but the thing didn't budge. Nick wondered if the row of jars was attached somehow to the railing. They would have to have sat there for seventy years or so through a whole series of earthquakes.

"There's no one here," said Glen Pendergast.

Nick, remembering Nadia's wacky hypothesis that the slaves of Kali-Ra were after her, said, "Nadia Wentworth strikes me as kind of impressionable. Maybe it was an accident and she imagined seeing someone."

"Someone was here all right," said Glen, who had now reached the section of balustrade from which the jar had tumbled.

"How can you tell?" said Quentin. He was surprised. He wouldn't have expected Fontana's thuggy companion to have bothered to come all the way up here to terrorize people when he could have been perfectly effective at ground level.

"Just look at this!" said Glen, pointing at the railing. There, next to a large circle with a length of iron bolt in its center where the jar had once stood, sat a sandwich with one bite taken out of it. From the look of it, it was peanut butter and jelly.

They spread out into the abandoned servants' rooms, turning on lights, checking rooms and closets, but no one was there. They certainly hadn't encountered anyone coming up. "God, I wish we could have caught the bastard," said Glen Pendergast fiercely as they clomped back downstairs. "We started too late. We stood around chatting and he got away."

"Melanie or someone will have called the cops by now," said Nick reassuringly. Something about the whole scene had given him a strange sense of déjà vu.

Quentin clutched the banister on the way down, feeling weak at the knees. Should he tell them about Fontana and his threatening chauffeur, who had been away from the car at the time the jar was pushed off the balcony? If he did, would the police grab him as an accessory to assault or extortion or something? It was all Maurice's fault.

Margaret was right. He should just quit, start over somehow, get out of Maurice's clutches. First, though, he had to pull together this deal, *somehow or other,* or Maurice was going to throw him to the dogs.

In his second-story bedroom, Duncan Blaine removed the headphones of his portable CD player, through which he had been blasting Mahler, and read over the scene he had just polished, eagerly scrolling through the lines on his laptop. God, it was good! It was the best damn thing he'd written in years. You could cut the sexual tension with a knife, yet it dealt with the ambiguities of sex in an insightful and sensitive way. It would be visually stunning, with an over-the-top operatic look that would work on many levels.

At the same time, it actually managed to be true to the repulsive spirit of that demented old hack, Valerian Ricardo, but with the addition of a humanity and wisdom the old boy had never suspected existed. Blaine thought dreamily that it was almost as if—he quickly pulled himself together and harshly suppressed the thought that something *other* had taken over and polished the scene in such an extraordinary way. God, he was starting to think like that old bat Lila Ricardo! There were no spirit guides or dead pulp writers doing his job for him. It had been his *own* skill and imagination that had fashioned that scene, polishing it like a precious jewel in the girdle of a goddess.

Like a precious jewel in the girdle of a goddess? Where the hell did *that* phrase come from? Maybe the ghost of Valerian Ricardo *was* trying to take possession of his mind. This material was definitely getting to him. He had to get a grip on himself.

He went to the window, flung it open and lit another cigarette, blowing the smoke out into the night because Nadia had made it very clear that her home was a smoke-free zone. He was now sober enough to know he'd been pretty drunk, but not too drunk to write the best damn scene of his life. Seized by a sudden panic, he turned to the laptop. He had better save his surefire Oscar material, and make a backup disk.

CHAPTER XX

PLUNGED INTO DARKNESS

The members of the attic expedition had just returned to the living room and the circle of expectant faces that awaited them there, when Nick suddenly realized where that feeling of déjà vu had come from. "God, that's it, the jars! He was in one of the jars! It was in one of Uncle Sid's books. The Nubian guy with the trained asp who steals the sacred dagger seems to have vanished but he's in a big Moorish jar."

"You're right!" said Glen Pendergast. "*The Cave of Kali-Ra*! Straight steal from Douglas Fairbanks in *The Thief of Baghdad*. Why didn't I think of that? Let's go!"

Suddenly, the room was plunged into darkness. There was a collective intake of breath and a few shrieks.

"We've got to get those candles going again!" said Melanie. Finally, Vince Fontana produced a lighter and began this process, joking about his early career as an altar boy. Their faces were now half-illuminated by flickering light, and they instinctively drew together around the coffee table.

"I don't like this at all," said Melanie. "If the power is off that means the alarm system is off."

"But someone already got in," said Nadia. "We pay Tom Thorndyke all this money and look what happens."

"I wonder where the hell Kevin is," said Melanie. "Tom said he was a highly competent guy."

"You mean the new pool man?" said Nadia. "What's

going on around here? People aren't telling me things." She looked around the room with an expression Melanie knew well. She was looking for something else to complain about and someone to pick on, so as to indicate that there was a gross pattern of inefficiency and disloyalty. "And who is this guy?" she demanded, pointing at a cowering Quentin. "Did we invite him here?"

"No," said Melanie. "He represents something called Maurice Fender Associates. Look, we'll talk about this later. First of all we have to—"

"I know that outfit," shrieked Lila, pointing at Quentin. "It all becomes clear. He tried to kill me because he stole the copyright and I know it. He pushed that jar over!"

Just then, Kevin came into the room with a powerful flashlight. He still waddled, but his wimpy persona seemed to have vanished. "Sorry, folks," he said. "We had a problem but it's under control. I want everyone to stay right here until I get back. I'm going to get the lights back on and reset the alarm and I'll let you know what happened." He went over to Nadia and put a hand on her shoulder. "You're out of danger, Ms. Wentworth."

"Someone was up there on that high balcony and tried to kill Nadia! We found a partially eaten sandwich up there," said Glen Pendergast frantically.

"There may be a guy in one of those jars up on the balcony," said Nick.

"There *was* someone up there in a jar," said Kevin. "But I've taken care of him. The police are on their way to pick him up." He turned to Glen Pendergast. "And I'm afraid that was my sandwich. I didn't even drop it after I heard the crash, I was running so fast. I'll tell you all about it when I come back. Remain calm." He sprang out of the room toward the kitchen with a light step.

"Thank God!" said Melanie. "I thought he was kind of a jerk, but he seems to know what he's doing."

"Well, he's not very attractive," said Nadia sulkily. "He has a bad haircut and he just breathed peanut butter in my face."

"So that was *his* sandwich and he got there before us," said Glen Pendergast. He sounded disappointed he hadn't made the collar personally.

"Where's the guy he caught and who is he?" demanded Nadia of no one in particular. "I'd like to see the bastard for myself."

Quentin began to tremble and sidled over to Vince Fontana. "May I speak to you for a moment?" he whispered. "It's about your chauffeur."

"Bruno? What about him?" he said in a loud voice.

"Crooks," continued Lila, pointing at Vince and Quentin. Nick thought she was looking particularly witchlike by candlelight. "They're conspiring, like when they stole Valerian's copyright." She turned to Callie. "You're part of it, aren't you?"

Just then Duncan Blaine, carrying a Bic lighter in front of him, stumbled into the room. "What the hell's going on?" he said. "I just lost the best scene I've ever done in my life. *This place is under a foul curse, I tell you!*"

As he said this, the lights came back on. Duncan Blaine was horrified to realize that his last utterance, which by flickering candlelight had seemed within the scope of sane conversation, hung in the air like the most wretched example of Valerian Ricardo's prose.

Fortunately, no one seemed to have paid the least bit of attention to him. He headed quietly to the black lacquered liquor cabinet in the far corner of the room.

"I don't get it," Nadia was saying. "Why is anyone talking about the rights to Kali-Ra? It's in the public domain. Right, Glen?"

"As far as I know," he said.

"Look," said Melanie decisively, "we can discuss this

later. Meanwhile, it looks like we might have had some ma-
niac running around loose. Let's concentrate on that first,
shall we?" She turned to Quentin and Vince Fontana and
said icily, "I can't help but notice that you guys were threatening me just when this happened."

"Hey!" said Vince. "I wasn't threatening you. I was tip-
ping you off. Don't mess with Quentin here come negotiating time. It's healthier."

"There's nothing to negotiate," said Nadia. "Is there?" She
turned to Melanie.

"That question aside," said Quentin nervously, "I'd like to
make it perfectly clear that I'm not sure what Mr. Fontana
was getting at. I do not represent him. He is a friend of the
person I *do* represent, and insisted on coming here tonight,
for some reason of his own that is obscure to me, but
please don't think that he represents in *any* way the views
or interests of the client I *am* representing. In addition, let
me state unequivocally that if his chauffeur, Bruno, has
tried to harm or frighten anyone here, it is completely without my knowledge or consent."

Just then Rosemary came in rubbing her shoulder. "That
Bruno's got a real touch," she said.

"Did he hurt you?" demanded Melanie, rushing over to
her, and looking at Quentin in angry horror.

"No, no. We had a bite to eat and I mentioned some of
my aches and pains and he straightened out that kink in
my back and got rid of the pain in my shoulder. What happened to the lights, anyway? And before that, was someone
screaming a while back? I was down in the laundry room,
but I swear I heard someone scream."

Before anyone could answer her, Kevin came back in
carrying his flashlight and giving everyone ·a reassuring
smile. "The breaker just tripped. It should be fine now. And
the police are on the way to pick up the intruder I captured. Also, the alarm is reset." He frowned. "I'll have a talk

with Tom about how he got in. There must be a weakness in the security system somewhere."

"Well, who the hell is this guy you caught? Is he the guy who was writing letters to me?" demanded Nadia.

Kevin shrugged. "Can't say what his motive is. The fact is that when I put a choke hold on him, he passed out. It happens sometimes. But his vital signs are normal."

"What!" said Melanie. "Didn't you call for medical help? Where is this guy, anyway?"

Nadia looked alarmed. "Yeah. I mean, if the guy croaks can he sue?"

"The dead can't sue," said Quentin. "But his heirs could."

"The police are arranging for medics," said Kevin brusquely. "Excuse me for a moment." He unclipped a walkie-talkie from his belt and listened to it for a while. "That's Tom. I'm meeting him out by the gate and we'll take a look around the grounds and see if there are any indications of how this individual gained entry. I'll be back as soon as possible."

"When the police get here, where shall I tell them the intruder you caught is?" asked Melanie, slightly bemused.

"He's under restraint in the garage," said Kevin, bounding off again, clearly happier in his role as a security specialist than as a pool man.

"I feel very uneasy about this whole thing. I mean we can't just leave some guy trussed up in the garage, can we?" said Melanie.

"Never mind that," said Nadia in a menacing tone. "I need to talk to you privately." She turned to her guests. "The rest of you can eat dinner or whatever," she said. "Melanie, you come with me."

"Let me wait for Tom," said Melanie.

"I am feeling majorly stressed out," said Nadia through clenched teeth. "I need to talk to you now."

The two women left, and Duncan Blaine sidled over to Callie. He had produced a couple of gin and tonics and he handed her one. "What the hell is going on?" he said. "The lights go out and next thing I know Rambo the pool man is running around taking charge. You seem like an intelligent girl. Tell me all about it."

Callie began to fill him in and Nick went over to where Lila was haranguing Vince Fontana and Quentin Smith. "I was just about to prove that you guys were crooks when my husband's books went out of copyright. So now are you saying they're back in?"

"Are you Mrs. Ricardo?" asked Quentin. "Did you inherit the rights?"

"I sure as hell did," she said. "He died intestate and I am his sole heir."

"Well," said Quentin in a kindly tone, "sometimes when there is some area of dispute, and the courts would take a long time to sort it all out, the wisest course is for both parties to compromise a little. My client might well consider an offer suitable to you that would allow him to negotiate directly with Ms. Wentworth's production company. Do you have a lawyer, Mrs. Ricardo? I can draw up something for you to sign. Maybe we can work out some arrangement agreeable to both parties."

"I'm not sharing with anyone," said Lila. "Valerian wants *me* to profit from his genius. Nadia understands that. You'll get the rights to his works over my dead body. I guess you already tried once tonight, but you missed."

CHAPTER XXI

THE HEIRS OF KALI-RA

Back in Melanie's office Nadia was pacing the floor. "What does Uruguay have to do with it? This is America. Since when does Uruguay tell me what kind of a deal I can make?"

"The Uruguay Round," explained Melanie, consulting the memo George had just faxed over. "In 1994, President Clinton signed the Uruguay Round Agreements Act. It was part of an international trade agreement."

Nadia scowled and looked as if people were deliberately keeping things from her. "I don't get it," she said in a threatening tone.

Melanie shrugged. "Uruguay is the place where they met to negotiate, I guess. Like the Treaty of Versailles or the Congress of Vienna or the Diet of Worms."

"A diet of worms!"

"It was some theological convention or something."

"Okay, okay, forget all this intellectual *Jeopardy!* stuff, please." Nadia gnawed on her knuckle as she so often did when overwrought. Melanie thought she looked kind of like a squirrel when she did it, baring her teeth in an odd way.

"Anyway," said Melanie in a calm, kindergarten-teacher voice she hoped would soothe Nadia, "the treaty says that if something is still in copyright outside the U.S., then the U.S. has to allow it to be in copyright here too. And apparently Valerian Ricardo's books, technically, are in copyright in England. These guys say he published them there first. You see, England just signed a treaty with the European Union so that all their copyrights would have the same length of time. On the first of January 1997, a lot of English copyrights were restored to match German ones, including Valerian Ricardo's, which means the U.S. has to recognize them too under the Uruguay Round."

"God! It's so unfair. Why should these fucking Uruguayans and Germans tell me what I can or can't do?"

"It's a bitch, isn't it," said Melanie. She knew when to stop explaining. Nadia seemed to be slowly getting the fact there was a copyright holder.

"But those books haven't been in print in years," said Nadia. "No one knows about them but me."

"Apparently the owners of the copyright know about them," said Melanie. "Their attorney has written us a strong letter. We'll have to negotiate with them. This Quentin Smith character seems to be trying to do that. Although what Vince Fontana is doing here beats me. He seems to be implying that the copyright holder, this company in the Caribbean somewhere, is part of the Mafia and they'll break our legs if we don't pay them whatever they ask."

"Get George on the line and set it up on the speakerphone," said Nadia pacing. "I want to hear from him who fucked this up and why and what he's going to do about it."

As Melanie made the call that she knew would chill George's bones down to the marrow, Nadia shouted, "Kali-Ra is *mine, mine.*" Her arms were rigid, her hands were in fists, her eyes were cast upward as if she were laying down the law about this with God. "I will never swerve from my course until I have secured my prize *completely.*"

Melanie wasn't sure, but she was pretty certain the phrase came from *The Island of Kali-Ra.*

Back in the living room, Rosemary came in and looked at the buffet table with disapproval. "You hardly ate anything," she announced to everyone. "It's not getting any warmer." Glen Pendergast apologetically helped himself to a plate of dinner and Nick refilled the plate that he had hastily abandoned earlier when he heard the crashing jar and the scream. Rosemary sighed and left.

Lila was still haranguing Quentin. Nick thought sadly that if Uncle Sid hadn't married this nutty old babe years ago, he would be the sole heir, and he'd be the one deciding if he wanted to go for the max or cut a sweet, simple deal that would put him through graduate school in style.

"Listen to her," said Glen sadly. "She put me through hell and now she'll put poor Nadia through hell with her phony claims."

"Is there anything to this stuff about these guys being crooks?" Nick glanced over at Fontana. "I've always heard the Mafia made his career and he's done errands for them ever since."

"I don't know anything about that, but there is some doubt in my mind that Lila was ever actually married to your uncle."

"Really?" said Nick. "Wow."

"Did you read that book of hers?" Glen rolled his eyes.

"I found it kind of heavy going," said Nick. "There was all that occult stuff, and the writing was terrible. It was all about her, not him."

"Yeah, well, there's a lot of crap in there about how they were brought together in a pure union of two souls, blessed by the Enlightened Ones on a mountaintop in perfect harmony with the universe. Nothing about a marriage license. Valerian Ricardo always made a big point about flaunting convention."

"Interesting," said Nick, his heart leaping with hope.

In the kitchen, Bruno sat at the kitchen table finishing his herbal tea while Rosemary wiped down the counters and told him her life story. "So after Jerry died, I was in a weird space. I needed a place to grieve and regroup, a comfort zone, somewhere where I could do the kind of food I believe in and have some time to work on my memoir of the years I spent on the road. I'm one of the only ones who goes all the way back to the very birth of the Grateful Dead."

"Wow."

"It's important that younger people know how it all went down."

Bruno nodded. "For sure. My generation is so cut off from the past."

Rosemary adjusted a long Indian earring. "Yeah, it's turning out to be so much more than a memoir. It's like a way for me to get in touch with who I am and I'm sure that's what will make it so moving to others. I thought after it comes out I could do a cookbook as a follow-up."

"Great idea." he indicated his empty plate. "This was a really good meal."

"Thanks. Hey, I don't know what you did, but my shoulder hasn't felt this good in ages. My naturopath hasn't been able to do anything. I was thinking of going to a chiropractor."

"I'll give you my card," said Bruno. "I put in about ten hours a week as a massage therapist, but I'm working on my degree from Long Beach State in physical therapy."

"So you don't work full-time for Mr. Fontana?"

"No. I just drive for the old guy as needed and check in on him once a day. His family is worried about him getting in trouble."

Rosemary gave the base of the blender a polish. "Drugs and booze, or sex—or both?"

"His problems are more interesting than that," said Bruno.

Quentin, overwhelmed by Lila's harangue, had made his

escape and come into the kitchen, ostensibly to use the phone. He was surprised to see Bruno there. "Oh, thank God," he said. "I thought you were all tied up in the garage."

"The car's fine," said Bruno, looking puzzled. "Are you and Mr. Fontana ready to go yet?" He checked his watch. "It's getting a little late for him."

"Maybe I'll just call a cab," said Quentin, eager to part company with Vince as soon as possible. He'd let Nadia Wentworth and her assistant figure out how to get rid of the old crooner by themselves, and he'd leave as soon as the two women emerged from their conference. He wanted to try for a little more damage limitation and a friendly departure.

"Just out of curiosity, Bruno," said Quentin, emboldened by the fact that he was about to break free of Fontana and his hired muscle, "where were you when Miss Wentworth screamed?"

"I was down in the basement with Rosemary," he said. "I carried down the laundry for her because she has some inflammation in her shoulder and should definitely give her deltoids a rest." He shrugged. "It's pretty far away and the dryer was going but I did hear what I thought could have been a scream. I wanted to come up and check it out, but Rosemary told me that Miss Wentworth yells all the time."

Back in the living room, Nick noticed that Duncan Blaine was practically sitting in Callie's lap, with a hand on the incredibly smooth knee that had emerged from the slit in her sarong. "Did it hurt much when they punched that hole next to your belly button?" he was asking as he drained his glass. "Maybe I should freshen these up, my dear. Same again?"

Nick didn't like her relaxed posture, or the fact that she seemed to be giggling. While Duncan was busying himself

over by the liquor cabinet, he leaned over the back of the
sofa and whispered, "Need rescuing?"

"Sure," she said, offering him a lazy arm, indicating she
wanted to be pulled off the sofa. He obliged, and she fell
onto his shoulder, then took his hand. "Come with me," she
said. "Into the moonlit garden. I have much to reveal, Raymond Vernon, things that will astonish you."

"Maybe we should wait until the police come," he said.

"It is my wish, the wish of Kali-Ra," she said throatily.

"Okay," said Nick. "Your wish is my command. Fresh air
will do us both good." Nick himself had been drinking
wine throughout the eventful evening, and it was clear he
would be doing the driving later.

She led him back out onto the dark but balmy and
flower-scented terrace and past some dense shrubs, then
opened the little woven pouch she wore strapped to her
torso and took out what appeared to be a fat joint and a
Zippo lighter. "This has all been a pretty weird couple of
hours," she said, lighting up with a practiced hand. She
stared up at the stars, exhaled in a series of parsimonious
puffs, and handed it to him. "This is some good shit," she
said. "Your uncle Sid would have loved it."

Quentin Smith sat in a corner of the living room trying
to look tiny and remain unnoticed. Fortunately, Lila had decided to babble away at Glen Pendergast. Meanwhile,
Vince Fontana and Duncan Blaine seemed to have patched
things up and were busying themselves over at the end
of the room with the liquor cabinet, drinking and chain-
smoking like a couple of fifties rat packers.

Things were about as bad as they could possibly be.
Quentin saw nothing but obstacles to his goal of securing
Maurice a million plus for the Kali-Ra rights.

First of all, there was Maurice's operation itself, which
was a criminal enterprise, and ripe for a RICO prosecution.

Years ago, as a lawyer representing a lot of people in show business, Maurice had arranged to buy up rights, collect the fees and royalties they generated, then pay his clients under the table in cash, saving them a bundle in taxes. A liberal and flexible tax policy in his offshore hideaway, which also offered citizenship for a flat fee, eliminated any tax problems Maurice himself might have encountered.

His hefty income was based on his commissions as a cutout. Every once in a while he got lucky and a rock star died of a drug overdose. Then, Maurice, the legal owner, could keep all the royalties, leaving the ignorant heirs high and dry.

The whole thing had worked smoothly for years, saving some of the biggest names in show business a lot of money. The customers, people like Vince Fontana, whose tax problems had been enormous before they "sold" the rights to Maurice, weren't about to complain. But now that Carla Lomax of Carla and the Cleartones was on the job, and until she could be bought off, things in Maurice's empire were pretty shaky.

Even if they managed to get Carla in line, Lila Ricardo was ready to do battle. As far as Quentin could tell, she had neither evidence that Maurice was running a scam nor deep pockets. But she could raise a lot of hell, which could be dangerous, especially with Carla Lomax on the offensive at the same time. And Nadia Wentworth seemed tight with the old woman. She might finance a suit for Lila.

Quentin looked over at Lila now, nattering away at the professor. If only that gigantic vase *had* hit her! He wouldn't have minded helping it along himself. This was as low as he'd ever sunk. Yes, it had come to this. He was ready to kill old ladies to keep Maurice off his back.

CHAPTER XXII

A MESSAGE OF DOOM

✗

Nadia was still yelling at George on the phone when Melanie decided to leave the office and check to see if the police had arrived. It seemed to be taking them a while. Tom and Kevin weren't back either.

In the living room, Lila was carrying on to Glen Pendergast about Valerian Ricardo and how tragic it had been that his genius had never been acknowledged in his lifetime. "Your book could have done something about this terrible injustice," she said in an accusing tone.

Melanie had had it. Lila was going to bed right now. She went over to her and said in a bossy voice, "The doctor says you need your rest."

"Yes," said Glen Pendergast hastily. "He gave her some sleeping pills too."

This was good news. "Where are they?" demanded Melanie.

"I don't know," said Lila vaguely. "Maybe Nadia has them."

"I saw her put them in her purse," said Glen, pointing at Lila's big handbag. "The doctor was very worried about you. You better take those pills and go to bed," he said sternly to the old woman.

"After what's happened, I'm a little nervous about sleeping in the guest cottage," Lila said.

"I understand," said Melanie. "You can sleep in the Blue

Room." With Duncan Blaine and Glen Pendergast both in residence, this was the only free bedroom.

"Is the bed on a north and south axis?" asked Lila suspiciously. "The Enlightened Ones told Valerian long ago that it's psychically dangerous for highly sensitive people to sleep at an angle to polar magnetism."

Melanie was beginning to feel as if she were trying to get an obstinate five-year-old to tuck in for the night. She mentally reviewed the orientation of all the beds in the house and realized that only one of them would meet the Enlightened Ones' criterion.

"Fine. We'll put you in Nadia's room. You'll love it. There's a swan bed on a raised platform and a fireplace and a private balcony and a Jacuzzi and everything." If Nadia protested, Melanie would simply say they had no choice because the Enlightened Ones wanted it this way. Maybe that would accelerate the process of disillusion.

"Well, all right," said Lila.

Melanie grabbed Lila's handbag and clicked it open. She removed a bottle of pills, and went into the kitchen for a glass of water. There, she was surprised to see Rosemary watching a baseball game with a young man who looked like a bouncer or a loan shark's enforcer.

"This is Bruno, Mr. Fontana's driver," explained Rosemary.

Melanie nodded warily. "Listen, Rosemary," she said, "I'm sorry we've kept you working so late. If you could do one last thing before you go to bed, I'd appreciate it. Lila needs to be settled in for the night in Nadia's room."

Rosemary raised her eyebrows. Melanie handed over the pills. "And give her a couple of these too. Make sure she takes them." As far as Melanie was concerned, if Lila never woke up it would be too soon.

*　　*　　*

Like everything else about the place, the pool looked exactly as a movie star's pool should look, vast, trimmed in Moorish tiles, fringed with palm trees. At one end, there was a kind of covered patio area with a tiled fireplace and masses of wicker chairs and settees; at the other were what looked like changing rooms.

"Oh, God, it's so beautiful," said Callie, staring at the darkness of the pool. "The stars are reflected in the water." She turned to Nick, gripped his shoulder and said in an excited voice, "Being rich must be the most wonderful thing in the world. You can even buy stars to float in your pool."

"Stars should be free," he said, puzzled. But she was right. They were for sale, weren't they? In Minneapolis they were often under cloud, but if you bought a house here you could buy clear skies, reflecting bodies of water to capture them, and balmy evenings in which to appreciate them.

"Let's swim," said Callie.

"Do you think it's okay?"

"I don't care if it is or not," said Callie fiercely. "When else can we have a private moonlight swim in a huge garden? Maybe never."

"Maybe there are some suits in the changing rooms," said Nick, trying the door handle. It was locked. He walked over to the next one, but was interrupted by the sight of Callie flinging off her little purse, and stepping out of her sandals. A moment later, she had shed her bikini top and cast it aside, untied her sarong and let it slither to the ground, and stepped out of a sliver of white lace.

She gave a wild little laugh, then ran naked to the edge of the pool and stood there in a diving pose for a second. He had just a glance of her pale body gleaming in the moonlight before she executed a perfect dive, scattering the stars in the pool. Nick scrambled out of his own clothes and dove in after her.

*   *   *

Nadia had slammed down the phone after firing George
and stormed back into the living room. There was no one
there but Duncan Blaine and Glen Pendergast. "Where's
Melanie?" she demanded.

"She's seeing Vince Fontana and that wet guy out the
front door," said Pendergast.

"Nadia, darling," said Duncan gushily, "I've just written
the most beautiful scene for you. It makes the whole story
come alive." Suddenly his expression changed. "Oh, hell,"
he said. "I lost the whole fucking thing in that power out-
age. I've got to recapture it!"

"Listen, Duncan," said Nadia, with a curl of her lip.
"Don't bother me with your stupid problems. Why don't
you get back upstairs and get to work? That's what we're
paying you for."

Glen could see that Duncan Blaine's face had taken on
a look of pure hate, but Nadia had already turned away
from him and flung herself sulkily into a chair. She had
sounded pretty harsh, he thought, but of course the poor
woman was under such pressure. With what looked like a
great effort of will, Duncan regained his composure and
left the room with an air of quiet dignity.

"Boy, you sure have been stressed out today, haven't
you?" said Glen in a kindly voice.

She closed her eyes, allowed her head to fall back and
ran her hand across her brow. "I've been through hell. As
if almost getting killed weren't enough, now some creeps
from Uruguay are fucking me over."

"I gather that there's some confusion about the rights."

She sighed. "Those bastards will probably try to hold me
up for really big bucks. It might even jeopardize the project."

"That would be terrible," he said solemnly. "You were
born to play Kali-Ra."

"Yes, I know I was," said Nadia.

"I know this sounds kind of weird," said Glen, earnestly, "but I first thought that a long time ago, when I was doing my research on Valerian Ricardo and read all the books. I kept seeing *you* as Kali-Ra. To me, you *are* the Queen of Doom."

"Really?" said Nadia. Her eyes opened, her lovely head resumed its upright position, and she looked over at Glen with a softened expression.

"Hang in there and do whatever you have to do to get the picture made," he said in tones of deep conviction, staring at her intensely with his babyish eyes. "It will become a great contribution to popular culture."

"Sometimes I feel so weak," she said. "I'm surrounded by sharks and bloodsuckers. But I guess you wouldn't know anything about that, being a professor and all. It must be such a peaceful life."

Actually, Glen Pendergast felt that his department at Badlands State College was full of bloodsuckers and sharks, but he sensed that Nadia didn't want to hear this.

"A life of the mind is not always peaceful," he said, breaking off the eye contact and gazing soulfully across the room. "It can be tremendously exciting, but all the excitement goes on inside you." He tapped his chest as if to indicate that his inner life was one of the heart, not simply the mind.

"Sometimes," said Nadia sadly, "I wish I had developed my own, like, intellectual part, a little more. My career has taken all my energy. I was voted Wenatchee Apple Blossom Queen right out of high school and things took off right away. I never had time to go to college."

"It's never too late," said Glen Pendergast, refocusing on Nadia. "Learning is a lifelong commitment." This was the motto of Badlands State College, and appeared between quotation marks on all its promotional literature.

"You know," mused Nadia, returning his gaze thoughtfully, "I always thought that Marilyn Monroe hooking up with Arthur Miller was really great."

"I was always very moved by that relationship too," Glen replied, strolling over to the chair next to hers. "I think she had a fine mind but no one really appreciated it because she was so beautiful and sexy."

"Exactly," said Nadia. "It's so unfair when that happens."

"It must be awful," he replied, his voice trembling with sympathy.

After showing Vince Fontana and Quentin Smith the door, and hinting strongly that she saw no need for Mr. Fontana to play any part in future negotiations, Melanie went back into her office to see if Nadia was still there.

She had gone. Melanie was about to leave the room when she spotted a piece of paper dangling from the printer. She picked it up and glanced at it. There were two lines of text in a font she never used, some kind of cheesy-looking Ye Olde Gothic. The lines read:

"Nadia Wentworth has invoked the wrath of Kali-Ra. We, her loyal slaves, will carry out the will of our mistress and smite the little bitch. To inflict pain in service of the will of Kali-Ra is a labor of love."

Melanie let out a scream and dropped the paper.

Where the hell were the police? And were Tom and Kevin still patrolling the grounds? She needed them now!

Someone had been, or was, *in* the house.

CHAPTER XXIII

A SEARCH OF THE GROUNDS

Nadia had to be taken somewhere safe. Melanie rushed back to the living room but there was no one there at all. A quick check of the other downstairs rooms revealed that Melanie was entirely alone. What was going on?

Melanie ran upstairs and knocked on bedroom doors. There was no answer from the Rose Room, where Glen Pendergast was staying, and no light under the door. She slowly opened the door to Nadia's room. In the sliver of light from the hall she could see Lila, all tucked into Nadia's huge carved bed. Her mouth was open and she was snoring lightly.

Maybe Nadia had discovered Lila there and gone to bed in the Blue Room—the only one left in the house. She wasn't there either. Melanie checked her own room with its demure twin beds and flowery curtains. Empty.

Finally, she rapped on Duncan Blaine's door, through which she heard tapping computer keys.

"What is it?" he snarled from behind the door.

"Can I talk to you for a sec?" said Melanie.

Melanie now heard the sound of a chair scraping and the door opened a crack, revealing a few inches of Duncan Blaine. His eyes were unfocused and he seemed to be weaving slightly from side to side. A cloud of blue cigarette smoke emerged into the hall. "What the fuck is it now? I am trying to work. This is impossible! I can't believe I'm being treated this way!"

"Sorry to disturb you," Melanie said. "I'm looking for Nadia." Melanie had a horrible fantasy that Duncan, pushed off the rails by a creative collaboration with Nadia, drunk and enraged, had tried to kill her and Lila with that big jar. Maybe he'd tried again and succeeded. She stood on tip-toe, trying to look into the room over his shoulder to see if Nadia was there in a strangled heap on the floor.

"Well, I haven't got her. I wouldn't want her! Why are you peering into my room? Checking to see if I'm smoking and drinking? Well, I am. I removed a bottle of gin from the liquor cabinet so I could finish this fucking rewrite, but I can't work here if you're going to come pounding on my door and carrying on."

He clutched his forehead with both hands like a scream-ing ingenue in a cheap monster movie and said, "I cannot work under these appalling conditions!" Melanie took ad-vantage of his histrionics by opening the door wider and taking a look inside. Nadia clearly wasn't there.

"Sorry to bother you," she said, stepping back to avoid his slamming the door on her feet.

Melanie was now in a state of panic. She had to find Nadia. She went out onto the terrace and heard the sound of splashing and a laugh from the swimming pool. She ran down the steps to the lanai. Now her paranoid thoughts about Duncan expanded to include practically everyone in the house. Okay, so Kevin found the man on the balcony, but now it seemed the intruder had a confederate *inside* the house who had left another message, this time in per-son, right in her office. How much did she really know about any of these people, really, other than that they all had some connection with Kali-Ra, Queen of Doom?

The pool was surrounded by shed clothes. Two naked people were floating on their backs in the middle of the water, their hands lightly touching. Melanie knew they were staring at the stars and the palm fronds. She often did that by herself during moonlight swims. On closer inspection, the couple appeared to be Nick Iversen and his girlfriend.

Nick Iversen claimed to be Valerian Ricardo's relative. But how did she know if that was true? All she knew was that he'd been buying Kaliana at some bookstore in the Midwest. God, how could she have been so dumb! He might be a nutcase who was stalking Nadia. Melanie felt a horrible, sinking feeling. He seemed so pleasant and normal. He couldn't possibly be a crazed stalker. But he also had that snaky-looking girlfriend in tow. She seemed to know a lot about Kali-Ra herself. And Lila had turned on the girl as if she knew her. Melanie had thought at the time that Lila was simply nuts, but maybe there was more to it than that.

Suddenly, Melanie remembered the central plot, in as far as Valerian Ricardo ever actually came up with a real plot, of *The Gong of Kali-Ra*. All the weekend guests at Lord Basingstoke's country house turned out to be slaves of Kali-Ra, with the exception of Raymond Vernon and the drab governess, who turned out to be Kali-Ra herself.

The moon made a silvery path across the bathers, who continued bobbing lightly in the water. Well, whoever Nick and Caroline actually were, they seemed too preoccupied to be stalking Nadia. The couple, apparently blissed out and floating with their ears below the waterline, hadn't reacted to Melanie's presence.

She ran back up the stairs from the pool, her heart racing, determined to get some kind of help. What is happening? she asked herself. Am I going mad, driven to depths of despair by the unrelenting presence of the Queen of Doom, drawn into her evil web by forces, which are outside the realm of normal humdrum life?

Yes, she must be. The thoughts forming in her mind seemed to have come from the twisted mind and depraved pen of Valerian Ricardo.

Melanie's morbid mood was broken by the sound of Nadia's voice drifting over the tall hedge surrounding the rose garden.

"Oh, Glen," she was saying, "I can't tell you how exciting it is to meet someone who gets the whole Kali-Ra thing. Let's face it, Hollywood isn't an intellectual town. Sometimes it gets pretty lonely."

Melanie went through the carved entryway in the hedge. Nadia was bending tragically over a rose, and sniffing it with her eyes closed. Dr. Pendergast, leaning on the base of a statue of Aphrodite, was gazing at her with a stupid, devoted expression.

If he had ever intended to harm her, he had apparently changed his mind. But what did they know about him, really? He seemed pretty normal, but maybe he was mad. Professors could go mad, couldn't they? Working for years on a Ph.D. thesis could push people over the edge, and his thesis topic had been Kali-Ra. Maybe he'd flipped after close reading of the complete works of Valerian Ricardo. Melanie thought this could very well tip a normal person over into a descent into madness. In fact, just a moment ago she'd felt as if she'd been losing her grip herself. Melanie coughed and they turned to her like startled animals.

"What is it?" snapped Nadia.

Still slightly paranoid, Melanie didn't want to go into details in front of Glen Pendergast. She'd just try to get Nadia out of here and check her into a hotel or something. "Um, did you forget about the benefit tonight? The limo's here."

"What benefit?"

"It's all my fault. I didn't post it on the schedule. But we talked about it. It's for a disease."

"Oh, forget about it," said Nadia. "It's too late."

"But they're honoring you," said Melanie. "Just come on up to the house for a sec and I'll show you the invitation. There are some really big people involved."

"Hey, forget about it," snapped Nadia. "I'm the only woman in this town besides Demi and Julia who gets more than five million a picture. I don't need to kiss up to anyone at some stupid benefit. Glen and I are talking. Call them up and have them FedEx the award or whatever it is. Make some excuse. Tell them I caught their disease."

Melanie gave up. "Okay. There's no benefit. But I'm worried. Tom and Kevin are missing in action, the police never arrived and we got another threatening message from the slaves of Kali-Ra."

"You mean I'm not really being honored?" said Nadia peevishly.

"Maybe you should call the police and see if they're on their way," said Glen with a worried look.

"I was just about to," said Melanie.

"Leave them out of it," snapped Nadia. "That's Tom Thorndyke's job. I don't want a lot of paparazzi making my life hell."

"Maybe the police are over at the garage with Tom and Kevin, arresting the intruder," said Glen.

"You're so smart," said Nadia.

"I'll go over and check," he said, squaring his shoulders.

"We'll come with you," said Melanie.

Nick couldn't believe he was running naked through the shrubbery under a starry sky. At least he'd had the presence of mind to grab a towel, which he carried as he ran. Branches from some prickly shrub were slashing at him, but he could still see the white gleam of her about thirty yards ahead across a darkened lawn.

While he felt exhilarated, gasping in the warm, flower-scented night air, he also wondered if he was doing the sensible thing. But what else could he have done? Callie was crazy and wonderful and beautiful, and when she'd slipped out of the pool after that chlorinated kiss, laughed wildly, and said, "If you catch me, you can have me," grabbed her sarong, and leapt into the darkness, carrying it over her head like a banner, he felt he had no choice in the matter. He'd look like a real jerk if he just treaded water.

And of course the thought of catching her and collecting his reward was delicious. However, the rational part of his brain, considerably feebler since he'd arrived at LAX ten hours ago, flickered into action long enough to tell him that the reason he'd better catch her was so she wouldn't run amok here and embarrass them both.

He didn't know how much her outrageous behavior was attributable to the gin and tonics that sleazy Englishman had poured down her throat and the megajoint she'd smoked most of, and how much to simple high spirts and an exciting personality, but he felt responsible for her. In fact, what he should do was catch her, get her dressed and bundle her off home, wherever that was.

Somehow, he imagined it as the Temple of the Chosen, in the special bedchamber, described so movingly in *The Island of Kali-Ra.*

> It was decorated with incense burners putting forth a queer and hypnotic blue haze, bowls of fascinating and rare fruits, lush, ripe and round, from every corner of the globe, and alabaster vases of orchids, roses, and lilies. All these things were tastefully arranged in a room with walls of lapis lazuli, jade, and amethyst and carpets of tiger skin. The chamber was dominated by a massive onyx bed trimmed with sapphires and emeralds and shrouded with pearl-embroidered, violet-hued draperies of gossamer-fine silk as soft and delicate as the pale, strangely yielding flesh of the Queen of Doom herself.

CHAPTER XXIV

A GHASTLY DISCOVERY IN THE CARRIAGE HOUSE

The garage, although built in the post-horse era, but just barely, was constructed like an old carriage house. It was a large, square structure set some distance from the house and covered with heavy vines. There were chauffeur's quarters on the second floor, and the windows there indicated that the lights were on upstairs.

Glen pulled open one of the heavy wooden doors, which should have been locked, and said in a loud voice, "Hello! Is anyone there?" There was no reply from the cavernous gloom.

Melanie felt Nadia's hand reach for hers and hold it tightly. She squeezed back, as much for her own reassurance as Nadia's. "There's a light switch to your left," she said.

The garage sprang into light. The Jaguar and the BMW were sitting there as usual, which gave a sense of normalcy to everything. Melanie felt her courage returning.

"How do you get upstairs?" asked Glen. "Maybe they can't hear us."

"Over here," said Melanie, making her way past the workbench and around the BMW. At the bottom of the stairs, her foot encountered something large and alive. She screamed and leapt backward. Nadia's scream echoed her own and Glen rushed to her side.

She looked down and saw the pitiful figure of a man in

the fetal position, hands behind his back, tied up with coils of strong rope. Across his mouth was a strip of cloth that seemed to split his face in two. She looked away, but turned back again when she heard a muffled moan coming from the prisoner. She screamed again when she realized with horror that the bound and gagged man was security expert Tom Thorndyke.

"This is so humiliating," said Tom, once they'd removed his gag. "I can't believe this!"

Glen Pendergast busied himself untying knots.

"What happened?" said Melanie. "Where are Kevin and the police?"

"All I know is that when I pulled up here, there was a huge wheelbarrow right in front of the gate full of what looked like peat moss. I got out of the car, surveyed the area to make sure there was no one around waiting to jump me or anything, and then started to move the wheel-barrow. Someone leapt out at me from under the peat moss and went right for my throat. A second later, they'd pressed a cloth soaked in some chemical into my face and knocked me out."

Tom was now shaking off the ropes and rubbing his arms and legs. "I came to here about a half an hour or so ago, I guess."

"Did you recognize the guy who attacked you?" asked Melanie.

"No. He was covered in peat moss."

"It's straight out of *The Secret of Kali-Ra*," said Glen excitedly. "Except that was a cart full of sawdust. The slave of Kali-Ra breathed through a reed while he waited to waylay Raymond Vernon outside the gates of Baron Santini's villa in Monte Carlo."

"Kevin was coming out to meet you," said Nadia. "But he never came back. And he said he'd captured the guy and tied him up here in the garage. But you were here instead. Maybe the intruder escaped and now he has Kevin."

"We'd better conduct a search immediately," said Tom, rubbing his wrists and ankles.

"Could there be more than one of them?" asked Melanie with a shudder.

"Maybe," said Tom. "I weigh two hundred pounds and I didn't walk here."

"You came in the wheelbarrow, I bet," said Glen. "That's how Kali-Ra's faithful slave Achmed did it in *The Secret of Kali-Ra*."

"I'll call the police," said Melanie.

"Maybe we'd better," said Nadia reluctantly.

Tom had gotten back up on his feet, and was assuming his familiar take-charge persona. "I'll handle that. I've got some good contacts with the Beverly Hills police. That way we can get control of the PR fallout. Meanwhile, you ladies should get back to the house and lock yourselves in one of the bedrooms. Glen here can escort you back and stay with you until I come back. Who else is on the premises?"

"Duncan Blaine is working on the screenplay in his room. Lila's asleep in Nadia's bedroom. Rosemary went to bed too, and Nick Iversen and his girlfriend were swimming in the pool just a little while ago," said Melanie.

Tom clenched his jaw in a determined way. "I want everyone inside. I'll round them up and call the Beverly Hills police from the pool phone. Then I'll find Kevin."

Melanie said anxiously, "I hope Kevin's all right."

"He will be," said Glen. "Minor characters in the Kali-Ra books get tied up and shut up in closets and cellars, and they're threatened with unspeakable torture, but Ricardo mercifully never followed through with the details."

"Well, this is one story that's going to end with the bad guy getting apprehended, prosecuted, and incarcerated," said Tom resolutely.

*   *   *

Back in his hotel room, Quentin had been tossing, frightened and angry, on the bed, trying to sleep for an hour. Just when he began to relax and believe he could fall asleep, the phone rang and the sound of Maurice Fender's demanding voice plunged him back into anxious despair.

"So how'd it go?" Maurice demanded. "I got a kind of garbled report from Vince. What's happening?"

"I'm not sure," said Quentin. "We did review the fact that the properties are back in copyright. There's a new wrinkle, though. The last copyright owner, Valerian Ricardo's widow, was there. As I mentioned before, she's living with Nadia Wentworth. She believes she has a shot at getting the rights back from us."

"We gotta make sure that doesn't happen," said Maurice. "You gotta."

"Well, I'll do what I can," said Quentin, exasperated, "but with all this stuff about Carla and the—"

"Not on this line, you idiot!" said Maurice.

"Good point," said Quentin, seeing a way of getting off the phone. "Maybe we'd better discuss this in the morning."

"There's not much to discuss. All you need to know is you have to take care of the old lady and get Wentworth's signature on the dotted line in the next forty-eight hours. Or else. And you know what 'or else' means, don't you? Your hottest career move could be wangling a transfer from the rock pile to the warden's typing pool."

"I don't think the old lady will settle."

"She's gonna have to," said Maurice. "We can make it happen."

"Well, short of throwing her under the wheels of an oncoming truck, I'm not sure—"

"Not on this line!" screamed Maurice.

"Give me a break," said Quentin, painfully aware that his voice was shaking. "I can only do so much."

"Stop whining! I want results! Mike might need some backup from you. He has this number and he knows where you are. If he gets in touch, give him whatever he needs to take care of this matter!" screamed Maurice, slamming down the phone.

Quentin stared up at the ceiling and wondered what could save him. The phone rang again. Presumably, Maurice had a few more thoughts to add. "Hello," he said in a melancholy voice.

"Quentin? Is that you?"

His heart leapt.

"Margaret! My angel! Oh, Margaret! I was imagining you in the arms of that federal prosecutor. You can't imagine how I've suffered!"

"Sam isn't that interested in me. He was more interested in talking about you. And then when I got back, I heard your message. We have to talk. Can I come over?"

Nick stood in the middle of the sweep of lawn and adjusted the towel around his waist. Callie had completely vanished. There was a lot of dense shrubbery around the place, so he couldn't search every inch of it in the dark, but he'd looked everywhere accessible and she was nowhere to be found. She'd probably stopped playing and had gone either into the house or back down to the pool to get the rest of her skimpy wardrobe.

Tentatively, he called out her name, making sure he wasn't loud enough to be heard up at the house. "Callie," he said. "Come out. Callie, where are you?"

Suddenly, he felt a powerful arm around his neck, his legs were kicked out from underneath him and he was pinned facedown on the ground by what felt like two hands and a knee. His face was pressed into the grass, and the wind was knocked out of him.

CHAPTER XXV

THE THING IN THE SHRUBBERY

✗

"What did you say?" demanded a rough voice at his ear.

Nick found it difficult to answer with his face squashed into the lawn. His assailant, hearing him mumble, seemed to understand this. He grabbed Nick's hair and twisted his head sideways, freeing his mouth.

"I was looking for someone," Nick said. "Who the hell are you?"

"You said 'Kali,' didn't you?" the voice barked.

"That's her name."

"Identify yourself."

"I'm a guest here. My name is Nick Iversen. Let go of me."

Suddenly, he was released, and the voice, now contrite, said, "Oh. Sorry." Nick sat up warily and turned to see the powerfully built, square-jawed man who'd attacked him. He was now extending a hand to Nick, but Nick chose to get to his feet without help.

The attacker addressed him in reasonable tones. "I'm Tom Thorndyke, Nadia Wentworth's security advisor. There may be an intruder on the grounds, and when I heard you call 'Kali,' I thought you might be this nut who's obsessed with Nadia's new project."

Nick attempted to straighten out his towel. Thorndyke looked puzzled and slightly disturbed that Nick wasn't wearing clothes.

"We were swimming," said Nick. "I was just about to go and get dressed. Maybe Callie's down by the pool."

"Kali?"

Nick spelled it. "Callie's my, um, girlfriend," he said, trying to make it sound natural. "It's short for Caroline."

"Well, I'd like both of you inside the house," said Tom. He followed Nick down the steps to the lanai, and watched him retrieve his clothes and put them back on. Callie's bikini top, tiny purse, sandals and white lace panties were still flung around in a wanton way.

"Where did your girlfriend go?" he asked.

"I'm not sure," said Nick. "It's been a confusing evening." Feeling self-conscious, he began to gather up Callie's things. "I guess we got a little carried away," he said apologetically. He'd had only two hits off that joint Callie had offered him, but he felt pretty disoriented. "Um, the changing room was locked so we just—"

"It was?" Thorndyke seemed to find this fact of some interest. He strode over and tried the knob carefully, then astonished Nick first by producing a large black gun, and then by running at the door and planting a foot firmly beneath the knob in some kind of kung-fu move.

A second later, he'd turned on the light and was staring into the doorway, then rushed inside. "Oh my God. He looks bad. I'm going to call the medics." He jogged over to the bar area and picked up a phone. "You go back to the house and wait for them, then bring them down here."

"Who is it?" asked Nick.

"It's Kevin. And he's unconscious."

Nick grabbed the pile of Callie's things, ran back to the terrace and tried the French doors. They were locked. He pounded frantically on them, and wondered if he should run around the house trying other doors or wait for someone to come and open up.

Finally, a head popped out of a window on the second floor. It was Duncan Blaine's. "Would you *please* stop making all that noise? I'm trying to work. Bloody hell!" He slammed the window shut.

"Let me in," pleaded Nick. "It's an emergency."

Now another head popped out of another window. It was Melanie. "What's going on?" she asked.

"Tom found Kevin locked in the changing room by the pool and he's in bad shape," said Nick. "The medics are on their way."

"I'll come down and let you in," she said.

Nick tried to pull himself together. The events of the evening were piling up in a startling way. So many incredible things had taken place in such a short period of time and his mind seemed unable to keep up. Why had he taken those hits off that joint? His stoned feeling made it all so much worse. He felt seriously as if everything were out of control, as if he had stumbled into some parallel universe created by the pen of Uncle Sid.

Just then he heard a thrashing sound in the shrubbery a few feet away from him. He turned to see some low branches slowly parted and then a stealthy figure creeping on hands and knees out onto the dark lawn. The thing made strange panting sounds.

No, he thought, I can't take any more. He put his hands over his eyes for a second and asked himself if he were imagining this.

He remembered how it felt being attacked by Tom Thorndyke. Maybe this creature was going to attack him too, like Zuma, the strange catlike beast, baffling to zoologists and personally trained by Kali-Ra herself to lunge at people and tear at their throats with razor-sharp claws. His eyes flew open. It was coming toward him.

Behind him he heard the French doors unlocking, but he continued to stare in horror as he realized that the thing that had emerged from the shrubbery was Callie. He ran toward her, just as she managed to drag herself upright. She stood weaving on the lawn, her sarong tied around her waist, her breasts exposed. The left one seemed to have a small tattoo.

"My God," said Melanie, as Nick, still managing to hang on to her bikini top, underpants and purse, clumsily rearranged her sarong under her armpits and tied it firmly. The thing was now a reasonably respectable knee-length strapless dress.

Nick faked an indulgent chuckle and said, "She's not used to so much excitement, I guess. And she normally never drinks. I don't know what happened."

"Weird stuff," murmured Callie, her head drooping on his shoulder. "Unspeakable horrors. The sacred temple. Horrible. I must flee this hellish place."

"Is she going to be all right?" asked Melanie.

Nick hoped he didn't appear as out of it himself as he felt. "I'm really sorry," he said. "That Duncan Blaine kept plying her with drinks and I guess—"

"If she drank what he spilled she's well over the legal limit," said Melanie impatiently. "What's the deal with Kevin?"

"Tom found him locked in the changing room by the pool. And said he was in bad shape. He called the medics."

Melanie put a hand to her forehead. "I think I'm going crazy," she said. "Too much is happening."

"I know," said Nick, stepping toward her as he pulled Callie along. "It was nice of you to ask us to dinner," he added, realizing how ridiculous this must sound. "I hope we didn't abuse your hospitality. We got a little, um, over-enthusiastic, and took a dip in the pool. I'm not sure I should drive, to tell you the truth. Maybe I should call a cab." He shifted Callie's weight a little, and accidentally dropped her underpants at Melanie's feet. They both looked down at them for a second, and then Nick scooped them back up.

"I'll call," said Melanie, with barely disguised eagerness. Nick felt ashamed that he and Callie had turned out to be such boorish guests. Half dragging Callie, he followed Melanie inside.

Melanie had the cab company on the line in an instant. "Where do you want them to take you?" she asked Nick.

"Um, what's your address?" he asked Callie, who looked at him with a glazed-over expression and murmured, "The Temple of the Chosen."

"Just a sec," Nick said, fumbling with her pouch. Hours ago, before she'd taken the wheel of his rental car, she'd claimed to have a driver's license on her.

There it was, next to a ten-dollar bill and the Zippo lighter. He read off the address to Melanie, who repeated it into the phone.

If the medics' sirens hadn't become audible just then, and Melanie hadn't rushed off to the front door to let them in, she might have noticed how shocked Nick was to see the words, right above the address on the driver's license, "Name: Cunningham, Kali-Ra."

As Melanie led the medics down to the pool area, two questions came into her head. The first was, how had the medics' car gotten through the security system? Kevin had said he'd reset it after the breaker tripped. The second question was, why did Nick Iversen have to look up his girlfriend's address? And if he lived in Minneapolis, how come she lived here? Melanie had definitely seen a flash of a California driver's license.

She forgot about both these questions, though, when she got down to the pool. Tom was there, propping up a tall, blond man who was half sitting, half lying on the tiles by the pool. He looked haggard but conscious.

"He's coming around," Tom said. He held up a coil of

thick rope. "He was tied up and gagged the same way I was."

"Who is he?" demanded Melanie as the medics bent over the victim.

"Why, Kevin, of course," said Tom.

"That's not the Kevin I know," she replied.

CHAPTER XXVI

A NIGHT OF PASSION

"So you *will* do it?" said Margaret, sitting next to Quentin on the bed in his hotel room. "I wasn't sure you would." She was as beautiful as he remembered, and wore a soft blue dress and smelled like violets.

"Yes, yes. Of course I will." He seized her fingertips and kissed them.

She withdrew them hastily and folded them primly in her lap. "They might want you to wear a wire and get him on tape."

"Fortunately, I've never adopted Maurice's Speedo dress code, so that should be no problem," he said.

"It could be dangerous."

"Of course it will. Maurice employs some pretty heavy muscle. Not to mention Vince Fontana's pals, who are prepared to run around breaking arms and legs." He arranged his features in a look of noble resolution and said with solemn dignity, "But I don't care, Margaret. All I want is the chance to redeem myself in your eyes.

"And of course," he added in more businesslike tones, "I'd also like immunity from federal prosecution for any criminal activities of Maurice Fender Associates in which I may have been involved."

"We can do better than that!" Margaret clapped her hands together and bounced enthusiastically on the bed. "Sam says they'll forget about the McCorkindale matter."

"They will? What did you tell him about it?"

"Just that I might be able to persuade you to help, but only if you felt secure that anything Maurice tried to peddle about you wouldn't be used against you. Sam said that was no problem, and they'd forget about anything you might have done in the past, short of murder, which isn't a federal crime anyway."

"Wow," said Quentin.

"Sam is really eager to be the one to nail Maurice Fender. His boss has made kind of a crusade of it. Even if Maurice becomes an official fugitive and manages to avoid extradition, Sam would like to shut him down and prosecute some of his money-laundering clients. The IRS has had some bad publicity lately, hounding widows and orphans, and they're particularly interested in making an example of some high-profile tax cheats in the top bracket."

Quentin's heart soared. After the humiliations of this evening at Nadia Wentworth's, nothing would be more satisfying than seeing Vince Fontana in deep shit. Let his mob connections try to help him! Quentin looked forward to watching old Vince hawk his schlocky tapes on TV in a desperate attempt to raise enough cash to stay out of jail.

"I can hardly wait to start," he said. "What do I have to do first?"

"Meet with Sam. He said it might be helpful if you had some preliminary information to hand over. Something that would show your good faith."

"I've got some hot stuff in my briefcase," he said eagerly. "Real paper-trail stuff that shows how Maurice works his little scam."

"Terrific. Bring it along."

"Oh, Margaret, you've saved me! I can't believe it. You *are* an angel. You're much too good for me."

"I know," she said.

Very gently, he placed a chaste kiss in the middle of her

smooth, intelligent forehead. She didn't flinch, so he caressed her hair reverently, and stared solemnly into her clear hazel eyes until she shut them, tilted her head sideways, and allowed him to kiss her mouth.

It was about half a minute later, right before they fell back onto the bed in a tangle of arms and legs, that the last rational thought Quentin Smith would have for several hours flickered momentarily through his brain. He remembered that in his haste to get away from Nadia Wentworth's house, he had left his soggy briefcase with those incriminating documents there. He would have to get it first thing in the morning.

The real Kevin's eyes were focused now, and the medics had a blood pressure cuff around his arm. He was making a clear attempt to overcome his grogginess and tell his story. "I'd just let myself in the gate with the security code, when suddenly, someone jumped me and knocked me out. Someone pressed a cloth into my face with some kind of chemical, a sickly sweet smell, that made me want to throw up."

"Chloroform," said Melanie. "I thought it was only used in old novels."

"After that, I don't remember much. Just occasionally coming round and being fed a chocolate-flavored liquid." He rubbed his arm at the memory. "I was never fully conscious."

Tom looked grim. "There are a whole mess of empty chocolate Slim Fast cans in there," he said, gesturing to the changing room. "At least the bastard kept him alive, but he probably drugged the stuff."

"What bastard?" demanded Kevin.

"Sounds like your assailant impersonated you," said Tom. "Someone calling himself Kevin has been running around here for a couple of days."

The real Kevin ran a hand along his jaw where there appeared to be a few days growth of beard. "How long have I been out of commission?"

"About seventy-two hours," said Tom.

"I can't remember much," said Kevin. "Except once, the guy mumbled something about waiting for the gong."

"My God," said Melanie. "The summons of the gong. Kali-Ra travels everywhere with one and when the slaves hear it, they gather. This idiot may still be running around the grounds," said Melanie to Tom. "Where are the police? And did you know the security system is down? The power went out. I bet the fake Kevin went down into the basement and turned off the power earlier this evening in order to shut down the system. Maybe there are more of these crazies he wanted to let in! Later, he went down there and turned on the power again and said he was reactivating the security system, but the medics here got through no problem."

One of them nodded as he shone a small flashlight into Kevin's eyes. "That's right. The gates were wide open."

"I'd hoped to keep the cops out of it," Tom said, clenching his jaw nervously.

"What?" demanded Melanie. "You said you were going to call them. We've got at least one and maybe more lunatics running around here chloroforming people and tying them up and dropping jars on their heads. Are you crazy?" But then it occurred to her that he wasn't crazy, just embarrassed. If it ever came out that security expert to the stars Tom Thorndyke had let some clown run wild around Nadia Wentworth's property for several days, his credibility would be severely diminished.

One of the medics now said, "We think he should spend a night in the hospital under observation. We don't know what kind of drugs he's been on. And we'll have to file a report that there was an assault here."

Tom Thorndyke sagged visibly at this news, and Melanie knew that her suspicions had been right. "I want the cops here to flush this guy out!" she said. "Helicopters, dogs, heat-seeking missiles, whatever it takes. Meanwhile, I'm taking Nadia to a hotel."

Outside the window of the Blue Room, there were noises of sirens and crackling walkie-talkies and people shouting in the dark. Glen wanted to go find out what was happening, but he remembered that his job was to stay here in this locked room, guarding Nadia until Tom Thorndyke gave the all clear.

Despite the commotion from the grounds, it was strangely serene in here. It looked, he thought, like a boudoir in some old Ernst Lubitsch picture, high-ceilinged with a central chandelier, lots of satin and silk. The furniture was French provincial—a blue-and-white striped couch on dainty curved legs, a dressing table with a tall mirror and a collection of crystal bottles, chairs full of cushions in various shades of blue; and a massive canopy bed festooned with gauzy blue draperies.

"The police seem to be here," he said reassuringly to Nadia, who had curled up into a corner of the couch. She looked tiny in this big, dramatic setting, much smaller than she ever had on the screen, an adorable, vulnerable waif. "Everything should be all right soon. They'll probably even let us out of here."

"I don't want them to let us out," she said. "I don't want any more hassles. I'm completely maxed out, emotionally speaking."

"I know, I know," he said, feeling that he could never convey enough sympathy to this poor, fragile creature.

"Oh, Glen," she said with a little sob, "I'm scared!" Her face fell into her hands and she began to produce the heaving motion of weeping.

He rushed to her side and perched with one buttock on the sofa. "It's all right. The police are here. And I'm here. I won't let anything happen to you!" Tentatively, he touched her shoulder and then gave it an avuncular series of pats.

"Hold me!" she whimpered, opening her arms like a child.

He flung himself on her and embraced her enthusiastically and she clung to him in return, her famous breasts squashed against his chest, her hair, scented like some tropical fruit, tickling his nose so that he had to smooth it down.

"I hate it when the world gangs up on me like this," she snuffled. "Everyone thinks I'm so strong and a real ball breaker and everything, but I'm just an ordinary woman."

"I know, I know," he repeated. "Like everyone else, you need someone to look after you once in a while, don't you?"

"Exactly," she said.

She pulled away and placed her hands on his shoulders, staring into his face. "Oh, Glen, I feel so safe here with you. Ever since you came here, I've felt you were a special person. Intelligent and sensitive to my needs."

"I want to be there for you, Nadia," he said earnestly. "In whatever capacity you need me."

"I need you to kiss me," she said huskily.

He obliged, putting his hand on the small of her back, thrilled by the feel of her arching spine as their lips met and their tongues mingled. She pulled her mouth wetly away from his just enough to murmur, "I need you to make love to me."

He plucked her from the sofa and carried her with manly strides across to the gauze-draped four-poster while continuing to gaze into her eyes. Now, he thought, I'm in my own movie.

BOOK THREE

In Which the Gong of Kali-Ra Summons
the Faithful to the Temple of the Chosen

CHAPTER XXVII

COMES THE DAWN

✗

The first hint of light came through the curtains, and the birds had begun to sing. Melanie lay awake in one of the twin beds in her room, despite the fact that she was exhausted. After all of yesterday's excitement, she had managed only a few hours of intermittent sleep.

The police had come and searched the grounds. This was no mean feat, as there were huge overgrown areas of the garden that had been untouched since the time of Vera Nadi, who had lived here until the age of ninety-eight. By the end, the silent-era vamp had been impoverished and senile, and a jungle of rhododendrons and ivy had been allowed to engulf a hodgepodge of follies, gazebos, and fake ruins. Nadia had reclaimed and restored only about a quarter of the acre and a half.

The police hadn't found a trace of anyone. They had searched the carriage house, and taken fingerprints from the living quarters in hopes of identifying the Kevin impersonator. They had done the same thing on the balcony from which the huge jar had fallen, and even placed the peanut butter sandwich remains found there in a plastic bag and taken them away. They had also examined the message of doom left in the office.

Meanwhile, Melanie had pounded on the door to the Blue Room and begged Nadia to come out and check into a hotel. Nadia had refused to unlock the door, giggled coyly and insisted she was safe in there with Glen Pendergast. "Go away!" she had said. "Leave us alone."

"The police may want to talk to you," said Melanie.

"Forget it," Nadia had said.

Glen, sounding strained and as if normal speech were an effort, had added, "Um, I think we've got everything well in hand here. Nadia really can't take any more."

"Yes I can," squealed Nadia merrily. There was an odd creak, as of bedsprings, and more giggling.

At that point, Melanie had sighed and given up. Nadia would be safe enough busily occupied behind locked doors with the grounds crawling with cops and German shepherds. As for Professor Pendergast, well, he would just have to fend for himself with the demanding Nadia. It was a problem most men would kill for.

Nick was just waking up. He hadn't noticed much about the place last night when he'd gratefully accepted a pillow in a flowered case and a crocheted afghan and crashed out on the lumpy sofa that his allergic nose told him was full of cat hair.

He remembered thinking, right before passing out, that he had just had the most extraordinary day of his life. And then, he'd had a strange, vivid dream in which he and Callie were swimming and kissing in the water and then the cabaña around Nadia Wentworth's pool had somehow morphed into the temple of Kali-Ra and he'd been separated from her, and found himself pursued through marble labyrinths by strange, menacing figures.

For part of the dream he'd been trapped in a phone booth trying to call in sick to the movie theater in Minneapolis where he worked, but he couldn't remember the number, or the name of Jerry Lundquist, his boss. Then Callie had reappeared and turned to him with an evil glint in her eye, and he'd said, as the awful knowledge dawned,

"You are one of them," and she had replied, "I am the goddess to whom they are enslaved, and will spare you if you pledge your will to the Queen of Doom," and he realized she wasn't Callie Cunningham at all, but Kali-Ra, and then suddenly he was back at the toga party his sophomore year in high school in that motel near Dayton after the Junior Classical League convention where they'd all got busted for drinking beer. Then Melanie Oakley appeared and said she was Pallas Athena and she was speaking Latin and he kept trying to understand it, and realized she was speaking the language of the Ancient Ones from Uncle Sid's book, and suddenly it all made sense, but as soon as he woke up he couldn't remember what she had told him, even though it seemed so profound and enlightening at the time.

He sat up now, trying to shed the lingering imprint of the dream. He began to examine his surroundings by the clear light of day, for the California sun was streaming through Venetian blinds. He appeared to be sitting in a very ordinary living room, decorated in the style of some of his friends' parents who hadn't changed their taste for thirty years, and who bought their knickknacks at craft fairs—a mantelpiece with sand-cast candles and clunky pottery. A coffee table made from an old trunk, covered with magazines. A sickly plant hanging in a macramé sling. A framed print featuring orca whales and dolphins disporting themselves.

He got up, discovered he had shed everything but his underwear at some point, recovered his jeans and shirt from a nearby chair and put them on over his T-shirt and boxers, and went to examine the bookshelf. There were a lot of books about discovering the inner child, getting in sync with female deities, running with wolves, beating hot flashes without estrogen, learning to develop self-esteem and finding a decent man. To his surprise, there was also a long row of novels by Valerian Ricardo. It seemed to him that it must have taken years to assemble such a collection.

He wandered over to the coffee table and examined the magazines. *Prevention. Cosmo. Psychology Today. Money. Self.* And there was also a pile of mail, which he glanced at perfunctorily, until he saw something that made his heart begin to race.

It was one of those magazine sweepstakes envelopes that was sent to everyone in America. Through the little window it said in screaming, computer-generated letters: "Congratulations Kali-Ra Cunningham. You May Already Have Won A Million Dollars!" He grabbed the envelope and stared at it. No, it hadn't been his imagination last night when he read her driver's license. He sank down onto the sofa.

Just then Callie came into the living room. She was wearing a pair of khaki shorts and a white T-shirt and looked more like a sorority girl than the goddess he had chased through the moonlight.

"Hi!" she said. "Sleep okay?"

"Sure," he said.

She tossed her hair over her shoulder and said in a whisper, "Listen, don't tell my mom about last night, okay? She's massively overprotective. If she heard I drank all that gin and smoked that pot last night, she'd have me in rehab in no time." She glanced nervously over her shoulder.

"No problem," he said. "Is your mom here now?"

She shrugged. "Yeah. I'll be getting my own place pretty soon, but for now it's okay to live at home." She sat down heavily in a nearby chair and began massaging her temples. "God, I feel like shit."

He glanced down at the mail in his hand and then he held it up to her. "I thought your name was Caroline."

She waved at the envelope with a dismissive gesture. "I

always tell people that," she said. "Wouldn't you be embarrassed to have a stupid hippie name like Kali-Ra?"

"I see your point," said Nick. He remembered a kid in his fifth-grade class named Pinecone, for whom he had always felt deep pity. "But how come—"

She interrupted him. "I really freaked out last night. One minute I was running around feeling frisky and kind of crazy and happy because it was so cool up there at Nadia Wentworth's house with the pool and the moonlight and everything, and then suddenly it was like I was in a very weird place."

"You looked pretty wrecked crawling out of the bushes," he said. "What happened to you?"

"I'm not sure," she said. For the first time since he'd met her, something akin to doubt flickered across her face. "I was tripping really intensely. I almost wondered if I hadn't made myself crazy. You see, I've been trying to empower myself and—"

Just then, a woman in her late forties with a soft face, a big curly perm, and a terry cloth bathrobe and large fuzzy slippers came into the room.

"Hi, Mom," said Callie in a cheerful little-girl voice, her fears of self-induced madness apparently forgotten. "I hope we didn't wake you up coming in last night." She turned to Nick. "This is my mom, Gail. Mom, this is Nick. He brought me home last night, from this party, and he needed a place to stay. He's from Minneapolis and he slept on the couch."

"Oh," said Gail, looking suspiciously at her daughter and then at Nick. "You didn't go to one of those raves or anything, did you? Honey, the drugs they have today are much stronger than when I was a kid. You have to be so careful. Or a frat party? I read this thing about campus rape in the *Times* that said—"

"Actually," said Nick with dignity, "this was a fairly civilized little dinner party in Beverly Hills. At Nadia Wentworth's." At least it started out civilized, he thought to himself.

That stopped Gail in her tracks. "Nadia Wentworth's?"

"I told you, Mom. I told you I could make it all happen," said Callie. "It's working." She closed her eyes and said in her spooky Kali-Ra voice, "If I will it, so shall it be. The will of the Queen of Doom shall prevail."

Slightly embarrassed by Callie's apparent ease at slipping into a trance state, Nick turned to Gail. "Your daughter has an unusual name," he said. "How did you choose it?"

"These are painful issues for me," Gail said in a whiny voice. "There are trust issues and bonding issues and major identity issues." She settled down on the sofa next to him with the air of someone in a therapist's office, eager to get in a full hour's worth of monologue.

Callie bounced to her feet and jangled car keys. "Some other time, Mom, okay? I gotta go. I need to drive Nick back to his car." She gestured at Nick with her eyebrows to indicate they'd better make a fast exit.

He supposed he'd have to wait until later to find out precisely why the strange and beautiful creature he had pursued naked through the moonlight was named after his Uncle Sid's trashy character. He rose to go, then rebelled. "Before we go," he said to Gail, "tell me why your daughter is named Kali-Ra."

CHAPTER XXVIII

THE DAGGER OF KALI-RA

Melanie got up, showered, and dressed. There was something odd yet comforting in the fact that, despite the many sinister events of the day and night before, today seemed a day like any other. As was her habit, she made herself a cup of coffee and toasted an English muffin in the kitchen, then took them to her office. No one else seemed to be up, which suited her just fine. Perhaps she'd spend an invigorating hour or so with Virgil.

But first, she should check the e-mail. Melanie hit the space bar, and was astonished to see the screen saver of a bust of Ovid vanish, replaced by the message of doom she had found in the printer last night. It looked less menacing by daylight, but it was still pretty creepy to realize that whoever had written this had sat in her chair and tapped it out on her keyboard.

"Nadia Wentworth has invoked the wrath of Kali-Ra. We, her loyal slaves, will carry out the will of our mistress and smite the little bitch. To inflict pain in service of the will of Kali-Ra is a labor of love."

At a second reading it became clear that there was something not quite right about it. All the messages they'd received by mail had been written in the style of the Kali-Ra books. The phrase "the little bitch," however, was very un-Valerian. "Foolish unbeliever" would have been more like it. Perhaps this represented a transition from the political to the personal in the lunatic mind behind the note. Tom had said that celebrity stalkers grew more and more agitated as their delusions persisted.

Suddenly inspired, Melanie clicked on the undo button, which eliminated the last edit. An extra letter leaped into the phrase "labor of love," and a squiggly red line, indicating a misspelling, appeared beneath it. Whoever had typed this had originally spelled "labor" the British way—"labour."

"Aha!" she said, then heard the bell ringing indicating that someone had arrived at the front gate. A check with the video monitor indicated that it was that jerk from Maurice Fender Associates, Quentin Smith. At least he hadn't brought that horrible old singing mafioso with the overpowering cologne.

Melanie pushed the speaker button and said crisply, "I thought we agreed that you would negotiate with our attorneys."

"Absolutely," said an apologetic-sounding Quentin Smith. "I've sent a fax to Ms. Wentworth's business manager that explains all about it. I'm only here because I left my briefcase here last night. What with all the excitement and all."

Melanie sighed and pushed the button that would open the gates, then began a search for the briefcase. She would hand it to him on the front porch and make sure he left immediately. She found it sitting in the front hall on the hardwood floor, visibly oozing damp. Melanie was irritated to discover it had left a white oblong mark in the varnish.

Outside, she was startled to see a red Ford Fiesta parked in front, then realized it must be the car tipsy Nick Iversen and his drunken, sluttish girlfriend had left behind. No doubt she could expect a visit from them later too. All Melanie really wanted was a nice cup of coffee and an hour of Virgil.

Quentin Smith drove up and leapt out. "Wow! Thanks," he said as he accepted his briefcase. "I'm really sorry."

"No problem," said Melanie.

"Look, about last night," he began.

She was about to cut him off, but then it occurred to her that listening to him blather on might be smarter. Perhaps he'd say something damaging that she could pass on to the lawyers.

"Yes?" she said amiably.

"I'm really sorry about Vince Fontana. I mean he means well and everything, but I really want to make it clear that I have nothing to do with any threats or harm that might come to anyone in this house. What I mean is—Vince Fontana and I don't even know each other. In fact," blurted out Quentin, "totally off the record and in the name of human decency I feel compelled to tell you that the claim of Maurice Fender Associates—"

Just then, a bloodcurdling scream came from inside the house.

"Nadia!" said Melanie, rushing inside. Quentin followed her and stood at the bottom of the stairs, while she ran up. Rosemary was rushing down and the two women collided.

"Murder!" screamed Rosemary, clutching Melanie.

Trembling, Quentin reached into his pocket, removed a cellular phone, and dialed 9-1-1.

"Where? Where?" said Melanie. Rosemary began to sob and Melanie disentangled herself from her and ran up the rest of the stairs. Outside the open door of the master bedroom she saw the fallen breakfast tray, a poached egg still on its toast on the carpet, a teacup on its side.

In Nadia's huge swan bed, Lila lay on her back, looking more asleep than dead. From her chest protruded the jeweled hilt of what appeared to be a very large dagger. The doors to the balcony were wide open. A gentle breeze lifted the hems of the sheer white curtains that hung there, making Lila's incredible stillness even more striking.

"It's only in the last few years that I've really been able to come to terms with the parental betrayal that made me what I am today," Gail began. "My own marriage couldn't last because on a deeper level I wasn't cool with my own parents' bogusness."

Nick cleared his throat. "I see." Actually he didn't.

"Naming my baby Kali-Ra was an act of rebellion against my mother," said Gail. "You see, Valerian Ricardo was my read dad, so I named her after his character. It was the only way I could pass on my true heritage. Anyway, all my friends liked it."

Callie rolled her eyes and muttered, "You could have named me Valerie."

Nick looked over at Callie. "So we're, um, related?" he said.

She gave him a knowing little smile. "Kinda."

Gail looked surprised. "Yes, I guess we are related," she said. She gave Nick a cursory glance, then sighed and gazed over his shoulder at the mantelpiece in a dramatic way and got back to her own story. "Anyway, when I was seventeen it all came crashing down on me. I found out that my birth certificate said I was born in the Florence Crittenden Home, a place for unwed mothers, and where it said 'father,' it said 'Valerian Ricardo.' Mom had lied to me, and it took me years of therapy to deal with that trust thing. My adoptees support group helped a lot but I'm still in recovery. Survivors have to take it day by day."

Nick figured people who'd been in years of therapy and support groups didn't mind personal questions. In fact, they probably relished them. "Did you confront her?" he asked.

Gail clicked her tongue contemptuously. "Mom said Bud Vanderhof was my real dad, but he'd joined the army and been shipped to Korea without knowing I was on the way. She said she was scared and her very strict parents had already been worried about Valerian's inviting her in for candy and stuff. They thought he wasn't a wholesome influence, so they bought it when she said he was my father. Then, when Dad came home on leave and found out about me, he married her, and she took back her story about Valerian Ricardo and said Dad was my biological father."

Gail's face took on the stubborn look Nick had seen briefly on Callie's face. It looked less attractive on the older woman. "I never believed it for a minute. Bud Vanderhof was nothing like me. When I finally met Valerian Ricardo I realized I had inherited a lot of his creativity." She turned to Nick and said with a trace of smugness, "I do collages."

"So you actually met Uncle Sid? Valerian Ricardo, I mean?" asked Nick.

"Uh-huh. When I was nineteen, I found him in the phone book. It's an unusual name. I went over and met him. We actually got to be friends, even though he was pretty old. I didn't get along with my parents at all at that point. There was a real generation-gap thing going. I really related to my real dad. He let me and my friends crash there a lot in the basement of the apartment house he managed.

"We thought he was really fascinating. He was interested in a lot of things that were coming up in the sixties. Like altered mind states and new ways of looking at spirituality."

"He was a total drug pig," said Callie, rolling her eyes.

"He was misunderstood," said Gail. "He was way ahead of his time. Not that I'm into substance abuse now, of course," she added primly, "or chemical brain alteration instead of meditation and healthy spirituality. But in those days we saw drugs as a way to overcome some of the uptight values of our parents. It was before we understood about true wellness. Anyway, he'd done a lot of hash and opium in the twenties. He was happy to get reconnected.

"And he was happy to meet me and my friends. He was kind of a lonely old man, spending a lot of time trying to get away from Lila in this really depressing little boiler room lined with roach killer cans and greasy tools. He'd tried to make it kind of homey, with Oriental carpets and some of his occult-type books and furniture he built and designed himself."

"Yeah, like the thing they found him strapped to," said Callie with more eye rolling. "Yuck."

Gail frowned. "He had an unusual outlook on life. Why are you so judgmental?"

"Did he say if he was your father or not?" asked Nick.

Gail looked evasive. "Not in so many words. He said that we were spiritually linked. I said I believed he was my father and he said, 'Then it is so, my child.' He couldn't come right out and admit it because of Lila. My showing up caused a lot of tension between Lila and Valerian."

"I met Lila last night, Mom," said Callie. "She turned on me and said 'You're back' and that I was a sly little minx. I think she thought I was Grandma."

"I'm not surprised. You look exactly like your Grandma Betty Lou did when she was just a teenager and had that affair with my dad. She was a very mature-looking fifteen-year-old."

Gail sighed and shook her head sadly. "Lila had never

processed her anger and she was very negative and hostile. Especially when Valerian wanted to come with me and my friends to the country and start a spiritual retreat–commune thing. He felt that the world was ready to hear his message once again, and that me and my friends could set him up as a kind of hip elder Timothy Leary–type thing. Lila was not open to that, because she wanted him all to herself. She was a major control freak.

"Anyway, it never happened because he died suddenly right before we were all going to get into this big old school bus and take off. It was so sad."

Gail looked as if she were about to weep, and Callie said, "Tell him about the box, Mom. That's proof, isn't it?"

"Oh. Yeah. When we went to pick him up and go off to start our utopian community, he was already dead. I went inside and Lila was just coming out of the basement room where we used to meet. Some tenant had just discovered him and he was in there phoning an ambulance or something, but it was clear he had died. Lila hated me and she said, cold as ice, 'Valerian won't be joining you because he's gone beyond the veil. He'll be safe there on the other side and someday I'll join him.' Then she handed me this box, and she said, in a nicer, softer way that was really kind of moving, I'll never forget it, 'Here, he wanted you to have this. It's all that's left from his old life. Now leave me alone in my grief, or I'll tell the cops about you and your friends and your dope.'"

Gail went over to the bookshelf and took down a small, square, gold cigarette box with the initials *V* and *R* in art deco letters made of tiny diamonds on the hinged lid. "It's all I have of him," she said sadly.

"Actually, it's worth quite a bit," said Callie. "I had it checked out. It's all real. I think it proves that Mom was his daughter and he knew it and Lila knew it."

Nick opened the box. There was some whitish dust inside, probably cocaine dregs from Uncle Sid's last orgy. "So Callie is his granddaughter," said Nick, handing the box back to Gail.

"And Mom is his heir," said Callie. "But she won't do anything about it. There's a lot of money involved in the rights to the books, and I want to make sure we get what's coming to us."

Nick remembered how he'd told her about his own fantasy of inheriting the rights. "Why didn't you tell me this before?" he said.

"I thought you might be after the same thing. I wanted to scope things out up at Nadia Wentworth's," said Callie evasively.

"Is that what you were doing outside Melanie Oakley's office? Eavesdropping?"

She smiled. "I had already figured out the things were back in copyright. The Copyright Office has a website with all the rules about the Uruguay Round and everything."

Gail sighed. "Honey, I told you not to get your hopes up. First of all, Grandma was always in total denial, and now she's dead. Second, there's Lila. And finally, there's that company that owns the rights. We've been over all this. You made me pay for that lawyer's consultation and he said to forget it."

Nick cleared his throat. "Glen Pendergast says he isn't sure Lila and Valerian Ricardo were actually legally married. Would that make a difference?"

"That's what I think too," said Callie. "She didn't have the right to sell off the copyrights to those Maurice Fender people. They belonged to us."

Gail turned to Nick. "I'm afraid Callie's getting a little carried away by all this. She always sneered at my real dad. Wouldn't read the books or anything. Now, she seems obsessed. It really freaked me out when she got that Kali-Ra tattoo. I've tried to get her to talk the issue out with my own therapist."

"I hated Valerian Ricardo because you were always going on about how your life was screwed up because of him," said Callie. "I think that's what drove Dad away. And I hated him because you gave me this stupid name. But now that there's a lot of money involved, I feel differently."

She turned to Nick. "I told myself that if I got into the fact that my name was Kali-Ra, kind of turned into her, allowed her spirit to take over or whatever, that it would be a good way to stay focused on my goal and really believe, and that I would get what I want. A visualization thing, you know? That's how I met you. I was at the Scheherazade, soaking up power vibes, and I saw Lila's book and you led me right to Nadia Wentworth. If you believe, it will happen."

"Oh," said Nick. "But we can't always get what we want, even if we want it a lot, can we?"

"I believe that if you want something badly enough and never give up, it will happen," said Callie with conviction. Nick remembered hearing a similar philosophy from Big Bird on *Sesame Street* when he was a kid. Later he was told in grade school that you can be whatever you want to be, a major league pitcher or whatever, if you hold fast to your dream. He had felt vaguely guilty about not buying into it until he studied real philosophy at the University of Minnesota, and realized with some relief that it was crap.

"I brought her up to empower herself," said Gail. "But, honey, I meant it in more of a spiritual way."

"I want us to have a lot of money," snapped Callie. "What's wrong with that? God, Mom, you're so fucking *passive*."

Nick looked over at her as she glowered at her mother. She sounded pretty crass and greedy right now, but maybe it wasn't her fault. Her ditz of a mother had brought her up with a lot of fuzzy ideas.

CHAPTER XXIX

CLOUDS OF SUSPICION

A neat, bald man with a small, pale mustache and heavy-lidded blue eyes was sitting behind the desk in Melanie's office tapping a pencil. He was a police detective, conducting brief, preliminary interviews with all the members of the household in turn. He looked more like a banker than a cop, and his neutral manner irritated Glen Pendergast, who sat across from him. Glen was red in the face and slightly bouncy.

"You see, it's straight out of *The Dagger of Kali-Ra*. The beautiful, headstrong debutante, Madge Barclay, is found dead in her bed, the ceremonial dagger of Kali-Ra plunged into her snowy bosom. Actually, she's not dead, she just fainted because she's one of those rare people with their heart on the right instead of the left, but you get the picture. The dagger of Kali-Ra is described in detail. A cabochon emerald surrounded by rubies."

The detective nodded. Glen continued. "What's really interesting here is the motive. Madge Barclay's near fatal mistake was to impersonate Kali-Ra at a masquerade ball. You see, she was in love with Raymond Vernon, who had told her all about Kali-Ra. Of course it was all futile, because a close reading of the books makes it clear that Raymond Vernon is a fetishist of indeterminate sexual orientation who isn't really interested in women in any normal sense. But my point is that last night Lila was in Nadia's bed. The

181

killer or killers *thought* they were killing Nadia Wentworth, who was going to impersonate Kali-Ra in the movies!"

"Very interesting, professor." The detective leaned forward with a sympathetic air. "Or can I call you Glen? You seem pretty involved with this whole Kali-Ra thing. Would you say you were obsessed with it? I mean did it just seem to take over your life? Gosh, that must have been tough, Glen. Maybe the pressure to get something like that off your chest is just too much to bear sometimes."

Pendergast glared back at him. "Are you insinuating I'm some kind of nut?"

"Not at all. It's just that you seem pretty worked up about all this."

"Of course I'm worked up," said Glen, rising to his feet and pounding the desk. "Someone is trying to kill the woman I love! These fiends must be stopped!"

"Of course, of course. Now, could you describe the weapon again?" the detective said pleasantly.

"A cabochon emerald surrounded by rubies," said Glen.

The detective smiled. "Gee, Glen, how do you know that if you didn't actually see the weapon?"

Huddled in the corner of a sofa, Quentin Smith was whispering on his cell phone to Margaret. "I told Maurice that Lila Ricardo was in the house. I told him she was the only impediment to a settlement. Now she's dead. He said he'd take care of it himself. My God, Margaret, what if he did? What should I do?"

"Tell them the truth," she whispered back. "Otherwise, they might think you did it."

"I could have," he said. "Last night I actually thought about killing that old woman with my bare hands."

Just then a uniformed policeman room loomed up behind him. "The detective would like to talk to you next," he said. "He's finished with Dr. Pendergast."

"I gotta go," said Quentin in a panicky voice. Had the cop heard him say he'd thought about killing Lila?

By the time Nick and Callie arrived at Villa Vera to pick up the car, paparazzi and vans sprouting satellite dishes had massed outside the gates.

"What's going on?" asked Nick.

"I don't know. Maybe they're covering the stuff that went on here last night," said Callie nervously. "That jar falling and all that. Remember I told you I had a weird experience, like a hallucination? I'm beginning to wonder if some of it wasn't real. My visualization techniques are more powerful than I thought."

Nick wasn't in the mood for any more irrationality just now. "Well, we have to get in there. I have to return the rental car." They parked up the road and hiked up to the gates.

A couple of police officers, one male, one female, were standing outside. Nick approached them and said, "My name is Nick Iversen, and this is Callie, um, Caroline Cunningham. We left our car here last night and—"

"Iversen? Cunningham?" said the policewoman consulting a clipboard. "I'll escort you in."

"What's going on?" asked Nick as he and Callie followed her up the drive. The officer didn't answer. She was speaking into a walkie-talkie. "I got those two witnesses we're interested in," she was saying.

"Oh my God," said Callie.

"What's happened?" said Nick after the officer had replaced the walkie-talkie in its holster.

"A homicide," she answered.

Callie clutched Nick's arm. "Oh, no," she said. "God, I hope—who was it?"

"The detectives will tell you all about it."

"Who was killed? Was it Nadia Wentworth?" asked Nick.

"An older lady," said the policewoman.

"Lila!" Callie said softly. She had the same strange look he'd seen in her eyes last night when she'd said that Lila might not last the night.

"I see," said the detective after Quentin had finished outlining his theories. "So you're saying you think this voodoo assassin guy flew in last night from the Caribbean and killed an old lady in bed with a machete under orders from your boss. Interesting." He jotted a few notes in a spiral-bound notebook. "If you knew this was going to happen, why didn't you warn the victim?"

"No! I'm not saying I knew about it for sure, or even that it happened. I'm just saying you should check it out." Quentin lowered his voice. "I feel it is my duty to tell you that there is also a possible Mafia connection here."

"Okay."

"My boss was using Vince Fontana to threaten Nadia."

"You mean the guy who sells those tapes on TV. Yes, I understand he was here last night."

"With a scary-looking enforcer-type guy named Bruno, trying to shake down Nadia Wentworth. Apparently, he has mob connections."

The detective nodded. "We'll look into it."

"Explaining it all will take some time, but I have an important appointment this morning. A federal prosecutor is interviewing me about a complex and ongoing conspiracy."

"I'm sure you'll have lots to tell him."

"It actually relates in a strange way to what might have gone on here last night."

The detective nodded solemnly. "I wouldn't be surprised. A lot of people think all conspiracies are really one big one. Like the Kennedy assassination or whatever."

"Yeah. Well, I could get back to you later," said Quentin. "I want to cooperate."

"We appreciate that."

"I'll call you," said Quentin.

"No, don't do that. We'll call you." After Quentin left, the detective wrote the word "fruitcake" in his notebook next to Quentin's name, and picked up the phone. He was still waiting to hear the autopsy report. It should be ready now.

In the kitchen, Melanie was cooking masses of scrambled eggs and bacon in case anyone was interested in breakfast. Rosemary had fallen completely apart, and after she had been questioned by the police, Melanie had arranged for her to take a few days off and stay with her sister in Anaheim. Nadia was mercifully out of the way, collapsed in the Blue Room. There, she was being comforted by Glen, as well as her massage therapist, her aromatherapist, and her stress management therapist, all of whom the Beverly Hills Police had obligingly allowed across the crime-scene tape.

Duncan now wandered into the kitchen with his hands in his pocket. Although he looked hung over, with little red eyes and a general puffiness, he seemed quite cheerful. In fact, he was whistling. "Oh, good. A proper breakfast. Good idea," he said. "I couldn't face mangos and muesli this morning."

"I was kind of surprised to find bacon and eggs in the fridge," said Melanie. "Maybe Rosemary has a secret carnivorous and ovolactarian life."

"Actually," said Duncan, "I bought the bacon and eggs and hid them behind that big bowl of soaking grains. I've been feeling a bit weak lately, and I thought maybe an animal protein stash might come in handy for a midnight feast at some point. Is there any coffee?"

Melanie pointed to a pot on the counter. "Help yourself."

He resumed his whistling as he poured, and Melanie was shocked when she recognized the tune. It was "Ding Dong, the Witch Is Dead" from *The Wizard of Oz.*

She had broken the news of Lila's death to him earlier, knocking on his door and waking him up to do so. Duncan, half asleep and bleary-eyed, had been silent for a moment, then said, "How extraordinary," and gone back to bed. Now she planned to tackle another matter.

"Did you use my computer last night, Duncan?" she asked.

"What do you mean?" Duncan said. She detected fear in his eyes.

Melanie quoted, " 'To inflict pain in service of the will of Kali-Ra is a labor of love.' " Duncan flinched and she continued, "Whoever wrote that note on my computer spelled it the British way first, then revised it after the spell checker picked it up. Naturally, I suspected you."

"Oh, Melanie, I would never—"

"Your secret is safe with me. This project needs a good script."

"All right, maybe I did get a little carried away," said Duncan. "But if you'd heard how incredibly rude she was to me, dismissing me like a menial. I went quietly back to my room but I couldn't resist just one little gesture on the way. I know it was petty and not worthy of me."

She sighed and arranged plates and cutlery on a large tray with the platter of bacon and eggs. "Okay. I'm glad we sorted that out. I'll tell the police that little mystery is solved. But don't pull any more stunts like that. Nadia will fire you immediately."

He rushed solicitously to her side, and picked up the tray. "Oh, let me help you with that, Melanie. God, I really am sorry. I couldn't help it. The fact is I was blind drunk. I wasn't responsible for my actions. I'd been under a lot of pressure, what with Lila ruining my script and all that. I'm afraid I let myself get too worked up about it all. Silly, really. Um, do they have any idea who killed the poor old thing?"

"Not really," said Melanie, who took a malicious pleasure in his groveling. "Put it on the sideboard in the dining room, will you."

A few moments after he left, Nick walked into the kitchen, where Melanie was removing a pitcher of orange juice from the fridge. "Duncan said you were in here," he said. "I came back to get my car and I heard the news. This must be a terrible shock for you." She turned and looked at him with her level gray-eyed gaze and suddenly he remembered dreaming about her as the gray-eyed goddess Athena and was overcome by a desire not to have her think he was an oaf. "I'm sorry about last night too. I'm afraid we weren't ideal guests. I guess I don't get out enough," he said with a self-deprecating smile he hoped was charming.

"Neither do I," she said wearily. "All I do is look after Nadia and I don't seem to be doing a very good job of that, either. Grab that coffee pot and bring it into the dining room, will you please?"

"Is Nadia all right?"

"She's not too hysterical, considering she was normally the one sleeping in that bed." Melanie gathered up a stack of juice glasses and led him out of the kitchen to the dining room.

"Wow," said Nick. "You know, it was a very strange night all round. I've never experienced anything quite like it. The police want us to stay," he added. He didn't want her to think he was hanging around on his own without an invitation. God, the food smelled good. He realized he was starving.

Duncan had left the tray on the sideboard without bothering to unload it, and could now be seen through the archway into the living room, where he was chatting cozily with Callie. Melanie began transferring the bacon and eggs to silver chafing dishes, while Nick arranged the plates and silverware.

"Your girlfriend seems to have made a quick recovery," said Melanie. "Did you find her house all right?"

"Oh. That. You must have wondered why I didn't know where she lived."

"The thought did cross my mind," said Melanie, giving him a sidelong glance.

Nick couldn't come up with any plausible explanation for not knowing this, so he sighed deeply and said, "Well, the fact is she isn't really my girlfriend. I just met her and she wanted to come along and—"

"And you wanted to impress her by introducing her to a movie star," finished Melanie. "Are you hungry? Help yourself."

"Thank you," said Nick gratefully, heaping scrambled eggs on his plate. "It wasn't like that at all. It turns out she was really interested in Uncle Sid. She saw me holding Lila's book in front of the Scheherazade Apartments where Uncle Sid lived, and she started talking to me and tagged along here. It's kind of a weird story. In fact, her name is Kali-Ra."

Melanie stared over at the girl, who seemed to be flirting with Duncan. "What?" she said. She turned and looked at Nick with wide eyes. "Were you with her all evening?"

"Well no, not exactly. These eggs are great."

"There was a tattoo on her breast," said Melanie, whispering now. "Did you see it?"

Nick began to blush. "Well, actually I've never seen her breasts except in the dark when we were swimming and then when she crawled out of the bushes topless for just a sec, but you're right, there was—"

Melanie leaned over and whispered in his ear. "I thought

it might have been a rose or something. I couldn't see it clearly, but it could have been a scarab. The slaves of Kali-Ra all have a scarab tattooed on their left breast. My God, she must be the person who's been stalking Nadia!"

"Oh, Callie isn't a stalker or anything," protested Nick. "There's a perfectly plausible explanation for her being named Kali-Ra. Her mother, Gail, believes herself to be Uncle Sid's daughter, the result of a union between Uncle Sid and his teenage neighbor."

Melanie stared at him. "Really? There was a statutory rape charge in 1952, but it was dropped."

"There's some question about paternity, apparently. Callie is kind of hoping she might be entitled to some money for the rights to her grandfather's books."

"I see," said Melanie.

"She wouldn't want to stalk Nadia or harm her. That would ruin her chances at getting money for the movie rights, because without Nadia, there would be no movie."

But as Nick reassured Melanie, he had another thought. Now that Lila was out of the picture, Callie had a much better shot at the rights money. He wondered if this would occur to Melanie too. He didn't want her to think he'd brought a cold-blooded killer into Villa Vera. And then he wondered if it could possibly be true.

CHAPTER XXX

SAVED FROM THE JAWS OF DEATH

He glanced at Melanie nervously to gauge her reaction, and saw she was now staring into the living room. "Oh my God, not *him* again," she said. The same policewoman who had escorted Nick and Callie into the living room had just arrived with Vince Fontana and his chauffeur, Bruno, in tow. "I told the police that he was here last night but if I'd known they'd bring him back here, I wouldn't have mentioned it."

She left Nick's side and went into the living room to announce that breakfast was available. Fontana, Callie, and Duncan all trooped into the dining room, but Bruno sidled over to Melanie, and twisted his uniform cap nervously in his large hands. "I'm kind of worried about Mr. Fontana," he said, maneuvering her to a quiet corner of the room partially obscured by a large potted palm.

Melanie said defensively, "Look, I had to give the police the names of everyone who was here last night. Your boss isn't going to hold that against me, is he?"

"No, no," said Bruno. "I was just worried when I heard about the terrible tragedy here last night. And now I hear there was some kind of assault on Miss Wentworth while we were here too."

"Someone tried to kill her," said Melanie indignantly.

Bruno looked horrified. "I'm sure Mr. Fontana didn't have anything to do with it. Okay, I understand he pushed

Mr. Smith, who was with us, into a pond or something. Sometimes he gets a little carried away. But he's harmless, really."

"I see. Um, actually, he implied some harm might come to Miss Wentworth," said Melanie carefully.

Bruno leaned toward her and said in a confidential tone, "I hope you can understand. Mr. Fontana is an elderly man and sometimes he isn't completely in touch with reality. Did he talk about the Mafia?"

"Well, sort of."

Bruno sighed. "Please try to forget about it. For the sake of his family. They're lovely people and they're worried about him. You see, Mr. Fontana doesn't have anything to do with the Mafia at all. Years ago, when his career was kind of sagging, some publicist put that story around to make him sound more interesting. Unfortunately, in the last few years, Mr. Fontana has grown to believe it. It's a shame really."

"Are you sure?" said Melanie. "He seemed awfully certain."

"I hope you'll keep this in strictest confidence," said Bruno. "The fact is Mr. Fontana isn't even Italian. When he started out, he didn't think anyone would listen to love songs from someone named Horace Bloggs." He shook his head sadly. "I'm sure sorry if he's been a nuisance."

"Oh, not really," said Melanie, managing a little smile. "Would you like some bacon and eggs?"

"Thank you," said Bruno, "but I already ate, and anyway, I mostly do carbs."

The detective who had been using Melanie's office appeared and told her he was leaving for a short while due to a new development, but would return soon and interview the others. "I want everyone to stick around until I come back," he said. "Meanwhile, feel free to use your office."

"Great," said Melanie. She had turned off the ringer on all the phones to avoid the tons of media calls she knew were coming in, but she was looking forward to a chance to check the e-mail. She had rehired Karen, Nadia's publicist, and was expecting a draft of a statement about last night's crime at Villa Vera.

Karen's statement wasn't there yet, but there was a message from George, Nadia's recently fired business manager. It was titled "Interesting News about the Rights!" and the gist of it was that Quentin Smith had sent an early-morning fax to George saying that he no longer had anything to do with Maurice Fender Associates, and adding the name and number of a lawyer representing Carla Lomax, formerly of Carla and the Cleartones, who was said to have some interesting information regarding Maurice Fender Associates that he was willing to share in the hopes that increased pressure on Maurice Fender Associates would strengthen his cash-poor client's position. A call to him had revealed that Maurice Fender Associates was almost certainly a criminal money-laundering enterprise in a precarious bargaining position. "In fact, our guy says we can tell them to forget about it or we'll join Carla in blowing their operation sky high."

"Of course," the e-mail went on, "according to our lawyers, this doesn't put the rights back in the public domain. We must now determine who does own them. Shall I get on it, or am I still fired? Some family history would help."

She e-mailed back, "Get on it right away. We start shooting in a month, for God's sake," and went into the dining room where it appeared Nick had finished breakfast. She caught his eye and beckoned to him. "I need to ask you some questions about your family," she said as he came into the living room.

"It looks like we can get these Maurice Fender folks off

our back, but we need to know who might own the rights if they don't. Valerian Ricardo was your uncle. Are there a bunch of relatives out there? How many are there?"

"I don't know," said Nick, feeling the dawning rays of hope. "I mean, Lila was his widow, but she's dead. And there is some question whether or not they were legally married. They never had children. I have a letter from Uncle Sid that says my grandfather would inherit the rights, and just recently, my grandfather left everything to me, so theoretically I could own them. But Gail Cunningham, Callie's mom, thinks she's his kid. I guess that would take precedence over my grandfather and me. If illegitimate kids can inherit."

"It sounds complicated," said Melanie. And expensive, she thought. The way this would probably shape up, the lawyers would throw cash at everyone until they shut up. Nick Iversen didn't seem particularly greedy, but that hard-bitten Kali-Ra bimbo looked like she would hold them up for whatever the traffic would bear. Lila, of course would have been just as bad. At least she was out of the picture.

Tom Thorndyke, who had been gone all morning, presumably ashamed that he had completely botched his job protecting Villa Vera, now came into the room, flapping his arms dramatically. "I have an announcement to make," he said, rushing over to Melanie and guiding her and Nick into the dining room, where the others, now at the table, looked up at him with curiosity. "I have some wonderful news. Lila hasn't died at all. She was unconscious because of some sleeping pills she took last night, but she isn't dead. It was a medical miracle."

Melanie ran upstairs to tell Nadia. As she ran, she realized that this bizarre development would change everything. Now, Lila was probably first in the running to be bought off. And she'd start messing with the script again, although maybe the old girl would need a long period of recuperation and would be too weak to ruin it completely.

Down in the dining room, everyone in the room had fallen silent at Tom Thorndyke's startling news. Only Vince Fontana continued to eat.

Nick looked over the table at Callie and saw an expression he'd never seen there before. She looked like a sullen child about to stamp her foot, and her mouth was pulled into a mean little frown.

Duncan Blaine broke the silence by getting up from the table and heading into the living room toward the liquor cabinet. "This calls for a celebration," he said through clenched teeth.

"I've spent the morning with the police and the doctor and it's an amazing story," said Thorndyke. "Apparently, Lila's pacemaker deflected the blade just enough to make the incision perfectly harmless. Her vital signs were very low because of the sleeping pills, but now she's conscious and everything. The doctors say it's a one in a million shot."

Melanie, Nadia, and Glen now rushed into the room and Glen said, "My God! Is Lila's heart on the right side of her body like Madge Barclay's?"

"Does she have a heart at all?" asked Duncan Blaine, who had made himself what appeared to be a Bloody Mary.

"Can she talk? Has she said anything about what happened?" asked Melanie.

"She's made a statement but it's a little incoherent," said Tom with a puzzled frown. "Something about someone named Betty Lou conspiring against her. It may mean nothing. Meanwhile, there's no sign of the guy who impersonated Kevin anywhere on the grounds, but it's pretty clear he's our guy. We think he's been leaving weird messages on the Kali-Ra website too. He's lost his grip completely. Says he's waiting for the final summons of Kali-Ra. Thank God he didn't actually kill anyone!"

Nadia ran over to Tom Thorndyke and began to drum her fists on his chest. "You son of a bitch," she said. "He *could* have killed someone. He stabbed Lila, and it's your fault. My God, that could even have been me! I can't believe you let this happen. I swear to God I'm going to make sure you never work in this town again." She wheeled over toward Melanie. "This is all your fault! Why did I think *you* could handle anything? Everyone lets me down." She ran into the living room and flung herself on the sofa, followed by everyone except Vince Fontana, who appeared to be in a world of his own and was helping himself to more bacon and eggs.

Melanie rushed to Nadia's side. "It's okay, Beanie," she said. "It'll be okay." She stroked her hair.

Nick was stunned. Lila had said Betty Lou had attacked her. No one else in the room knew who Betty Lou was. No one but Callie. Callie's mother had said that Callie was the spitting image of her grandmother, Betty Lou. Was Lila saying Callie had stabbed her?

Horrified, he looked over at Callie to see how she was reacting. But Callie had her back to him and was in deep discussion with Tom Thorndyke. Something about her posture and Thorndyke's own attentive, grim-faced pose indicated that she was speaking urgently to him and that he was listening with great interest.

Now he had his arm on her elbow and was guiding her to the door. What was going on? A phrase flashed into his brain.

Strange forces were at work, forces with a power so alluring yet terrifying that they could only come from the beautiful evil one, the Queen of Doom.

"Glen, I need you," wailed Nadia, rising from the sofa. He now rushed to her side and embraced her as Melanie stepped away and stood beside Nick while Nadia sobbed on Glen's shoulder.

Nick must have looked surprised because Melanie whispered, "They seem to have fallen in love last night."

"Oh," said Nick. "Um, what did you just call her?" he asked Melanie. "Was it Beanie?"

Now Melanie blushed. "Oh that's what Nadia used to be called when she was a kid. Her real name is Brandi but she couldn't pronounce it until she was about three. For God's sake, don't tell anyone. She'd be so embarrassed."

Nick was struck by Melanie's loyalty. Nadia didn't seem to deserve it. "She doesn't seem to be the easiest boss in the world," he said. "She was pretty rude to you just now."

Melanie shrugged. "She's maddening, but she needs someone to look after her and no one else would put up with her. Anyway, I didn't know what else I could do with a B.A. in classics."

"Well, I guess Lila owns the rights again," Nick said, trying not to look disappointed.

"God," said Melanie, "First the script problems and now this. We're supposed to start shooting!" I hope we can sort this out. Sometimes I wish I'd never heard of Valerian Ricardo. There's been nothing but trouble since I found that damn book! Lunatics running around stabbing people, death threats! And now we don't even know who owns the rights to those rotten books."

"I'm sorry," said Nick.

"It's not your fault," she said, looking ashamed at her outburst. "I'm sorry I trashed your uncle's work."

"But his work *is* trash," said Nick. "The guy was obviously a sicko, and his so-called philosophy, a lot of crap about evil really being part of the greater scheme of things, was a lot of cheap claptrap and an excuse for him to pander to prurient interest. I mean an honest pornographer wouldn't have thrown in all that theosophy or whatever it is."

"I'm glad to hear you say that," said Melanie, glancing nervously over at Nadia. "I'm exhausted from pretending the stuff has any literary merit at all."

"The creepy thing is, there's something kind of potent about his prose. Lately, some of my thoughts have been phrasing themselves in Uncle Sid's overripe style. It's unnerving," said Nick.

"The same thing's been happening to me," said Melanie, with a relieved air. "God, it's good to be able to tell someone."

"It's horrible to think we're so easily seduced by sleazy prose, isn't it?" said Nick.

"The other day," confided Melanie, "I almost felt as if I were slipping into some other reality where cheap sensationalism was standard operating procedure. I've been trying to clean out my head by reading Latin poets. It helps."

"Maybe I'll try it. I'll start with Lucretius," mused Nick. "Reason. Lucid thought. Intellect instead of cheap emotion. I'm afraid my Latin isn't that great, though. I've only read him in translation, but for the full antidote effect I could see that the original would be better."

"I've got the dual-language edition in my office," said Melanie. "Want to borrow it?"

"Yes," said Nick, and he followed her down the hall. "The sooner the better. I'd hate to crack up like the fake Kevin."

"When we hear the gong of Kali-Ra summoning us, we'll know we're doomed," said Melanie with a laugh. Just then, Nick heard a faint, metallic-like sound from outside. He grabbed Melanie's arm. "Did you hear that?" he said, alarmed.

She giggled. "Stop it," she said.

God, maybe he *was* going around the bend.

But a second later, he heard it again. Melanie did too. "Oh my God!" she said, clutching him back.

CHAPTER XXXI

IN THE TEMPLE OF THE CHOSEN

Although it was midday, the dense canopy of branches and the heavy vines and tangled vegetation above the milk-white temple shut out the light, giving the scene a dusky, emerald glow. The structure was simple but striking in its austere beauty, a perfect frame for the exquisite Kali-Ra.

It was made of marble and consisted of a circle surrounded by steps, a ring of fluted columns, and a roof that cast in shadow she who stood there tall, proud and beautiful. Her green eyes glowed in a queer, trancelike gaze that seemed to penetrate all of time. She wore a plain garment of some white, finely-woven stuff draped to reveal a beautiful shoulder. In her hands was a brass gong and she struck it once more, producing a thrilling but alarming tone, a tone that lingered and beckoned like the evil summons it was.

Soon, the summons was answered.

A wretched, bulky figure clambered noisily down from a large eucalyptus tree nearby, panting with exertion and trembling with excitement at his nearness to his mistress.

"Oh, Queen of Doom," he murmured, casting his eyes on the woman before him. "You rang?"

"Slave!" she said cruelly, her tone tinged with just a hint of the rare benevolence that when mingled with her mighty power incited his passionate loyalty.

"Is it really you?" he whispered. "I had dared to hope for so long, yet—"

"Have you no faith?" she shrieked, tearing at her garment and exposing her left breast. "You see, I bear the sacred scarab."

"Oh, beloved mistress," he replied, fumbling with the buttons of his shirt, which bore the embroidered name KEVIN in a small oval above the left pocket. "I too bear this mark." Clumsily but eagerly he removed half his shirt and pulled up the white cotton T-shirt beneath it to reveal a similar tattoo on his chest.

"Prostrate yourself," snapped Kali-Ra, readjusting her garment as the slave fell on his face near the bottom step. "What have you done in my service since we last met?" she demanded.

"I have entered the house where she who would profane your name slept, and plunged the dagger of Kali-Ra into her breast," said the slave proudly. "I used the dagger I fashioned years ago in shop class, crafted to the exact specifications of your own sacred dagger."

"Describe to me the deed and how it was done," said Kali-Ra with an impatient snap of her long, slim fingers.

"Um, well, I climbed up on the balcony, using a ladder I found in the garage, and I just went into Nadia's bedroom and did it. The door wasn't locked or anything." He paused and added, "It was the most exciting thing that has ever happened to me, except of course for coming into your presence, oh great queen."

"You fool! You stabbed another. Nadia is alive," said Kali-Ra. "Could you not see?"

"I did? Gosh. Well, it was pretty dark," he stammered. "And I lost my glasses last night in the tree. I just assumed. I mean I know it was Nadia Wentworth's bed and everything."

"Ah yes, the tree," she said. "I am pleased you followed

my orders about the tree, so I will spare your life, but I am displeased with your clumsy mistake, which has brought the attention of the authorities to us. You must be punished."

"Oh, Kali-Ra, be merciful," the pitiful creature whined. "Let it be you personally who metes out the punishment. And could that punishment possibly be the sacred lash of Kali-Ra?" he added with a shudder of despair and delight.

"Silence! How dare you tell me what to do! Are you my slave or are you not!"

"Oh yes!"

"Shut up!"

The slave began weeping, and facedown, began crawling toward her.

"How can you be so cruel?" he sobbed. "I have devoted my entire life to your service, and you have ignored me. When at last I fall down before you, you mock me."

He had made his way to her feet now, and she stared down in horror as he stroked her bare feet, then grabbed her ankles.

"Hey! Let go!"

"But I love you," he said. "And you should appreciate that."

She tried to pull free of him, but he held her more tightly, then gave her ankles a smart yank, sending her sprawling on her back on the floor of the temple.

"You little jerk!" she shouted. "Let go!"

The slave, less humble now, scrambled into a sitting position, pinned Kali-Ra down by her lovely shoulders and said, his voice now filled with anger, "You bitch! You're just like all the girls back in high school. I knock myself out for you and you treat me like this. I've had it with women!"

"Seize him," shouted Kali-Ra in a frightened voice.

"Raymond Vernon was right about you," the slave went

on. "You're no damned good! Why, I ought to—" He raised his hand as if to strike and she screamed.

Just then, with much thrashing of foliage, a figure leapt from the bushes, wrapped one beefy arm around the slave's throat, and pulled him off the Queen of Doom. She scuttled out of his reach, her hair falling over her face, her white robes falling from her body, her face beautiful in its terror.

"Great job," said Tom Thorndyke, as he pulled the slave's arms behind his back and whipped out a pair of plastic handcuffs with which he bound the dazed man's wrists in a practiced movement. "Most inspiring undercover work I've ever seen."

"Thanks," said Callie with a happy grin. "It was kind of fun, to tell the truth." She rewrapped her garments, stood up, and picked up her gong and mallet, which closer examination revealed to be a large frying pan lid and a hammer.

"Just cooperate and it'll be easier on you," said Tom to his prisoner. "Listen, pal, you've caused everyone a lot of problems. Grab the camera, will you, honey, and let's turn this wacko over to the cops."

Callie scooped up a camcorder, which sat in the grass nearby. "Did you get it all?"

"Every second. Great stunt with your breast. I bet that little move will get us an extra twenty thou from *Inside Edition.*"

"We should have got some stills for the *National Enquirer,*" said Callie with a little frown.

"No problem, we can restage the whole thing," said Tom. "Maybe get a better-looking gong."

"This sheet kind of sucks too," said Callie, fingering the fabric swathed around her body.

"Well, this guy bought it," said Tom with a smile. "Now maybe I can get Nadia Wentworth off my back."

Tom Thorndyke hustled the prisoner into the house, and after a frantic phone call, the two detectives rushed back from the hospital to arrest him. They had planned to take him to headquarters for questioning, but he seemed anxious to tell them all about himself immediately.

His name turned out to be Winston Goodlet, a native of Moose Jaw, Saskatchewan. He listened carefully as his rights were read, said he didn't want a lawyer, made a full confession, and was delighted to hear that there were TV cameras outside the gates of Villa Vera. His only regret, he said, was that he had been taken in by a cheap impersonation of Kali-Ra.

"I just wanted to believe," he said sadly, "but I know the real Kali-Ra is out there, and someday, I will hear her gong."

He had been lurking in the shrubbery the night before, when he thought he saw Nadia running naked across the lawn. Seizing the chance to punish her, he grabbed her and carried her off to the temple he had found in the overgrown part of the garden. He had selected the site earlier as a suitable spot for some unspeakable tortures that he hadn't thought up yet, hoping to get guidance from Kali-Ra herself.

When he discovered he had captured someone else entirely, and saw the scarab on her breast, he begged forgiveness, and asked if his captive was a fellow slave of Kali-Ra. "I was pretty excited because I'd never met a fellow slave of Kali-Ra," he explained. "I even fixed the security system last night in case any of them were out there and wanted to join me. It's been pretty lonely."

"No, you fool, I am no slave," the young woman had said, wrapping her sarong around her hips, striding to the center of the temple and raising her hands above her head. "I *am* Kali-Ra."

"I told her how I had devoted my life to her service, ever since I was thirteen and found a couple of Valerian Ricardo books in my gran's attic. I knew immediately that they were real, even though everyone told me they were just made up. I asked her what I could do for her and said I was trying to kill Nadia for her, and I missed with that jar.

"She said that was fine, but as penance for carrying her off, I must first climb to the very top of a huge eucalyptus tree that happened to be right near the temple there, so I did. When I came down again, she was gone, but I thought I better get on with the job. Afterwards, I went back up there, figuring it was a pretty safe place. And it was. I guess the strong smell of the eucalyptus leaves is what fooled those dogs I heard barking around here last night. Anyways, when I heard the gong I came down."

At the end of his story, the detectives stared at him for a second, slightly slack-jawed, and he said, "I know my sacrifice will not be in vain and that my mistress will reward my loyalty. Can I talk to the press on the way out? You never know. *She* might be watching CNN."

After he had been carted away, along with a duplicate tape of his surrender to Kali-Ra Cunningham, Tom Thorndyke having kept the original, Melanie decided that there were a few more loose ends to be tied up.

Approaching Vince Fontana, she addressed him in the Italian she had picked up on her junior year abroad studying Roman inscriptions. "Sí, sí," he responded, and she smiled and gave him another dose. When he pinched her cheek gaily and said, "Sí, sí. Bella ragazza! Say, you don't look Italian, honey," she relaxed, and said, "Bruno says it's time for you to go home now. Ciao, Vincenzo."

"What did you say to him?" asked Nick as they left.

"I asked him if he was really Italian and didn't he agree that fire was cold and ice was hot. When he said 'sí, sí,' I followed up with a suggestion that his mother and sister were prostitutes and he agreed to that too. I guess Bruno's story checks out and we don't need to expect horse heads in our beds. Don't go away, I have to check on one more detail." She excused herself and went over to Duncan Blaine.

"So when's the old girl coming back from hospital?" he asked morosely.

"Very soon, apparently," said Melanie. "Listen, Duncan, the police told me that Kali nerd they captured is from Moose Jaw, Saskatchewan."

"I guess I'd go mad up there too," said Duncan.

"The point is," said Melanie, "that it's a lucky break for you, because in Canada, they spell labor with a *u*."

Melanie glanced over at Nadia, who was holding hands on the sofa with Glen Pendergast. "Her disposition may improve," she said with a little smile. "But no more scary stuff. We've been through enough."

"I promise," said Duncan.

Tom Thorndyke and Callie, who had been conferring with the police, now came into the room with a triumphal air. Callie was still wearing her bedsheet, which seemed to be slipping a little so that she had difficulty avoiding stepping on her hem. Melanie said acidly, "Who taught her to tie a toga?"

"Tell us all about it," said Nick. "What happened?"

"With the help of Callie here," said Tom, "I caught the son of a bitch and he's in custody. We got the whole thing on tape. It's sensational." He went over to the VCR hidden in a cupboard near the liquor cabinet and set up the tape while Callie explained.

"Last night that creep grabbed me because he thought I was Nadia, and I realized the only way to get away was to pretend I was Kali-Ra. Which was pretty easy because I've been doing that anyway as an empowering visualization thing that I'll explain to you all later. Anyway, I didn't know how to get rid of him, so I saw this big old tree and told him to climb to the top. Then I ran away and staggered back through the bushes."

"Wow," said Nick. "But why didn't you tell anyone?"

"Well this sounds nuts, I know," said Callie, blushing. "But the whole experience was so weird that I thought I might have imagined it. I mean this guy said he was my slave and stuff. It was bizarre. It was like posttraumatic stress denial or whatever." She neglected to mention the killer joint and the gin, thought Nick. "I was so freaked out I thought maybe I'd done more stuff I couldn't remember, like stabbed Lila or something. I mean this Valerian Ricardo stuff can make you crazy."

"I know," said Melanie, Nick, and Duncan Blaine in unison.

"It's all cued up," said Tom, flapping the remote. "Great publicity for the movie, Nadia." he gave her a winning smile and Nick figured he hoped she'd forget her threat to ruin his career.

They all watched in silence, and when the tape ended, Tom said, "We'll have to release this in conjunction with your own promotional needs, Nadia. We can liaise with your publicist."

"Hold on," said Glen Pendergast with a frown. "I'm not so sure this should be made public."

"What do you mean? It's sensational," said Tom.

"It'll probably be good publicity for you, Tom," said Glen. "But I'm not sure that anything that detracts from Nadia's interpretation of the character is a good thing." He looked over at Callie. "There can be only one Kali-Ra in the public's mind. A basic rule in promoting a legend. She must be unique."

"Glen's right," said Nadia. "We can't let this out."

"Wait a minute," said Tom. "It's nice to hear your opinion, professor, but this is a professional decision that Nadia's going to have to make."

"Glen is my new manager," said Nadia. "And my fiancé."

Duncan Blaine appeared to perk up at this news. He rushed over to Pendergast and shook his hand. "Wonderful news," he said. "Nadia needs a firm hand on her career. I hope you'll address the script problems that Lila has been causing. With your knowledge of the works of Valerian Ricardo—"

"Wait a minute," said Callie suddenly. "There's another issue here. Whoever owns the rights to the Kali-Ra books owns the rights to the character I portrayed just now. And I have a good reason to believe the owner of those rights is my mom, Gail Cunningham." She turned to Nadia. "But frankly, I'd rather be rich than famous. Go ahead, buy the tape from me, and if you can match an offer I might get from *Inside Edition,* you've got a deal."

"Hey!" said Tom Thorndyke, "we had a deal too, remember? We were a team, a great team, babe!"

Duncan Blaine had drifted back to the VCR, rewound, and was fast-forwarding to the place where Callie had flashed her breast. In viewing it again, Nick could understand why Nadia might not want a rival Kali-Ra.

"I'm going nuts," said Melanie to Nick. "My lawyer says the stuff is back in copyright, Glen's told me Valerian Ricardo didn't have a will, and Maurice Fender's own lawyer says he doesn't have a legitimate claim. I want to find out as much as I can about who owns the rights to these damn things so I can turn all the information over to the lawyers at the start of business tomorrow morning. I'm starting with you. Come into the office with me and draw me a family tree."

CHAPER XXXII

A BAFFLING LINEAGE

"But I don't know that much about it," said Nick as Melanie sat him down at her desk and handed him a pencil and paper. "I mean I never met Aunt Lila until yesterday."

"Here's what we know about her," said Melanie, slapping down Tom Thorndyke's report in front of him. "I'm afraid it doesn't paint a very attractive picture of your uncle Sid."

"Then it's probably pretty accurate," said Nick, beginning to read. "The family back in Minnesota always figured him for a real lowlife. At first I thought they were just jealous, but I'm beginning to think they were right."

"I'll leave you to it," said Melanie. "I have some filing to do."

When Nick had finished reading, he glanced up at her bending over a file cabinet drawer, a frown of concentration on her face. She looked so competent and conscientious. Suddenly, he asked her, "How on earth did you end up in this job?"

"A lot of people wonder that," she said, straightening up and turning to face him. "I don't usually tell them, but you don't know anyone in show business, so I'll tell you. Nadia is my cousin. We grew up together in this small town in Washington state, and went to the same school and everything.

"When she first came to Hollywood a lot of people jerked her around and she trusted me, so she asked me to

208

come and take care of her. I used to take care of her when we were kids, even though she's a few months older. You see, Beanie was the pretty one, but I was the smart one. I helped her get through remedial math and wrote her speech when she ran for Apple Blossom Queen."

Nick wondered how he could get across to Melanie that she was very pretty herself without sounding patronizing. "Why do you keep it secret?" he asked.

"Because people wouldn't take me seriously. I mean Elvis had a bunch of cousins on the payroll, for heaven's sake. I understand there was one guy whose job it was to hand him a glass of water every now and then." She resumed her filing, and he stared at her for a second. He didn't like the idea of this smart, sweet-faced girl devoting her life to high-strung, selfish Cousin Beanie.

She seemed to sense he was looking at her and she returned his stare. "You're feeling sorry for me, aren't you?" she said with a touch of hostility. "That's another reason I keep it secret. But you don't have to feel sorry for me. I know what I'm doing. She's paying me a lot and I'm saving and investing, and after her career peaks and she starts playing moms, which will be soon enough in her line of work, I'll be able to go back to graduate school. I already own an apartment building back home in Wenatchee that's a nice little earner, and some mutual funds that just keep growing. It helps that I live rent free."

"Wow," said Nick. "That's great. I'd like to go back to graduate school myself. All I really want to do is be in school forever, as a student or a teacher or whatever. That's all you can do in philosophy anyway."

"The same thing with classics," said Melanie. "I figure I'm good enough to get a doctorate but there's no guarantee I can get a university job or tenure. I can always teach high school Latin, though. There are signs it's coming back in fashion."

"Really? That's great, especially if it means more people start studying philosophy," said Nick. "I didn't stick with Latin after high school, but for me it was a gateway to classical philosophy. The trouble with schools today is there's so much undisciplined thinking." He thought about the grim selection of books at Callie's mother's house, and her mushy worldview.

Melanie's eyes took on a happy gleam. "What I'd really like is to do research. Did you know there are three hundred thousand known Latin inscriptions throughout the ancient Roman Empire, and a thousand more are discovered every year? We're learning more all the time. It's so exciting."

They smiled at each other like a couple of kids who had just made friends at camp, and then Melanie said self-consciously, "So how are you related to Valerian Ricardo exactly?"

Nick drew a quick family tree, and explained that his grandfather had left him everything, and that as far as he knew, his grandfather would have been Valerian Ricardo's heir if Lila hadn't been in the picture. "But maybe they weren't married," he added.

"Even if they weren't, and if that meant she couldn't legally inherit his copyright," said Melanie, "she could muddy the waters for years. One thing I've learned in this job is that you can keep things tied up with lawyers even when you don't have a case, and hope people buy you off. We just don't have that much time."

"And then there's Callie and her mom," said Nick, drawing a dotted line on his chart from Valerian Ricardo to Gail to Callie. "Can illegitimate kids inherit?"

"I don't know, but the same thing applies. They could keep the whole thing going for years, and in the end the lawyers would get rich and the picture wouldn't get made. Both Callie and Lila are stubborn and avaricious as far as I can tell," said Melanie, then looked nervously at Nick as if she'd insulted his girlfriend.

"I'm afraid you're right," said Nick. He picked up the report Tom Thorndyke had written. "Although interestingly, Lila did one generous thing, according to Callie's mother. Gail was one of the hippies doing drugs with Uncle Sid in the boiler room. They were about to cart him off to some commune in the hills the day he died. Gail went over to pick him up and Lila broke it to her that he'd had a heart attack and gave her something that belonged to him. Something valuable too." Nick described the diamond-studded monogrammed box and quoted Lila as saying, "He wanted you to have this."

Melanie looked thoughtful. "Sounds like something he would have kept his stash in. Apparently, he was a coke-head."

"That's exactly what it looked like," said Nick. "In fact, there were some traces of whitish powder inside. Gail's mom said they did hash and opium, but she wouldn't have admitted to Callie they were doing coke too. Now that she's a middle-age parent she's on this clean and sober kick. Anyway, Lila's gesture gives some credence to the idea that Gail was his daughter."

"No, it doesn't," said Melanie. "Do you think Lila would have liked the idea of her dear Valerian knocking up some teenage neighbor? The last thing she would have wanted was to admit it was true or condone it."

"You're right," said Nick. "Remember how she turned on Callie? Apparently she looks just like her grandmother Betty Lou, who charged Valerian Ricardo with rape. Lila seemed pretty hostile."

"I find it especially interesting that the box was actually valuable," said Melanie. "That makes it even weirder. As far as I can tell, Lila's a greedy woman.

"Anyway, a DNA test can probably tell us if your uncle

Sid fathered Gail. We could match her against Betty Lou's husband if he's alive. Or you, probably, because you're some kind of a cousin. But they might not cooperate. This is all pretty complicated."

Suddenly, Nadia came into the office. "Wonderful news," she said. "I just called the hospital, and Lila's in such great shape they're releasing her! We have to hire a private nurse, though. Get one over here right away, will you? Glen is driving me down to get her. It was be wonderful to have her back. I talked to her and everything! She says she's strong enough to start work on the script right away. Isn't it wonderful? And oh, Melanie, isn't it exciting about my engagement! I haven't even had a chance to talk to you about it. He's perfect, absolutely perfect!"

The two women embraced and Nadia danced out of the room.

Melanie smiled, and said, "I know it's sudden, but he seems sweet and solid." A second later, she was back in businesslike mode. "Listen, I have an idea. Do you think you can get Callie's mother up here? I'd like to hear what she has to say about all this. The more I know and can tell the lawyers, the faster we can sort this out."

"I'm pretty sure I can," said Nick. "I know I can get Callie to try to convince her to come."

"Ask her to come in a couple of hours, and tell her to bring that box," said Melanie, who had picked up Tom Thorndyke's report and was rereading the last page.

CHAPTER XXXIII

A SHOCKING SECRET REVEALED

Tom Thorndyke drove Glen and Nadia slowly through the jostling flock of photographers clustered outside the gates. There were shouts of "Nadia, Nadia." Glen blinked furiously, and felt slightly jangled, but he also felt a great welling-up of excitement, and a strange sensation of familiarity. He had seen this scene in so many films.

Nadia put her hand on his. "Get used to it, honey," she said. "Stop the car for a sec," she said to Tom, touching the button that rolled down the window.

"Talk to us, Nadia," said a man with a big smile leaning into the car. A brace of microphones was thrust through the open window around his face. "Were you harmed? Did you know the guy they arrested? What's up with this dagger thing?"

"I've been majorly stressed by recent events, but in a way, they all tie in to the power of the themes of my next film, *The Revenge of Kali-Ra*," she replied. Glen felt claustrophobic as hands pressed against the glass and more faces peered inside the car.

"I'm putting it all behind me," Nadia continued, "and I hope the alleged individual responsible for the criminal acts that have gone down will receive humane and caring treatment. It's like, there but for the grace of God goes us."

Glen recognized a reporter from *Entertainment Tonight,*

one of his favorite shows, and a great source of material for his academic work. "We understand you were terrorized by the suspect," he said with a grim look of concern.

"My fiancé, Dr. Glen Pendergast, was very supportive," said Nadia, placing her hand on Glen's shoulder and smiling at him, holding the pose for a second as more shutters clicked and the press produced a chorus of "Wows" and "Aw rights."

Glen tried to look worthy of Nadia's hand, and gave her a dignified yet affectionate smile as they took the pictures. Then, Nadia turned away, looked pensive, and said, "In a way, it was a learning experience. It really made me understand at gut level what Salman Rushdie must have gone through, you know? But now we're going out to celebrate our engagement." She looked demure and said, "If it wasn't Sunday, we'd be going down to City Hall to pick up the license. Life goes on."

Glen leaned over and said to the reporter, "Nadia and I are totally committed to artistic freedom, and we are opposed to any form of censorship of the arts, especially when it is based on delusional interpretation of texts, valid as they may seem to those operating under the delusion."

Nadia flicked the window button again and gestured to Tom to drive on. "Oh, baby, great sound bite," she said, squeezing Glen's thigh affectionately.

Lila had seemed a little miffed when the starry-eyed Nadia and Glen had wheeled her into the living room in her wheelchair, introduced the nurse who would tend to the maintenance of the dressing of her superficial chest wound, and dashed off. Melanie had warned Duncan Blaine of Lila's impending arrival, and he had scuttled back up to his room, announcing that he would put the final tweaks on his latest draft, and Callie, after phoning her mother, had gone upstairs to change out of her sheet, so there was no one with her except Melanie and Nick.

"I thought there'd at least be a press conference," Lila said.

"We don't want to put you under any strain," Melanie replied. "Although I hope you won't mind meeting Gail again. The woman who says Valerian Ricardo is her father?"

"What? Gail? That hippie?"

"Yes," said Melanie smoothly. "There's some confusion about competing claims on the rights to the Kali-Ra books. I take it you have heard there's a possibility they're no longer in the public domain."

"You better believe I have," said Lila with spirit. "First thing tomorrow morning, I'm calling a lawyer. I'm sure Nadia and I can come to a swift agreement. Of course, I can't sell the rights without script approval."

"I kind of thought you'd say that," said Melanie.

"I'm afraid there is much Duncan does not understand. He is a young entity, and will need many more lifetimes to develop a higher level of sensitivity. By weaving the strands of fate so that I am in complete control, the Enlightened Ones have worked behind the scenes to ensure that Valerian will be able to direct the project from a plane beyond earth." Her blue-veined hands fluttered at either side of her face and she tilted her head to one side and gave Melanie a sappy smile, meant, apparently, to convey spirituality. Instead, Nick thought, Lila just looked smug.

Nick didn't know what Lila's views on the script were, but he felt sorry for Melanie. Letting this crazy woman have creative control over a project costing millions was a pretty scary thought. If Callie and her mother managed to get their hands on the rights, Nick was pretty sure they'd squeeze every last dollar out of Nadia, but they wouldn't care about the content of the movie.

Callie, dressed once again in her khaki shorts and T-shirt, came into the living room with her mother.

"You remember Gail, don't you, Lila?" asked Melanie pleasantly.

"I'm afraid I do."

"I don't know if you knew that Caroline here, whom you met yesterday, is actually Gail's daughter," she went on.

Lila glared at both women. "I never thought I'd see you again," she said to Gail. "You have a lot of nerve coming here. You tried to corrupt Valerian and ruin his last days. It was disgusting. You kids were down there having orgies and stuff in the boiler room. The tenants complained."

Gail blushed. "Maybe a few of the things we did were kind of inappropriate, but it was an experimental time."

Lila rolled her eyes. "Drugs, naked girls, God knows what all. The excitement killed him. And it was a blessing, because he was just about to completely go off the deep end."

None of this had been covered in Lila's autobiography. The last days of Valerian Ricardo had been described as a time of spiritual preparation for life beyond the veil, with Valerian becoming more and more saintly in aspect and an inspiration to all those who met him.

Lila turned to Melanie and Nick. "What kind of young girls would fool around with a man in his eighties? They were depraved."

"The little mind-expanding rituals we did didn't involve actual, you know, *sex*," Gail said earnestly, glancing nervously over at her daughter. "I mean there was some nudity and he liked us to dance around in these veils he had, and we did kind of trust exercises involving, um, restraints and, um, being vulnerable. He was really into that."

"God, Mom," said Callie. "And you gave me a hard time when I pierced my navel."

Gail was blushing now. "Really, you have it all wrong, darling. Lila is making it sound much worse than it actually was. I've done similar things in the team-building exercises they make us do on the phone company middle-management retreats."

Lila turned to Callie. "You look just like your grandmother, that little tramp Betty Lou. I thought you were a reincarnation of her."

"Don't you dare call my grandmother a tramp! She was a sweet little teenager and your perverted husband tried to lure her into his evil web." Callie turned to her mother. "No offense, Mom, but I think your real dad was a phony loser, who seemed incredibly cool to a bunch of white-bread kids from the valley. But that's not the point. The point is, you're his heir. And we could use the money."

Lila paid no attention to Callie's outburst and turned to Melanie. "Betty Lou was a little tramp who lived with her parents on the fifth floor at the Scheherazade. He'd shown a kindly interest in the girl. When she got knocked up by her pimply boyfriend, she tried to saddle Valerian with a statutory rape charge. She backed off when the boyfriend agreed to marry her. Even if, God forbid, Valerian had actually done the deed, legally, Betty Lou's husband is the father."

"The man who pretended to be my dad married her *after* I was born," said Gail.

"Your family has been a curse on me for three generations," said Lila to Gail. "First Betty Lou, that sly little bobby-soxer with her scuffed saddle shoes and her tight sweaters and false accusations and scandal! Then, twenty years later, you and your friends moved in and polluted his soul." She pointed to Callie. "And now her!"

"I hear your anger," said Gail with a solemn nod.

Lila ignored her and went on. "Anyway, even if he was your father—which is highly unlikely considering Valerian's pure and spiritual approach to the sensual side of life, different than other men's in some very basic ways—as his widow I'm the heir."

"Ah," said Callie with a smile Nick found a little chilling. "That's the interesting part. I don't believe you are his widow."

"That shows how much you know," snapped Lila.

"Glen Pendergast said he couldn't find a record of a marriage between Lila Lamb and Valerian Ricardo for when and where your book said you got married," said Nick.

"Of course he couldn't," said Lila scornfully. "Neither of us ever changed our names legally. The names on the certificate are Sidney Olav Gundersen and Ethel Mae Lasenby. Ours was a sacred union of souls that never required the seal of earthly authority. It was a marriage on a much higher plane than normal people have. But we got legally married in 1963, because of some legal problems we had having to do with the damned IRS. I have the certificate in my safe-deposit box at Golden West Savings on La Brea."

"Oh," said Callie, momentarily taken aback.

As far as Nick was concerned, that probably cinched it. Lila might have to share some of her money with the Cunninghams, but as Uncle Sid's widow, she clearly had a strong claim.

He realized too that any little hopes he'd been harboring about cashing in on Uncle Sid's legacy were dashed. As for poor Melanie, she'd have to negotiate with greedy Lila and maybe watch *The Revenge of Kali-Ra,* and Nadia's career, go down the tubes due to the old woman's horrible meddling.

Lila narrowed her eyes at Callie. "You're a grasping, materialistic girl, aren't you?" she said. "Well, you won't get a dime from me." She laughed.

"Kids still count. Are you denying that Mom is Valerian Ricardo's child?" said Callie.

"I certainly am."

"Well, what about the cigarette box then?" said Callie.

Gail rummaged in the bottom of her large purse and produced the gold diamond-trimmed box. "Lila, when you gave me this, you practically admitted Valerian was my dad," she said.

"That doesn't prove a thing."

"It's a beautiful box," said Melanie disingenuously.

Lila gazed at it and said wistfully, "It was from Cartier. When I first met Valerian he had lots of nice things left over from when he was a rich and famous author. The ruby cuff links went first. Then the gold candelabra and the Egyptian antiquities. Finally, we sold the sterling silver cocktail shaker and the handmade golf clubs. That was about all that was left from the old days."

"So it was especially generous of you to give it to Gail," said Melanie.

Lila looked at her with an expression Nick couldn't interpret. She seemed startled.

Melanie turned to Gail. "Tell me, Gail, was it a spontaneous gesture? Did she say 'I've thought about it and I think he would have wanted you to have this?' Or did she just grab it and hand it to you?"

Gail said, "I don't know. She was leaving the boiler room as I was going in. And it was already in her hand. Then she told me he was dead. And she gave it to me."

Melanie leaned forward. "Did she know you were there, Gail?"

"No." Gail closed her eyes and said, "I remember it very clearly. No one I had ever known well had died, and it all kind of etched itself on my mind. She opened the door and came out with the box and seemed as surprised to see me as I was to see her."

"And then she handed you the box," said Melanie.

"Yes, and told me to clear out."

"Because the police were coming."

"That's right. She said we might get busted. We were very paranoid about the police in those days."

Melanie turned to Lila, who was now shrinking back into a corner of her wheelchair and staring at Melanie with a horrified expression. "The boiler room seems like an odd place to keep such a valuable thing," she said.

"Oh. Well," said Gail, "um, I think it's where he kept his stash." She turned to her daughter. "He did a little cocaine now and then. It was very fashionable in the twenties, and no one realized until the eighties how bad it was for you."

Melanie said, "She didn't plan to give it to you, Gail. She didn't even expect to find you outside the door. I think she was cleaning up before the cops came."

Gail looked over at Lila.

"That's right," said Lila. "I didn't want the police to find the cocaine. I threw the hashish into the boiler."

"No you didn't," said Melanie. "You kept the hashish to show to the police, because you wanted them to bust Gail and her friends, didn't you?"

"No, no," said Lila.

"That's what the detective on the case said. He's retired now, but we spoke to him recently and he remembers it all very well. He talked you out of pursuing it because he felt sorry for you. He knew it would come out just what kind of person Valerian Ricardo was, and thought you were a sweet woman who wouldn't want sordid publicity." Melanie leaned forward. "You were cleaning up before the police came because that box didn't just have cocaine in it, Lila. It had something else. It had whatever killed him in it. Whatever you put in there for him to sniff so that he couldn't run off with Gail and her friends.

"You practically said so right now. You said it was a blessing he went when he did because he was just about to bail out. I don't think you wanted to be left behind to stoke the boiler and battle the roaches all by yourself."

"Roaches!" said Nick. He turned to Gail. "Didn't you say the boiler room was full of roach killer?"

"DDT," said Gail. "We even talked about it. We told him they had found out how bad it was for the environment, and that how it was going to be banned soon because it never goes away. Eventually, they did ban it."

"If it never goes away," said Melanie, "and it was in that box, then there are probably still traces of it in there."

Gail flipped open the lid. "There are little bits of some kind of powder down in the cracks."

"So what? Maybe there are," said Lila. "The place was lousy with cockroaches. Valerian was an old man. Maybe he made a mistake."

"I don't know a lot about inheritance law, or copyright law, other than that copyrights can be inherited," said Melanie. "I don't know if common-law wives or illegitimate children could have inherited the copyrights. The lawyers will sort that all out tomorrow. But I do know that murderers can't inherit from their victims. That's pretty universal. And I also know there's no statute of limitations on murder, Lila."

"But it wasn't really murder in the broad sense of the word," said Lila. "Death is an illusion. Valerian understood what I had to do and he's grateful. He's told me so from the other side. Anyway," she said smugly, "I don't think anyone could prove a thing, even if there are traces of something in there."

Melanie looked over at the nurse, who had been sitting quietly in the corner. "Did you get all that?" she said.

"Yes, I did," said the nurse, who appeared to be fiddling with some buttons on a small black machine.

To Lila, Melanie said, "There are five witnesses, including the nurse here, who is a disinterested party, and an employee of Tom Thorndyke's very respectable security firm, Lila. I doubt there are very many lawyers who will encourage you to pursue your claim after they hear what you just said."

Melanie turned to Gail and Callie and said briskly, "You're next on the agenda. I think we should arrange for some immediate DNA testing. I've taken the liberty of getting in touch with Grandpa Bud. He'll be glad to give a sample, Gail. He's very anxious to prove he's your real father. And I'm sure you'll want to settle it once and for all."

"Mom!" said Callie. "Let's think about this carefully. We should talk to a lawyer first."

Her mother seemed not to hear her, and said to Melanie, "Oh yes, I'd be glad to do it. I really need closure on this issue."

CHAPTER XXXIV

THE LEGACY OF KALI-RA

A year and a half later, at the party after the wildly successful Los Angeles premiere of *The Revenge of Kali-Ra,* Glen held Nadia's hand and smiled at his wife with pride as photographers snapped pictures of the couple. He leaned over and whispered in her ear, "You were sensational. Everyone adores you. I'm the luckiest man in the room."

"Nadia! Nadia!" said a reporter. "When's the sequel coming out?"

Nadia smiled up at her husband, who answered for her. "We're working on the Kali-Two script now, but we start shooting the Dionne quintuplets movie in Vancouver next month. It's a real challenge for any actress. Nadia will play five roles. She's been working on her French accent."

"We're hoping some of that fertility will be catching," said Nadia playfully. "Right, honey?"

Glen looked shy and said, "And we're still hoping to get the Sylvia Plath thing going. Nadia is looking forward to a role she can really sink her teeth into."

Across the room, over by the bar, Duncan Blaine sipped his drink thoughtfully and accepted the congratulations of his agent. The man had made a big point of rushing over to speak to him, a new and pleasant development. "Great work. Everyone loves it," he'd said, squeezing his arm. "We have to look at your next project very strategically. I've got

223

people in this room ready to sign you up for anything you want to do, right now. Call me tomorrow. Better yet, Duncan, I'll call you."

Across the room Duncan saw a couple who looked familiar. He realized that it was Tom Thorndyke and that strange girl he'd met that very odd night at Nadia's. The girl was wearing more clothes now, a beaded, silvery sort of dress with long sleeves, and she'd done something with her hair that made the whole package look more mature and expensive, and less as though she'd wandered off the beach. Duncan had liked her better as a nymphet of nature, and he thought fondly of her flat, golden stomach.

He caught her eye and waved. The two of them came over to his side. "You're looking marvelous, my dear," he said, giving her little Hollywood kisses and shaking Tom Thorndyke's hand. "I'm kind of surprised to see you here. After the results of that DNA test."

She shrugged. "Oh, well, actually, we're working. That DNA thing was a major downer at first, especially knowing Mom gave me that dumb name for nothing."

"Hey, no problem," said Tom. "We made out just fine on the home movie of my best little operative in action." He beamed at her.

"I've been back in Europe," said Duncan. "The last I heard, Nadia and Glen didn't want that footage shown."

"We worked a deal," said Tom. "They realized it was great publicity. The tape is running on all the tabloid news shows, but it's being timed to break during the opening week of the movie in major markets."

"And," Callie added, "we had to agree to disguise me with those little swirly video squares. Glen didn't want Nadia to have any competition, Kali-Ra-wise, but that's cool."

"We were okay with that," said Tom, "because now that Callie's working for me as a celebrity undercover agent, we wouldn't want anyone to know what she really looks like. Confidentially, that whole Kali-Ra thing has been a little gold mine for the business, PR-wise, on top of the massive bucks we got for the tape. With your new success, Duncan, you may be in the market for some security." He pressed a card into Duncan's hand. "Think about it. There are a lot of wackos out there."

"Business is great," confided Callie. "Thorndyke Associates no longer provides security for Nadia Wentworth, but we've added a lot more new clients. We're here keeping an eye on someone tonight."

Callie gazed over at Nadia's costar, who had played Raymond Vernon in *The Revenge of Kali-Ra*. The slim, handsome Englishman with a high forehead and flaring nostrils was a Royal Shakespeare alumnus billed as the new Leslie Howard. His date this evening was a twenty-three-year-old former child star just out of rehab who was making a comeback in a sitcom about a lingerie model putting herself through veterinary school.

Since going Hollywood, the actor had dumped his boyfriend of many years and engaged in a frenetic round of overtly heterosexual dating so as not to alienate Middle America. Duncan had heard in London that the spurned lover had threatened to publicly humiliate the star at the first available opportunity. Presumably, Tom and Callie were there to prevent any scenes that would damage his straight cred.

Duncan nodded and smiled. "I'm glad to hear things are going well." Now that his own career was back on track he felt vaguely pleased about the good fortune of others for the first time in ages. "You know, Tom, I think you should make her a partner."

"He's going to," said Callie. She held up her hand and displayed a large sapphire on her left hand. Tom simpered at her, then pointed to Duncan's glass and said, "Can I get you another drink?"

Duncan looked down into the glass. There was nothing left but a squashed lemon wedge. "Sure. Gin and tonic, no ice. And make it a double."

Quentin Smith, wearing a gray flannel suit and a white shirt, stood in front of the closet in his bedroom holding a necktie in each hand and looking at each in turn. Margaret, still tucked in, was watching coverage of last night's premiere of *The Revenge of Kali-Ra,* a benefit for a battered women's shelter. "I guess the idea is if some guy hits his wife, Kali-Ra will come around with her whip and flog him. A nice tie-in," she said.

"Speaking of ties," said Quentin, "which one shall I wear in court today?" He held up a subdued mauve silk number and a red-and-blue striped one.

"Well, the striped one is nice and sincere-looking for your testimony, but the tapes have nailed Maurice flat anyway. The mauve one is better for the ceremony. It will look good with my dress and it makes your eyes look fabulous."

"Okay, mauve." He came over to the bed and bent down to kiss her. "Are you sure you've got it all set up? Judge Withers is right across the hall, and he knows we're coming over at the noon recess?"

"Yes, darling, it's all set. Are you nervous?"

"Nothing Maurice Fender's lawyers can do could make me nervous after that breakneck taxicab ride through the hurricane to the airport to catch the last plane out with those goons with Uzis coming after me in the black Cadillac," he said.

Margaret hit the mute button. "No, you idiot! Nervous about getting married, I mean."

"Oh. That. Not a bit. But maybe you should be. I can't

believe a sensible, wonderful woman like you is marrying a flake like me."

"Neither can I. But I think everything is going to be just fine from now on."

"If it isn't, I'm sure you can fix it," he replied.

A much smaller contingent of the Hollywood press corps than had been present at the premiere attended the press conference called the next morning by Lila Ricardo and the lawyer who had successfully pled her assailant insane. This event took place at the lawyer's offices.

"My client, Winston Goodlet, couldn't be here tonight for obvious reasons," said the lawyer, an aggressive young woman with long blond hair and a lot of makeup. She leaned into a small microphone at the end of the conference room table. Lila, clicking and unclicking her cracked patent-leather handbag and gazing with glittery eyes and a strange half smile out at the handful of reporters, sat next to her. "But he wants me to tell you how touched he is that Lila has forgiven him. The two of them had a moving meeting up at the State Men's Institute for the Criminally Insane last week, which I was privileged to witness. They have decided to market their story in the interest of all who have been touched by mental illness."

"And," piped up Lila, leaning over the microphone while the lawyer looked on nervously, "for all the little people over the years whose lives have been enriched by the work of Valerian Ricardo. Winston truly understands and feels Valerian's work. He has loved it perhaps not wisely but too well."

"Yes," interrupted the lawyer. "And he *is* getting well too, with proper medication and sensitive, caring treatment. We are announcing tonight that we are selling the literary and screen rights to the extraordinary friendship that developed between assailant and victim, brought together in such dra-

matic circumstances. A percentage of the proceeds will go
to appropriate charities."

Now Lila burst in again. "Including the Valerian Ricardo
Foundation. Valerian himself has told me how pleased he
is about this, and says it was all part of a divine plan."

The lawyer grabbed the microphone and slid it out of the
old woman's reach. "Proceeds will also be used to defray
Mr. Goodlet's vast legal expenses. We will entertain offers
from all sincere parties, and expect that the bidding will be
lively for such sensational material." She cleared her throat.
"I will take questions now on the selling of the rights to the
story of Lila Ricardo and Winston Goodlet, but we are not
prepared to comment at this time on possible pending
homicide charges against Mrs. Ricardo."

"Is it true the DA said he wouldn't press charges if you
signed away the rights to Valerian Ricardo's works?" asked
a woman in the front row.

"We have no comment," said the lawyer. "Other than to
say that the district attorney's office has not filed charges
and we do not expect them to do so. Neither are we prepared to make any claim to the literary rights to the works
in question. We are much more interested in sharing with
the world the story of Lila Ricardo and Winston Goodlet,
an uplifting story of madness and wellness, redemption
and forgiveness."

About five hundred miles to the north, Nick came out of
the shower, and went into the kitchen where Melanie had
already toasted their English muffins and made the coffee.
She was wearing one of his T-shirts and looked adorable.
He kissed her, picked her up, twirled her around, and set
her down. She laughed and arranged plates and cups on
the table in the sunny breakfast nook of the airy arts and
crafts house in the Berkeley Hills that Nick had bought with

the rights money from Uncle Sid's works. It was secluded and peaceful, but still close to campus.

"Beanie called while you were in the shower," she said as she poured coffee in his cup. "The premiere was fabulous. It's going to be very big. They're talking at least one sequel. Thank God I got you points. And the merchandise tie-in is really going to be a little gold mine. Glen says the good word of mouth on the picture has really got the Kali-Ra doll back ordered."

"Are you sorry we missed the premiere?" said Nick.

"No," said Melanie. "I am incredibly happy."

"Me too," said Nick. "I am in love and in school. It's everything I ever wanted."

Melanie buttered muffins. "I used to be sorry I found those Kali-Ra books at the Hotel Splendide on Boola Lau, but I'm not sorry about that anymore, that's for sure."

"Ah," said Nick in a spooky voice. "We must be grateful for the strange workings of fate that drew you to those neglected volumes in the forgotten library of that tropic isle, for in doing so, you set off an extraordinary chain of events that—"

He sipped his coffee and Melanie picked up the thread, "—that unleashed the dormant power of the cruel Kali-Ra. But, while her evil ran amok at Villa Vera, strange forces of the cosmos deemed that things which are good and worthy were also to blossom in the strange, sweetly-scented realm of the Queen of Doom."